leisure & culture DUNDEE

LGBT

HARMONIOUS HEARTS 2018
STORIES FROM THE YOUNG AUTHOR CHALLENGE

Harmony Ink

Published by
HARMONY INK PRESS

5032 Capital Circle SW, Suite 2, PMB# 279, Tallahassee, FL 32305-7886 USA
publisher@harmonyinkpress.com • harmonyinkpress.com

This is a work of fiction. Names, characters, places, and incidents either are the product of author imagination or are used fictitiously, and any resemblance to actual persons, living or dead, business establishments, events, or locales is entirely coincidental.

Harmonious Hearts 2018
© 2018 Harmony Ink Press.
Edited by Anne Regan

Cover Art
© 2018 Paul Richmond.
http://www.paulrichmondstudio.com
Cover content is for illustrative purposes only and any person depicted on the cover is a model.

Trade Paperback ISBN: 978-1-64108-144-3
Digital ISBN: 978-1-64080-966-6
Library of Congress Control Number: 2018908786
Trade Paperback published October 2018
v. 1.0

Printed in the United States of America
∞

This paper meets the requirements of
ANSI/NISO Z39.48-1992 (Permanence of Paper).

Contents

Introduction

WELCOME TO the fifth annual Harmony Ink Press Young Author Challenge anthology, *Harmonious Hearts 2018*. It's always a thrill to read through the submissions to our short-story challenge aimed at young authors writing LGBTQ+ themes.

The authors selected for this year's anthology represent five countries across five continents. While demonstrating the universality of LGBTQ+ experiences, they also highlight the authors' individuality and unique perspectives. Whether related as science fiction, fantasy, or contemporary realism, the characters in these stories face challenges, doubts, and loss but also find strength, acceptance, and love.

Some of these writers have participated in previous Young Author Challenges; for others, this is their first professional submission. But they're all authors to watch as they continue to develop their storytelling skills.

If you're a young writer yourself, or know someone who is, you can find information about our ongoing Young Author Challenge at www. harmonyinkpress.com/submissions. We'd love to receive your stories.

In the meantime, it's my privilege to introduce you to our next group of young writers.

Anne Regan
Executive Editor, Harmony Ink Press

Just a Phase
by M. Caldeira

"JUST A phase, huh? Like when you were all for Meg and you were at my heels going 'This will pass, it has to pass'?"

Her tone is harsh, and I glance at her sideways. Rare are the moments where she employs that tone with me. The paper I'm writing on is the one to suffer the unfortunate consequences, as my hand trembles so much I poke a hole through the page. It's a wonder I can detect it; she must really be laying it on thick, as I'm kind of tone deaf.

"That was...." It's hard to think of an answer that will get me off the hook with Emme, so I look away as I rip the page from the notebook. I hadn't really written much anyway. I can easily start again. She's known me for so long that she must have been there for every crush, every attempt at something more. Because who am I but a girl who's obsessed with romance novels?

Of course, most romance novels feature straight protagonists, and the girl gets with the boy... but she kind of has me pegged on that one too. Something about "underrepresentation of other sexualities and gender minorities in popular media." That's what she would probably say.

Rather than tear away the page cleanly, I tug at it insistently, pulling it with all my strength, the tugging of the page mirroring the confusion in my head. Because one thing is very clear, but that's the thing I can't reveal.

But that's Emme, always looking for a cause to follow, always so passionate about things. It's actually kind of hard not to use the plural when she's discussing one of her crusades, one of her many fights for equality. Whatever minority it is, I always stop myself before "You should get your rights" becomes "We should fight for our rights." That would be complicated to explain.

The page gives, and I'm nearly knocked backward as the sheet of paper comes undone. I'm really not hiding that I like girls very well. But for that there is silence. She might be the one at Pride and raising money and fighting for equality, not only for her sake but for everyone else, but she won't get me to admit *that* to her.

She's my friend! And friends keep secrets from each other all the time. Including the big one. I think my mouth purses as I think of that one. I steal a glance at her.

She still awaits my answer, despite the silence that followed the first part of it. She's gazing at me, her deep hazel eyes glancing into my plain boring bluish ones. I hear that some girls desire girls with blue eyes. That hasn't happened to me, so far.

Of course, when I catch her staring, I blush. It takes the strength of a Titan not to get lost in those eyes. And with me caught staring, I don't really see what I'm doing. The paper I grabbed and ripped gets wrinkled and turned into a ball. To such an extent I don't think I'll be able to check the answer anymore. I bite my lip and come up with a reply rather halfheartedly.

"Different. That was different," I repeat, as if that will make it any less shaky, as if it will give it legs to stand on. Because if we're being honest with one another, she can make a whole list of examples. Like in those cartoons where a list scrolls down comically for meters upon meters. Meg hadn't been my first crush, and I doubt she'll be the last.

"Right." The way she rolls her eyes tells me the truth that my heart doesn't want to accept. She is definitely not convinced of my theory. Then again, if I were in her place I likely wouldn't be either. One time is curiosity, two is pushing it, three? Well, either I was really into girls and girls alone, or I was attracted to them and boys all the same. And so far most of my crushes had been on bright young women. The one or two boys I had gone out with fell short on the whole spectrum of manliness. If that was a thing. I didn't think it was.

She gently places a hand on my notebook and pushes the few sheets of paper it held. She does it so perfectly that it looks to the world, and to me, like there was never any ripping. She's gentle with her actions; she acts slow, in a controlled manner. But that is the personification of Emme, gentle but perfect.

My sexuality aside, I have a much bigger problem in my life than whether I like boys, girls, or both. Or none of those, or… anything else, really. Emme would have been perfect in this aspect. Like with the sheet of paper, she would have been able to address people by their preferred pronoun. She would be able to be cordial, perfect, and not judge people as odd or weird.

She would probably take them under her wing as she had done with me. Emme was mature like that, though we weren't any different in terms of age—we were both sixteen. But I sometimes saw her as wiser than any adult I knew. And this had nothing to do with the fact I was in that age where adults fall under the whole "flawed and awful" description. Yeah, sure, most adults weren't perfect, but then….

I sigh, which doesn't go unnoticed. How can she detect me sighing and yet not interpret my blushing? Maybe she's being willfully ignorant? Besides being probably the most accepting, understanding person I know, she is also very perceptive, something I have seen in action often.

I just have to hope that she won't catch me on the other thing I hide from her. Because while my sexuality, which I vehemently denied, might be obvious—not only to her, but probably to everyone—the other thing I struggle to keep better hidden than that.

And yet as I grab hold of my pen, I have to steady my nerves. I have to breathe and go to my happy place. Which unfortunately just so happens to feature Emme, but there's little I can do about that. I hold the pen, flipping it until it's steady. Then, making sure not to look at her, I speak.

"There's a reason most people who want help ask for it," I declare. I somehow manage to pronounce this with all the certainty I don't have. I manage to make it sound like a fact even if I personally don't believe in it. How many times has she uncovered someone in need and given them a helping hand, guiding them to the right path? Too many to count. Emme is like a saint on earth. And even when I'm not personally bawling at her feet, she is there.

She's always been there. A hand on the nape of my neck for support, resting my head against her head or shoulder. She somehow always seems to know when I need help. When I need, not only help, but *her*.

And thoughts like those do nothing to help alleviate my problem. If anything, instead of dispersing it, they make it more apparent. I am certain I'm getting red, that I'm blushing up to my ears. Not for the first time. And I can't exactly call it a side effect of rage. My tone has been far too casual, my smirk far too apparent.

This isn't the first back-and-forth about my feelings I've had with her. It's just that she shouldn't—couldn't know. That much is obvious to me. That's what I desire, that she won't take a second glance at who I have a deep passion for. More than all those other crushes I somehow find myself with. Someone I have fallen for years ago and I still wish for, years later.

And someone who has been there for me through thick and thin, through the hard times and the times that flew by like a breeze. Part of me is well aware that, though I could find other girls attractive or boys likable, there's never a chance of a relationship.

The pen still in my hand, I make sure to turn my face away from her. How can I not blush when I'm thinking about all her qualities, about my feelings, about everything that entails? And it's not like everything's perfect....

It still sucks when I'm rejected when putting feelers out there, but even If I had started a relationship, I wouldn't have been happy. That much I'm aware of. And maybe it isn't fair to those girls or boys that I would try to get with them when I'm longing for someone else. But what else can I do? My feelings are no less genuine just because I have a deeper crush. And going for what I know to be physical attraction might seem shallow, and indeed it's never worked, but it's as good a disguise as any.

I've heard of the term "beard" to refer to the wife of a gay man. I think the term somewhat applies here. No, I'm not married and maybe I'll never be, it's hard to tell. But all those failed relationships or attempts at one? Beards, all of them.

And yet I wish Emme didn't prod deeper. Hence why I try to ignore her sign that she didn't uncover just who I'm crushing on. Because more than awkward, more than embarrassing, that would be hard to explain. Even if we're sitting together under the pretense of doing our homework together. Even if it's just a normal, definitely boring school-related activity. We still discuss our feelings.

Or rather, my feelings. It's an uneven relationship in that I don't help Emme with her feelings at all. I don't know why, but she never speaks of how she feels in front of me. Maybe that's because I'm a poor listener, or maybe it's because she just prefers to help instead of burdening others, but it still feels unfair.

Any attempts at trying to help, to know her feelings fail, though. And I got the memo. I don't try anymore. If I have things I'd rather keep hidden... especially from her, then she has that right as well. Repeating her words and echoing the sentiment that "sharing would help"? Well, that would just be hypocritical, not to mention moot, when I don't share the target of my affection.

And how can I? Emme is perceptive, so much so that I have to try to do everything in my power so she doesn't figure out my feelings. Even then she's gotten around my supposed sexuality in a roundabout way. I trust her so much I admit things I definitely shouldn't or wouldn't want to share.

Even when we're doing the most mundane of tasks. Homework, there's not much to it, but she makes me feel all sort of emotions. Confusion of course, but also happiness. I enjoy her company. Even if she doesn't normally prod as hard, one can see why my homework still hasn't been done.

Not that I don't trust Emme. I do. She isn't a gossiper; it's only that to trace such paths, to create the precedent…. It's a dangerous game I play. At least if she isn't aware of just who I have that crush on, and I sure hope she isn't , then keeping it hidden is all the more important and hard, because of how much I've revealed freely.

I lightly bite the tip of my pen cap, as if having the blue plastic in my mouth will help me from revealing my hidden feelings. If Emme wants to know anything, she has her ways of getting people to speak. She can use a whole wide array of tactics, ranging from kindness to earnest friendship. The words that people reveal would come, not as something she plans, but as a side effect.

Not that Emme does much judging, or indeed any other activity that would put me in a bad light. In fact, she's managed to become the one most everyone goes to talk to and have a moment of friendship with. It's just the thought of rejection that keeps me from revealing anything. She wouldn't make fun of me, and if she says no (my mind corrects me to *when* she says no), she would offer me a hand in dealing with the issue. It's only that I don't want to compromise our friendship… and I'm afraid of the one word that can tear it apart. A simple "No."

"Sometimes people don't realize they need help until someone shows them the way…."

Emme speaks, and I spit the pen cap to the floor in shock. I should have realized she wouldn't let the issue drop, but it's been long enough that my thoughts drifted where they shouldn't, when with her. If she's just spoken now… I wonder why.

With a sheepish smile on my face, I drop down to my knees to look for the pen cap. There goes that plan to keep quiet. I'm aware that now I'll have to answer. Unless I put the pen tip on my mouth and bite it. But I don't want to ruin the pen. The cap had been enough, and now it has fallen and it's likely full of dust and other stuff.

I pick up the slightly wet pen cap and pocket it. Maybe that will dry it. Making a big pretense of still looking for it, I try to find an answer to what Emme said.

The big problem is… I knew what she said to be true. I agree with her. And while I can make a variety of arguments on why that makes no sense, they all ring hollow to my ears. And if they ring hollow to my ears, then surely someone as smart as her would see right through them.

Finding no suitable counterpoint to her argument, I decide to concede. Lifting myself up, as if I have found the pen cap just then, I have to admit to her that she has a point, as she often does.

"And don't you know it? How often did you find that to be true?" Maybe admitting she was right doesn't have to call for her personal experience or a (not so) hidden compliment, but those come out of my mouth either way, my body betraying my mind's vow to play it cool. Maybe she will take it as a sign of friendship and leave it at that. I sure hope that will be the case.

Should have known better than to expect a miracle, I guess.

"Not often enough, I find. For instance, sometimes even with me trying to help, people refuse to acknowledge their feelings."

The amused little smile from when she saw me rip out the sheet, only to fall, is gone. So is the positive outlook on life. Her words are downright negative. I've never seen her like this. Even when she's talking to someone who has no hope, she can bring a little bit of joy. Here, even the way she speaks—it's matter-of-fact, but it's devoid of that bubbly voice she normally employs—shows a different facet of her. It pains my heart that something would make her feel that way. Then I take notice of her words and alarm bells ring in my head.

If I still had the pen cap in my mouth I would have swallowed it, I'm so alarmed.

A single, shivering idea runs through me. *She knows.* All my efforts to hide it from her have been for naught. And now I'm set to hear the rejection.

I can pretend that what she says doesn't affect me at all. I could go "How so?" in an incredulous tone, as if I didn't know who or what she's talking about. But I don't think I can fool her. Even if I were to restore normality, I still don't want to see her sad.

So I simply ask one question, one that makes the color return to my face. Though I had gotten pale when I understood her answer, now the blush returns, as the question that hangs in the air is asked. "How lo...." I take a deep gulp and a breath to steady my nerves, and the pen I hold in my hand shakes once more, making a mess out of my homework. That doesn't matter now, not as much as this. I'll wipe the sheet clean and go over it again later. I just hope I can do the same with our relationship. "How long have you known?"

She glances at my eyes, those boring bluish ones, and smiles. I'm a pile of nerves. I feel like my every last attempt at subtlety has failed. And yet she smiles. Despite the way her words come out as sad, that smile is still dazzling.

"About your feelings? Ages. But then I hoped that you would come to me with them, instead of hiding under the 'it's just a phase' excuse."

She averts her eyes, and I glance down, abashed. If she knows and I know…. Does that mean I've been hurting her? I can't stand such a thought.

"It's not," I state, sure of it. If it hasn't gone away in four years, maybe even five, before I knew that what I feel is love, then it won't go away now.

"It's not a phase, it's just… I like you, like, *like* you, you know?"

My smile is tiny due to nerves, though I suppose it contrasts with my skin. Her smile, on the other hand, seems to increase even further, as if that were possible.

She places a hand on mine, steadying it. She holds me gently, the same way she rips paper. She doesn't even flinch when I get ink on her hand. And sure, we've held hands plenty of times. It's a common enough thing we do as friends, but never has the touch been so soft, never have I so freely admitted to it.

I realize this is the start of a whole new phase of our relationship. And this time, I hope it won't be "just a phase."

M. CALDEIRA is a Portuguese author who started writing even before they knew how to read properly. Their first story, about a squirrel turned boy and highly inspired by a certain animated movie, is still in their parents' safekeeping. Nationally published at age thirteen, M. Caldeira wrote their first ten thousand words, and many more, with someone else's characters. Artist, photographer, musician via computer, and creator of new worlds, they're never happier than when using their imagination to escape a dull day.

M. Caldeira is a survivor of the shipping wars, doodler of many sketches in class, and a fan and collector of both new and old video games. They currently study Translation because they often found themselves explaining what was happening on screen to younger siblings and friends, and they decided they might as well make a living out of it. M. Caldeira has a fascination with the past, even if they acknowledge things are better now and they keep getting better.

The Language Unspoken
by Chelsea Winters

IT WAS snowing the first time the stranger came into First Impressions.

Cody had been late for work. His car had refused to start, and Cody had frantically tried everything he could to give it a boost. But nothing worked, and his hands shook so badly he could barely grasp the keys. By the time he had gotten it started, he was on the brink of a panic attack.

It didn't help that he was already short of breath from the cold nipping at his face and fingers. He had hoped to get into his car and warm up before the telltale feeling of rope coiling around his chest started to suffocate him.

Of course, luck wasn't in his favor. It never was.

He had used his quick-relief inhaler, taken with fumbling fingers. The heaviness decreased as Cody attempted to calm himself back down with deep breaths, as well as he could manage. He knew it was a bad idea to start driving into work when he hadn't fully recovered from his asthma attack.

And he did anyway.

When he got to First Impressions, he hurried inside. The bell above the door chimed as he entered, a light jingling sound. Once he was inside, Cody became aware of how audible his wheezing was.

The girl who was sitting at the front desk glanced up. Elie, Cody's best friend from childhood, immediately realized what was happening and bounced out of her chair.

"'M fine," Cody puffed out. He wasn't.

"Uh-huh. Come here, sit down. Do you have your inhaler?" she asked, not missing a beat as she guided Cody over to the receptionist's desk.

That coiled feeling had returned, so Cody nodded instead of trying to respond.

"Good." She crouched beside the chair. She ran her hand up and down his arm, her golden bronze skin a contrast to his pale pinkish tone. Her warm hand chased away the chill in his body, and the cold, metallic taste in his throat started to dissipate.

After Cody used his inhaler, he tried to focus on Elie's breathing. She watched him with a reassuring smile, and it filled his chest with a soothing heat, driving away the last of the cold.

He gave her a thumbs-up when the vise grip around his chest loosened. Elie beamed up at him and her hand stilled. She gave his arm a final squeeze before she released him.

"I made you tea. It's probably cold now, but I'll go put some hot water in. Hey, weak tea is better than no tea, am I right?" Elie grinned at her own antics. Cody puffed softly in amusement as she waltzed away into the back.

What would he do without Elie?

If her presence wasn't comfort enough, the familiar window-lined, painted azure walls made him feel at ease. The shelves and racks that displayed all the colors of the rainbow in flowers brightened the mood.

The soft ivory sphere lights hanging above and bathing the florist shop in their glow also helped to ease his high-strung nerves.

He was settling down until the bell above the door chimed and Cody tensed all over again. Cautiously, he glanced toward the noise.

Standing just inside the entrance was a tall, dark-haired, brown-skinned stranger. His eyes roved around the shop curiously.

Then his gaze landed on Cody and caught him staring. Cody felt his heart skip a beat and his face heat in embarrassment, but he didn't look away.

He probably looked like a mess. If his cheeks weren't still colored from the cold outside, they were now from getting caught. His nose was probably red too. He was wearing a hat that he thought had looked cute when he left, but now Cody hated it. He wasn't a hat person; what was he thinking?

Oh, and then there was the asthma attack, and all the panic, and if that wasn't enough—

The stranger gave him a soft smile. Cody only blinked in return. By the time he came out of his daze, the stranger had turned away and wandered behind one of the display racks.

"Cody?"

He jumped, his heart beating wildly in his chest. Elie stood beside him, her expression concerned. In her soft pink-nailed hands she held a mug of steaming tea.

Cody glanced over to see if he could find the stranger again but found nothing. He turned back to Elie and tried to duck out of her gaze. "Mm… thanks," he mumbled, taking the offered mug. He curled his fingers around it, savoring the heat emanating from the mug and the hot tea within.

From the edge of his vision, he watched Elie narrow her eyes skeptically. "Are you okay?" she asked, mixed parts concern and suspicion.

"Of course," he assured hurriedly. The flush on his face darkened, and he tried to hide behind his gray-and-blue mug. It was just a stranger, for goodness' sakes. And here he was, all flustered. *A pretty stranger with a pretty smile.*

He made an unintentional, incomprehensible noise. Elie gave him an odd look before pulling out another chair to sit beside him. "All right. You're going to tell me what that entrance was."

At some point, while Cody was relaying to Elie what had happened, the bell chimed again. He paused midsentence to look up. The glass door was closing, but Cody could see the stranger from earlier. He didn't turn back around as he left, and it was silly for Cody to expect him to, but....

He's just a customer. Just someone browsing around a flower shop. Looking for flowers for someone. You shouldn't even be watching him like that.

THIS WAS the same thing Cody repeated to himself the next time he thought about the stranger.

It wasn't the first time Cody had gotten hung up on a person he had never talked to and would probably never see again. It wasn't likely to be the last either.

Elie called him a hopeless romantic. Cody argued that it was appreciating art. Elie countered that it was romantic to think of people as "art." Cody didn't have a good comeback to that.

Cody reasoned with himself that it wasn't the big deal he was making it out to be. To try to forget the stranger, Cody came up with a mental list of reasons. *He could be a jerk. He could be straight. He could be a serial killer. I shouldn't even be interested in him. I shouldn't even be thinking about him.*

The bell chimed, and Cody looked over, absentminded. His gaze was glazed, distracted, and it was only after he nearly got whiplash from whirling his head back around that he realized who had walked in.

Speak of the devil. Or an angel? *Okay, geez, Cody. Crush much?*

For a moment Cody's eyes met the stranger's, the same one he had just been thinking of. His whole body froze, like a deer caught in headlights.

Then the stranger glanced down at a sheet of paper, breaking eye contact. Cody cleared his throat and looked away as he scrubbed his face. Maybe if he scrubbed hard enough, he could erase the blush covering his cheeks.

Geez, this guy didn't even do anything.

When he peeked up again through his fingers, the stranger was gone. Cody exhaled through his nose, slumping back into the chair. He wished Elie had been working today.

He set his hands in his lap, looking down for lack of something better to hold his attention. So what if he was curious? *I shouldn't be.* Was that so wrong? *Yes.* It wasn't as if it would ever amount to anything anyway. It shouldn't amount to anything.

Someone cleared their throat, and Cody jumped in his seat. He jerked his chin up to look at the stranger, standing behind the counter and watching Cody.

The first thing Cody noticed was that he had gray eyes. Were gray eyes attractive? Cody had never thought they were particularly special. He was reconsidering.

Cody coughed nervously and scrambled to his feet, trying to collect himself. "Uhm. Can I, uh… help… can I help you?"

Brilliant.

The stranger watched him for a moment before giving him a soft smile that made Cody's heart skip a beat.

"I'm… I was wondering if I could put in an order? I have a list to order. Of flowers." He gestured to the piece of paper in his hand, glancing down only momentarily before gazing back up at Cody, almost curious.

He has a really nice voice. It was smooth and gentle, deeper than Cody's, and steady.

"Mm," Cody hummed, trying not to stare. Maybe Elie was right. Cody was hopeless. "Yeah, I can. We can. I mean, I can… no. I mean, yes." He resisted the urge to bury his face in his hands. *Please let the ground swallow me whole.* "What did you want to order?" he mumbled, avoiding the stranger's eyes.

When the stranger didn't immediately respond, Cody glanced back up. There was that soft smile again that made little butterflies take flight in Cody's stomach. Though he was bashful and flustered, Cody did his best to return the stranger's smile.

"Here." The stranger slid the piece of paper across the counter. Cody took it and scanned over the words written in beautiful calligraphy.

Honeysuckle, violets, bridal roses, angelica. Cody tried to envision this mystery bouquet, but he couldn't remember what half the flowers looked like.

"Oh!" the stranger exclaimed in a quiet breath. "I forgot to add the rest. I didn't have a pen with me. Add lilacs, crimson polyanthus, and sycamore. Please."

"Sycamore… like the tree?" Cody asked, a frown gracing his features as he slid the paper back across the counter. He turned away from the stranger, searching for a pen he *knew* had been there a moment ago.

The stranger looked down at the paper, as if uncertain what to do with it. Cody realized that giving it back to him did little to help, seeing as it was Cody who was supposed to be putting in the order.

"Well, yeah." The stranger chuckled, a soft rumbling noise that set Cody's butterflies off again. He found the pen and handed it over silently, already forgetting the list of flowers he'd been given. "Thanks. The trees, they have blossoms. But a tree with flowers around it would be a pretty cool arrangement too."

Cody snorted, warmth blossoming in his chest. The irony that he, a florist, knew less about flowers than his customer apparently did was not lost on him. "I think it might be hard to move."

The laughter that followed his comment caused the warmth to spread. The feeling stayed with Cody after he put the order through and told him to come back in a week to pick it up. It stayed with him after the stranger left.

It was even lingering into the next day, when Cody started to daydream about a soft smile and gray eyes.

THERE WAS a bouquet on the front desk one day. And it wasn't a part of their display.

Cody had come in to work early, drowsy and still not quite awake yet. It was bitterly cold outside, and Cody felt like an abominable snowman. He was wearing at least three extra layers, trying to find a way to cheat asthma.

He loved winter, but the feeling clearly wasn't mutual.

The florist shop was warm, and Cody was struggling out of his extra clothes as he approached the front desk. Leaning on the other side of the counter, propped on her elbows, Elie tapped away at her phone. Her hair was wrapped up in a tastefully messy bun. And she wore glasses.

Elie never wore her glasses. For all that she radiated confidence, she thought they made her look stupid. Cody told her that was ridiculous and that she was pretty either way, which was honest. Elie always brushed him off.

"You're wearing your glasses," Cody said as he shucked off one of his jackets, forgoing any formal greeting.

She glanced up at him, her eyes bright. She looked radiant, almost as if she was glowing. Cody had a sneaking suspicion it had something to do with her boyfriend.

For most of yesterday, Elie had been begging Cody to come to dinner with her and David. And it wasn't that Cody hadn't wanted to come. He hadn't formally met David and wanted to see who was making Elie so happy. But he also didn't want to be a third wheel.

He'd agreed, eventually. Because he had a weakness for Elie's puppy eyes, and because he genuinely wanted to be a supportive friend. And it had been a nice evening. Until Cody had gotten back to his apartment.

Alex, his roommate, wasn't home yet. Cody ended up almost drowning in a wave of loneliness, realizing how painfully single he still was.

It wasn't Elie or David's fault. He knew neither had bad intentions. It was his problem, after all. Cody didn't *need* a love life. He didn't even know why he was so worked up over this; he had enough to juggle without a relationship in the mix.

"You kind of look like crap," Elie pointed out instead of replying to his comment on her glasses. "Did you sleep last night?"

If he mentioned his restlessness, Elie would no doubt blame herself for his agitation. "Oh yeah, I just… I stayed up a little late studying. I had to play a little catch-up." He shrugged, placing the two other jackets in a heap behind the desk, out of sight.

Elie nodded, but her eyes stared downward, spaced out. Cody sighed, leaning up against the counter in front of her.

"Els, what's up?"

She chewed on her lip, then glanced up at him with wide brown eyes. "What do you think of David? I mean, he's really nice, yeah? I-I really… I really like him, Cody." Elie's lip tilted upward, a soft but hesitant smile. "But if you got any weird vibes from him—"

Cody held up his hand. "Elie, stop." He tried his best to give her a reassuring smile. "David's great. He's nice and funny and charming. And he's clearly enamored with you," he told her truthfully, patting her shoulder.

If there's one thing Cody knew about Elie, it was how much she struggled in the dating realm. She couldn't stand people who were "fake," and most of the people she met fell into that category, apparently.

She often trusted Cody to be honest with her about her potential matches. His social incapability made for a good test for possible boyfriends and their personalities, surprisingly enough.

For a moment Elie studied him, before a grin broke out across her face. "Geez, maybe I'll have to protect him from *you*. Can't have you stealing my boyfriend, can I?"

He glanced away from her, his stomach twisting. It was stupid, *so stupid*. Cody had known he was gay for years. Even though he thought about it a lot, it was still a little wrenching to hear it spoken aloud.

Elie had been a huge help to break him out of that mind-set, but it still wasn't perfect. He still slipped.

"Don't think you have to worry about that, even if I tried," Cody said without thinking. He saw Elie open her mouth to scold him for his "other bad mind-set," one of self-deprecation, so he quickly jumped in again, "See? He bought you flowers."

He gazed over at the flowers for the second time since he'd walked in. There were only three types of flowers in the bouquet: red daisies, white daffodils, and pink plumeria.

They stood out against the blues and greens of the florist shop like a glittering gem on display. David must have good taste in flowers or had consulted someone who did.

"Oh, those?" Elie asked, waving toward the bouquet. "Those aren't for me. You know I'm not really a flowery person." Cody glanced over in surprise, watching as a different, more playful grin split across her face. "Look at the tag."

Suspicious of both Elie and the bouquet now, Cody stepped forward and lifted a small plain white tag and opened it.

Inside, in blue ink and near perfect handwriting, it read *Cody.*

His heart made funny palpitations before swelling with foolish hope. Cody had to take a few deep breaths. Surely there was some error, some mistake. Who would give *him* flowers?

"They were dropped off here yesterday. Robyn said they went into the back, and when they came back out, voila. Bouquet," Elie explained. Her voice almost sounded fuzzy, as if Cody was underwater.

Why? Cody swallowed, his brow furrowing into a deep frown. No, no he couldn't get his hopes up. That didn't make sense. "Did Robyn see anything? Like who, or… um—"

Elie's phone buzzed, and Cody finally snapped out of his trance, looking away. He glanced around the shop as if his surroundings might hold the answer.

He was met only with rows of display racks showcasing their fresh flowers and arrangements. The full panel windows in the front seemed to taunt him, teasing at something he couldn't have.

"Not that they said," Elie replied after a moment. "The bouquet was just there. The shop was full of people, though, so it really could have been anyone."

Why me? "Oh," Cody said, trying to tuck away his disappointment elsewhere. Maybe it wasn't even someone he wanted a bouquet from. Maybe it was a prank or something. That made more sense.

"You know what this means?" Cody finally turned back around to see Elie beaming at him again, her dark eyes holding unspoken mischief.

Cody shook his head, narrowing his eyes. "No."

Elie laughed and patted his shoulder. "You, my friend, have a secret admirer."

Cody scowled, his cheeks dusting pink as he sat down in the chair behind the desk. He attempted to hide behind his phone screen while Elie continued laughing next to him.

Regardless, Cody was grateful for the comment, despite the embarrassment. He allowed himself to consider the possibility of a secret admirer, rather than the troubling path his mind had started to take.

He flipped the card in his hand again. The only difference he noticed as he reread it was a small *J* written in the bottom corner, which still gave absolutely no indication to who they were from.

Secret admirer. That was a weird thing to think about. Cody swiped his thumb back and forth on the home screen of his phone, gnawing on his lip with a fluttering sensation in his stomach.

He glanced back up at the bouquet and couldn't fight a small smile when he took them in for a third time. Roses may have been romantic, but there was something sweet about the simple variety of the floral choices. Unusual, yes, but sweet.

And yeah, he was already totally enamored with two strangers, both of whom he knew next to nothing about.

IT WAS a Not Good day.

Cody was tired, having stayed up late catching up on more schoolwork the previous night. Again. It felt like he was always staying up late to catch up on schoolwork.

Alex had found him hunched over his desk asleep the next morning. "Cody! You have to stop this! Please, God, you're killing yourself!" he had said, a wild desperation that was so uncharacteristic of Alex that it made Cody's stomach turn into a jumbled mess of knots.

He was fine, honest. He was only a little tired. But Cody had almost lost everything to get where he was after he came out and his mother cut ties with him, and he wasn't going to give it up for the world.

Then, after he had finally convinced Alex that, *Yes, I'm fine*, and *I have to get to the florist shop*, and *I promise I'll get sleep tonight in my bed*, Cody had managed to escape his roommate's fussing.

Of course, someone had been smoking moments before Cody had come outside.

It was a warmer day, which meant the worry about having a weather-induced asthma attack was low. Not that it wasn't there, but Cody was trying to be optimistic about the day after his confrontation with Alex.

He had frozen, his mind grinding to a halt and his body refusing to cooperate. Should he try to leave? Should he go back into the apartment until it was gone?

All too soon, that heaviness set in and the coils wrapped around his chest and he couldn't breathe. He couldn't breathe because he was *drowning* in air. Smoky, polluted air.

He had fallen over, or maybe he had just sat down, Cody wasn't too sure. But he'd ended up on the ground, and someone had shouted, and everything was too loud, and he was trying to breathe and trying not to at the same time.

Somehow, at some point, Alex had arrived at the scene. He had brought Cody back to their apartment—carefully, as not to upset him— and sat him at the kitchen table.

Alex gave Cody the inhaler he kept in his bedroom, and while Cody gradually recovered, Alex made him tea. Elie had made the suggestion of warm black tea and honey to help Cody when his asthma had gotten worse in high school.

After he had nursed the tea, enduring a worried stare from Alex as he did so, Cody got back up again. Alex argued against him going to work—Cody was already late, and he wasn't feeling well—but Cody brushed him off. "Elie's there. I'll be fine."

About an hour late to his shift, Cody dragged himself into First Impressions. If he had been tired before, it came down like a tidal wave now. And while the pollen and overall flowery smell didn't bother Cody's asthma, it didn't help the light headache it left behind.

He walked over toward the receptionist's desk, where Elie and Robyn, another coworker of his, were chatting animatedly. Elie was making excited hand gestures, while Robyn nodded along. She was talking fast and rambling about what Cody thought was a movie, but couldn't be sure.

She was on edge. When Elie was on edge, she gesticulated wildly, spoke a mile a second, and rambled.

Robyn was watching Elie politely, but it was clear they knew Elie was antsy too. When Cody approached, their eyes slid over to see him. Robyn gave him a soft smile, and Cody gave them a little wave.

It took a moment for Elie to realize she had lost Robyn's attention and turn. She made a disgruntled noise when she saw him. "*Cody*," she hissed.

Cody should've known it was too much to expect that Alex wouldn't call Elie to tell her what happened. The two of them often thought they had to put him in bubble wrap. It was endearing and weird and sometimes annoying.

"Elie," he sighed, burying his hands into the pouch of his hoodie. "Hi, Robyn." He leaned onto the receptionist's desk, tapping his foot anxiously as Elie glared up at him from the chair.

"Hey, Cody," Robyn greeted, their voice soft and raspy as they watched him with sympathetic blue eyes. "I have to go finish some transactions in the back. Don't be too hard on him, Elie. I hope you feel better, Cody."

Elie scowled as Robyn disappeared through one of the doorways. Cody felt his stomach swirl, bracing himself for a lecture. Still, even though Robyn had left, their gentleness was enough to let Cody settle down somewhat.

"Can we please not talk about this right now?" Cody asked, looking at Elie pleadingly.

She continued to glare at him, but her expression did soften. "I'm sure you know Alex told me what happened." Elie rubbed at her arm, glancing out at the displays. "Cody, you worry me."

Guilt ached in Cody's chest, and he bowed his head. He hated the way something that should only be his problem affected and hurt the people around him. They hadn't asked to deal with *his* setbacks. *His* obstacles. It wasn't fair to them.

"'M sorry," he mumbled, his eyes downcast. He opened his mouth to add more, but his chest tightened, and he only tacked on another "Sorry," hoping it would be enough.

For a moment Elie looked as though she still had half a mind to shout at Cody. But as she turned back to him, she sighed and shook her head. "You're okay now," she said, stepping forward to wrap her arms around his waist.

Cody hesitated before he hugged her back. A little voice in the back of his mind asked if he was worth her pain.

He tried not to think too hard about the answer.

CODY WAS clumsy.

Not all around, constantly tripping over concrete cracks or knocking over vases all the time. In fact, Cody had gotten pretty good at avoiding all that.

Maybe clumsy wasn't even the right word. He was... spaciously ungraceful.

He had a bad habit of getting distracted, both visually and mentally, and forgot about his physical body. As a result, he bumped into people and walls a lot, neglecting to look where he was going or suddenly turning to change his direction.

There was a coffee shop two blocks away from Cody's apartment, and since Alex's decade-old coffee maker had stopped working, well....

The place was a small and homely family-run business. The inside had splotched brown walls covered with paintings and other works of arts, with a recurring coffee theme. The seating was a combination of chairs around round tables and sofas next to armchairs.

It was Wednesday evening, which meant Cody was off from work, and he'd finished up classes hours ago. He had studying to do, but he wanted a soft buzz to keep him awake later.

The coffee shop was quiet when he got there, and Cody almost wished he had brought his homework with him. It would've been a rare opportunity to study there when it wasn't bustling with activity.

But he hadn't. So Cody walked up to grab his order when his name was called and then went over to the condiment station. Alex had asked him for a peppermint mocha, and Cody knew he liked cinnamon—a gross concoction, but Alex was not to be questioned.

He planned on going back to his apartment then, but instead decided to put a little experimental chocolate powder in his own coffee, if the milky drink could be called that.

Cody put the lids on, picked the two cups up, and turned to leave.

And bumped into someone.

He jerked back, his heart pounding rapidly as he lost what was surely most of both drinks onto the stranger's shirt. His eyes widened, and he froze, glancing up in surprise.

Not any stranger either. *The* stranger, from the florist shop. The one with the sycamore trees and the beautiful eyes. And Cody had just gone and *spilled coffee all over him*.

It took Cody a moment to realize he was standing there, two half-empty paper cups in his hands, gaping at the poor guy. He quickly set the cups down and grabbed a fistful of napkins.

"I'm... I am so sorry, I-I'm really sorry, I didn't even, I mean I didn't see that you were—" Cody let out a puff of air, standing awkwardly in front of the stranger with a handful of napkins and wide eyes.

His mouth was open again, working as if trying to speak. He shoved the napkins toward the stranger, his face turning pink.

"I'm really sorry! I should have—"

"What are you doing on Saturday?"

They both froze and stared at each other. The stranger must not have meant to ask the question because his cheeks dusted over with a rosy color.

It blended in with his darker skin, and Cody might have missed it if he hadn't been staring straight at him.

"Sorry, that was… that was not what I meant to say. Well, it was, but not… was that too forward?"

His voice was all the fantastic Cody remembered it from the first time. But if he had been flustered before, there wasn't anything that could describe how he felt in that moment.

Cody unknowingly tightened his grip on the napkins, the paper crinkling in his hand. "I'm… what?" He wondered if the stranger had even noticed that Cody had spilled coffee on him.

If possible, the red on the man's cheeks darkened. "I was… your friend, she said that… I was trying to ask you out," he mumbled, his expression falling into something of a distressed frown.

It took a moment for Cody to process this, only managing to continue staring and flapping his mouth like a fish. But Cody wasn't just clumsy physically. It was no secret that he wasn't good with his words.

"I just dumped coffee on you!"

They stared at each other in surprise again, before a soft smile spread across the stranger's face. Even though he was beyond embarrassed, Cody closed his mouth long enough to smile shyly back and make a soft noise of amusement.

He gestured with the napkins again, and that time, the stranger took them. Cody shrugged, but with the tension dissolving, he felt marginally better. "I-I don't even know your name," he said, much quieter this time.

The stranger paused from where he had started to pat his shirt with the napkins, glancing back up at Cody. He held out his other hand with that soft smile. "Jonathon."

"I'm Cody," he said, as Jonathon finished patting his shirt. Cody took Jonathon's offered hand. His hand was warm, and bigger than Cody's, and made his already pale skin look even paler.

"I know," Jonathon replied as their hands lingered together. Cody frowned and then blinked. Jonathon's smile dropped when he saw Cody's expression and cleared his throat. "Oh right, uh, I asked one of your coworkers. Sorry, that's kind of stalker-ish. I just wanted to make sure the bouquet went to the right person."

Cody blinked again, his eyes widening as he stared at Jonathon. He was highly aware that their hands were still clasped together. Could it even be considered a handshake anymore? Cody was pretty sure that wasn't how handshakes were supposed to go.

"You-you're the one who… you sent the bouquet?" he asked, thinking back on the mystery bouquet with the tag that read *Cody* in that lovely handwriting. It was sitting in his room on his windowsill, now partially wilted.

Jonathon seemed to remember he was still holding Cody's hand and quickly let it go, letting his own fall to his side. "Was that not… do you often get bouquets from people?" he asked, his gray eyes strangely disappointed.

"What? I mean… no! No." He laughed nervously, not quite sure why. "I mean, who would give me flowers?" *Could I have said anything more pathetic?* "I mean, *obviously* you did, and that's… I really like it, but I mean, *why*? Sorry, that's kind of stupid—"

"Cody," Jonathon interrupted him gently and reached out to brush his hand against Cody's arm. "It's okay. You're interesting, that's why. I'd like to get to know you."

Why? Cody didn't ask again, even though he wanted to. Jonathon didn't need to spell out his intentions to the letter. Not that it made any more sense than it had before. "Oh," he said instead. "I… oh." He tried to think of something else to say. Anything else. "Thank you. They're really pretty. And I mean, roses are pretty overrated, right? So… um, that was creative of you."

Excitement blossomed in his chest when Jonathon chuckled softly, scratching his ear and ducking his head. "Yeah." He glanced back up at Cody with that soft look again. "It's an unspoken thing," he said.

Cody tilted his head. "The flowers?"

Jonathon nodded. Cody didn't know what that meant, but he blamed his distraction on Jonathon's eyes. They did funny things to his stomach.

They stood in silence that quickly became awkward until Jonathon reached into his pocket and pulled out a pad of sticky notes. "Do you have a pen?"

He didn't. But Jonathon went over to the cashier and managed to get one anyway. He wrote something down before handing the pen back over and returning to Cody, who was still hovering by the condiment station.

Cody's curiosity grew as Jonathon tore off the note and stuffed the notepad back into his pocket.

Jonathon offered the sticky note to Cody, who glanced down as he took it. The paper was hot pink, and in that same beautiful handwriting as before, it read *Jonathon*, with a number scribbled below.

In retrospect, Cody should have guessed who had brought him the bouquet. He had seen Jonathon's handwriting on the list he brought in the first time Cody had met him.

"It's an option," Jonathon told him, stuffing his hands into his pockets and shrugging.

He was still smiling, and Cody felt his heart swell. He couldn't fight back a contented sigh, returning the smile. *It's an option.* Jonathon wasn't pressuring him into anything. But he was opening a door for Cody to enter if he wanted.

It's an unspoken thing.

SHIRLEY'S WAS somewhere between being cozy and being fancy.

Cody was settled in a booth, looking around in awe at the dark wood paneling and the golden lights that bathed the space in a warm amber glow. Paintings in various vague styles were scattered over the walls, and there were vases of flowers to accentuate the shelves and tabletops.

Soft jazz music echoed through hidden speakers, and the clank of silverware against ceramic and friendly conversation filled the air.

He couldn't help but feel a little out of place, sitting alone there at the booth. He shifted awkwardly as a waitress passed and sent him a curious glance. Cody smiled shyly, before ducking his head to look down at his phone. Again.

Twelve minutes ago, Jonathon had sent him a short text saying that traffic was rough, but he'd be there soon. Ten minutes ago, Alex had texted him, telling him jokingly to be safe and use protection—to which Cody had blushed crimson—and more seriously, to have fun.

Elie had sent him a text too, giving him advice like *Be yourself* and *Do whatever you did that attracted him before* and lots of heart emoticons.

This advice wasn't overly helpful. Cody still didn't know what had caught Jonathon's eye. And what did *be yourself* mean in the greater picture? Cody wasn't always one way or another. Sometimes he was a "hopeless romantic," as told by Elie. Sometimes he was a "goof muffin," something Alex liked to call him. Which *Cody* was Cody supposed to be?

"Hey. Sorry I'm late."

Jumping in his seat, Cody snapped up his head to watch as Jonathon slid into the booth. He had gotten so lost in his mind he hadn't even noticed Jonathon approaching.

Cody blinked as Jonathon gave him a soft smile and realized he was supposed to respond. "Oh, um. Yeah, I mean, that's okay." Regardless of which "Cody" he was supposed to be, the moment he opened his mouth, he became nervous, awkward Cody.

"Have you been waiting long?" Jonathon asked as he settled in. His gray eyes searched Cody, and Cody found himself lost for a moment as he watched Jonathon. "Cody?"

"Sorry!" Cody shook his head, scrunching his nose and then trying to compensate with an apologetic smile. "No, it hasn't been that long." He shrugged, sliding his phone back into his pocket.

Jonathon paused for a moment before he set his hand on the table. He held it open, still with that quiet smile, and Cody realized he was offering an invitation.

It's an option. Jonathon's voice echoed in his mind. Cody felt himself flush lightly as he set his hand on the table beside Jonathon's. Their fingers touched, and Cody's pinky wrapped around Jonathon's.

Even though they technically weren't holding hands, it felt surprisingly intimate. Cody, who had been on a grand total of three dates, wasn't used to this kind of affection. His ears burned.

One was back in high school, when he had asked a girl out because his mom had asked him why he didn't have a girlfriend, was he *a faggot*? Subsequently, Cody had freaked out.

That was before he had even figured out what *he* was, but he hadn't wanted her to get suspicious of his lack of love life. Female love life, in particular.

The next two were after he had moved in with Alex. They were blind dates with two guys Cody didn't know, set up by Alex. Only one had gotten him to a second date, which hadn't gone any further. Cody was "*too nervous*," according to the first guy.

The second guy had been looking for... something Cody wasn't interested in.

He'd never had a *proper* date. Was this a proper date? What constituted a proper date?

"I've never done this before," Cody blurted, eyes wide as he stared at Jonathon. "I mean, well, I've been on *dates* before, but not like this! Not that this isn't... this is great! I mean, I like this, but I just haven't—" He cut himself off.

He realized Jonathon was watching him with a soft, sweet smile and a sparkle in his eyes. Cody shut his mouth. Instead, he started bouncing his leg. He offered Jonathon what he hoped was another apologetic smile.

"I haven't done much of this either," Jonathon admitted. "This… is okay, right? You'll tell me if you're uncomfortable or anything?" he asked as his brow dipped into a soft frown.

Cody couldn't help but get lost in Jonathon's gaze again but managed to shake himself out of it. "No. I mean, yeah, I'll tell you." Cody ducked his head into his shoulders. "You'd be… that's okay?"

He hated how uncertain he sounded, but it was too late. It wasn't like he could take the words back now.

The soft jazz turned into something slower and mystical sounding as Jonathon raised his eyebrows at him. "You think I'd ask you out on a date if I didn't want to prioritize your comfort and security?" Jonathon wondered, almost as if the idea was hurtful.

Before Cody had a chance to open his mouth to reply—probably splutter and make a fool of himself because that was one of the kindest things anyone had ever said to him—the waitress came to their table and asked what they wanted to drink.

Jonathon asked for water. When the waitress turned to Cody, he cleared his throat and stumbled over himself trying to ask for iced tea. She waited, if only a little impatient, and gave them a quick smile once he had managed to spit out his order before she sauntered away.

"Do you mean that?" Cody asked Jonathon, his voice hardly above a whisper as he watched carefully for Jonathon's reaction. He cleared his throat again, his chest feeling a little tight. "Because, I mean, I come with a lot of, um…. Alex, my roommate, he calls it baggage." He shrugged, his leg still bouncing.

A couple sat down at the table beside their booth, carrying the bitter smell of perfume.

"I'm not looking for a one-time thing, if that's what you're asking," Jonathon told him. "Relationships are never easy… is that, ah, is that too soon to be talking about?"

Cody felt his throat constrict, but he tried to push it away to focus on Jonathon. His hand twitched, and he shifted it until he had placed his hand in Jonathon's. Butterflies exploded in his stomach, and he tried not to giggle and ruin the moment.

"Well, it's ground rules, right? I don't mind. Nobody has ever… I'm not really, like, the choice most people would make or anything, though." Cody watched Jonathon's expression soften as his eyes flickered down to look at their hands. "I wasn't really looking for anything, but I'm not… I don't really do the, um… one-time thing. Or anything else. Like that, I mean."

He coughed again, the nearby perfume tickling at his nose. Cody's heart kicked into overdrive when he realized what was happening. *Crap!* Why did the people wearing the strong perfume have to be seated *right* next to them?

Jonathon didn't seem to realize anything was wrong yet. "That's okay," he said, giving Cody's hand a gentle squeeze.

The familiar coils curled around Cody's chest and started strangling him. His face contorted, and the gentle smile faded from Jonathon's face as Cody's breathing turned to choked gasping for air.

"Cody?" Jonathon asked, concern coloring his voice. "Are you okay?"

Had he brought his inhaler? If he had, it was in the car. Jonathon didn't know about his asthma. Why hadn't he just said that? Would it have changed Jonathon's mind? Of course. Why would Jonathon want to be with someone like him? He was a royal mess of a person.

Tears prickled in his eyes, and he tightened his grip on Jonathon's hand. "Breathe," he wheezed, "I-I can't—" A strangled noise tore from his throat, interrupting him. *You're a fool, Cody Jensen.*

The clanking of the dishes and silverware suddenly sounded incredibly loud. Everyone talking, the music playing. The perfume was awful, and Cody wanted to get away, but he couldn't. He was stuck, and he couldn't *breathe*, and it felt like there was a grand piano resting against his chest.

Why now? Why does this always have to ruin every good thing I want?

"Cody, hey, is this a panic attack?" Jonathon asked, and Cody could still feel his hand. Jonathon was like an anchor. Maybe if Cody let go, he'd float away.

He managed to shake his head and tried to tug Jonathon's hand toward the end of the booth. It wasn't fair to make Jonathon deal with something that wasn't his problem, but Cody wasn't sure he could stand alone. *Just another person to pull into my problems.*

"You want to leave?" Jonathon guessed, gently rubbing his thumb over the back of Cody's hand. Cody nodded vigorously, stars sprinkling across his vision.

It felt like years before Jonathon managed to help him out of the booth. Cody's legs almost buckled beneath him when his feet touched the ground, but Jonathon caught him. He slung Cody's arm around his shoulder and carefully navigated him out of the restaurant.

Cody wasn't completely sure he wouldn't pass out on Jonathon. His heart felt like it was running a marathon, while his lungs felt like they'd been taken to a vacuum sealer. It had stolen all his oxygen, and now none could enter. And yet, there was *too much* at the same time.

"C-car," Cody coughed once they'd stumbled their way outside. He was starting to feel light-headed. With his free hand, he tried to point to his little dusty sedan.

Somehow, Jonathon interpreted his shaking signal and helped him over. Cody tried to dig into his pocket for his keys, but Jonathon got to them first, watching his reactions carefully.

His breaths were hollow and raspy now. Cody tried to rub at his chest, as if it might ease the strain. Might loosen the knots and the tangles that were suffocating him.

Jonathon opened the driver's door, and Cody collapsed into the seat. Just outside the car, Jonathon hovered, watching him carefully. Cody could feel his nervous energy. It did nothing to help his own state of mind, and he tried to ignore Jonathon as he fumbled in the cup holders for where his inhaler should be.

He found it and quickly stuffed it into his mouth. *One.* He relaxed his grip on the inhaler and let his head fall back against the headrest as he started counting to sixty.

The coils began to unwind, but Cody still took another puff after sixty. Then he set the inhaler back in the cup holder and let his shoulders slump, taking slow, deliberate breaths as his chest relaxed again.

At some point Jonathon had sat down on the curb just outside Cody's door. He was looking up at Cody with concern filling his gray eyes and spilling out onto his face. Cody almost wanted to cry at how genuine he looked. How worried he was.

He was stuck somewhere between *He cares, he's worried about me, that's so sweet* and *I caused that. I made him worried. I should never have agreed to do this.*

After several moments of silence, Cody heaved a sigh, looking down at his feet and the pedals to avoid Jonathon's gaze. "'M sorry," he mumbled.

"Don't be," Jonathon replied quickly. "Are you okay?"

Cody shrugged. Was he okay? Physically, he was okay now. But emotionally, he hated that he had tangled another person into his web of complications and problems.

More selfishly, he hated that Jonathon had seen him crumble and break down like that. Cody hated how weak and how dependent on other people he was.

"Yeah."

It was a wonder if Jonathon would be able to understand him. Cody was hardly articulating anything.

"Are you sure?" Jonathon pressed, and Cody finally looked over at him. Those soft gray eyes were still filled with so much emotion. Cody couldn't help it as his heart swelled. He nodded with slightly more conviction.

"I'm okay."

Jonathon watched him with a kind frown before he relaxed too. "That… that was an asthma attack, right?" he wondered hesitantly, his tone cautious.

"Yeah," Cody sighed. "I should have told you that I have asthma. I should have just…." Tears started stinging in his eyes again, and he looked at his hands folded in his lap. "I'm really sorry, Jonathon. I ruined the night you planned, and I just… I told you I'm a mess, didn't I?"

This time Jonathon didn't wait for Cody to come to him. Two warm hands grabbed Cody's own and squeezed them. Jonathon came to kneel against the car to be closer to Cody.

"Hey, no, don't think like that. It's okay. I told you I didn't expect this to be easy, didn't I?" Jonathon let go of one of his hands to gently grab Cody's chin and direct him back to look at him.

Cody looked down into his tender gray eyes, his vision blurred by tears. Jonathon brushed his thumb against Cody's jaw, and Cody couldn't help but lean into the touch.

"It's okay, I don't mind." Jonathon smiled at him again. "I get the feeling you're worth it. And besides, that place was a little too fancy anyway."

If possible, Cody's heart swelled even more, and he let out a soft, choked sob. Was there any feasible way Jonathon could be sweeter? He really wanted to hug him right now. Or kiss him. Kissing Jonathon would definitely be okay with him.

Except that he was crying and kind of gross and just had an asthma attack. Who would want to kiss *that*?

"I thought you… you said you hadn't done this before," Cody said with a soft laugh. He hiccupped quietly, smiling through the tears that dripped down his face.

Jonathon chuckled, grinning. "I haven't. Why, am I doing something right?"

Cody laughed again, pulling Jonathon's hand to his heart and covering it with both of his. He wanted to kiss Jonathon's hand. But even thinking about it gave his heart shocks, and he didn't want to push his limits.

Once their joviality had fallen back into silence, Jonathon spread his hand so that his palm lay flat against Cody's chest. Cody wondered if he was trying to feel his heartbeat. It was starting to calm again, at least.

Was this a normal thing? Was this something people did on dates? Cody was pretty sure there wasn't anything normal about this date.

"Do you want to come back to my place?" Cody asked, turning to Jonathon before he could chicken out. "I… only if you want to. I know, it's kind of soon. And my roommate is probably home, and I'm not sure you want to meet him—*ever*. He's great and everything, but like, he's also super blunt and he likes to tease *everyone*, and he can be a little invasive. You probably don't want to deal with that or anything—" Cody cut himself off again when he noticed Jonathon beaming up at him.

"I'd love that," Jonathon said once he seemed to be sure Cody was finished talking. "I would actually take a couch and movies over eating out any day."

Cody studied him for a moment. His gray eyes were somewhat hooded in the night atmosphere, but they still sparkled up at Cody. A nearby streetlight was bathing part of his face in a warm honey glow that highlighted his skin. But most of all, Jonathon's smile lit up the space around him.

"Okay," Cody agreed. For the first time since meeting Jonathon, even though his heart danced with giddiness, he felt relaxed. His mind wasn't swimming, his heart wasn't racing. He felt serene.

Maybe it would be okay to catch someone else in his web, even if it was messy. Maybe Jonathon could help untangle some things with him.

CHELSEA WINTERS is a quiet Midwest girl who was raised at dog agility trials. She sustained a love for animals through the years and never quite grew out of her horse phase. As a child she loved telling her cousins wild stories, devouring books, and filling black-and-white composition notebooks. She wrote tales about animals and adventures but hadn't quite realized she could actually be an author someday. Around the age of nine, her written words became her voice and a great way for her to spill out some of her overflowing imagination.

Now when she's not writing or at the stables, you can probably find her singing, playing the piano, or buying new video games to get part of the way through and never finish.

Chelsea can be found on Twitter at @kezwrites or email at qmmk21@ outlook.com.

A Boy Like Edgar
by Nick Anthony

I CONSIDER myself the type of person who knows what he wants. I also consider myself to be someone who believes in "love at first sight," or some variation of the concept. Not the cartoonish beating heart, googled eyes, slack-jawed version of love. To be truthful, perhaps it's not even love at all. Yet the fact that I had a deep, visceral feeling I when I locked eyes with Edgar was undeniable.

Before I met him, I found myself standing with a group of freshmen art majors that, like myself, were uncomfortable with being alone in such a loud new place. We were all shocked that we were at the first big college house party of our freshman year. The party was a celebratory (and unofficially sanctioned) mix and mingle between the art majors of all grades at our private arts college.

Matthew, the only other openly gay freshman art major in my class, practically clung to me, his eyes nervously scanning the room. I suppose he was cute in a sweet sort of way, with anxious tendencies and a seemingly good heart. We had flirted a bit when we first met a few days prior. We had gotten lunch a few times, watched a movie or two in my dorm room, and even kissed once or twice. But all in all, it was nothing serious. At least it wasn't something serious to me.

Matthew and I were accompanied by two other freshmen. One was Erica, and through the brief conversations we'd had, I could already pick up that she would be the "mom friend," someone whose maturity and levelheadedness would be both extremely annoying and incredibly invaluable. Violet, who was from the West Coast and felt extremely out of place in our prestigious little art school in northern Vermont, completed our ragtag little quartet. The four of us occasionally talked to a few upperclassmen as the night went on, but we mainly kept to ourselves, surveying the party.

We were having an in-depth conversation about our artistic backgrounds, who had studied *where* and *what*, when we were interrupted by a trio of sophomores who likely came to scope us out. One introduced herself as Amy, a sculptor and printmaker. She had piercing and intelligent eyes that scanned the four of us, and whitish-blonde hair cut into a sharp bob. Her obvious intellect and intensity terrified me. I liked her immediately.

With her was Ronny, a loud and friendly guy who had a slight Spanish accent. He was an international student from Argentina and had come to the United States to study drawing. I recognized him as the TA in one of my classes and smiled at seeing him in such an informal setting. When I peered past him, I saw Edgar for the first time.

Admittedly, it would have been easy to overlook him. He hung behind the other two, from shyness or aloofness I couldn't quite tell. He was about my height, neither tall nor short, but much more slender and lean. His skin, which was as pale as cream, seemed to almost reflect the colored lights that danced around the room. He brushed a strand of dark blond hair away from the chunky black glasses he wore and stepped forward to introduce himself, not looking any of us in the eyes, but rather at the wall behind us.

"I'm Edgar," he said simply, his voice an interesting and gritty mixture between high and low. His lips were very red against his pale skin and his brows and lashes thick and dark. I liked the subtle dips and planes of his face and the way they matched how both angular and curvilinear his frame was. There was a hidden sort of beauty to him; once I started looking at him, I couldn't stop.

"Edgar? Not Ed?" I asked, and his eyes flicked to me for the briefest of seconds before darting back down to the floor.

"No, not Ed."

I nodded, and Emma asked us to introduce ourselves.

"I'm Gabe Santiago," I said coolly, my eyes still on Edgar. I felt a twinge in my chest when he didn't look up.

After the rest of us freshmen introduced ourselves, the three sophomores excused themselves to go meet other freshmen at the event. Throughout the whole exchange, my attention never left Edgar, and I continued to watch him even as he slipped toward the crowd trailing behind his friends. I couldn't explain it, but something about him captivated me.

I knew in that moment how much I would like him. It felt like something was tugging deep inside me. To be honest, the phrase "love at first sight" was the first thing that came to my mind. It seemed silly, and love a gross dramatization, but I couldn't deny the feeling that something was beginning to change in me. I had the urge to know more about Edgar. I wanted to hold him, to touch him, to put my hand on his jaw, part his pink lips, and bring his face close to mine.

I was suddenly brought back to reality by a tug to my arm, and my few seconds of dreaming of Edgar's lips and face were over. I looked at Matthew, who had been watching me with a frown on his face. "Edgar was pretty cute, wasn't he," I said, more of a declarative statement than a question. Matthew nervously nodded and ran his fingers through his own frizzy brown hair. I felt bad and took a step away from him, but when I turned toward the crowd again, Edgar was gone.

As two weeks passed and classes commenced, I saw Edgar more and more. We never conversed, but he would occasionally be in the painting studio, working quietly and with headphones in the corner. If he talked to anyone, it was usually Ronny, Emma, or another sophomore. He didn't seem like the type to pry into the lives and gossip of the freshmen. He was too focused on his own work.

I got along well with the other freshman art majors, which I found surprising. In my past I've been surrounded by artists who were all hungry for praise and recognition. Thankfully my class here wasn't like that. We were a pretty diverse lot. There were about twenty of us, all from varied backgrounds, and all with a variety of interests. I was primarily interested in painting and portraiture. I had studied at a high school for the arts in New York before college, and some of the others in my class seemed impressed by this.

I wasn't like the rest of them. I had years of formal training in art and had broken it down to almost a scientific perspective. My work was heavy and precise, with dark, moody palettes, and obviously showing a lot of skill. I wasn't like some of my counterparts, full of energy and color, making strokes with abandon and whimsy. That had been bred out of me.

The first real freshman painting critique two weeks into the year had given me a glimpse of everyone's unique style, unique view on life. My paintings were always dark and heavy, but some of the others were light and airy; some were realistic, some abstract. Some had great technique, while others were messy and more painterly, throwing their emotions on the canvas brazenly and without consideration.

While we all had the same still life to paint, everyone's unique viewpoint was visible. I was proud of my still life. I felt like it was a good representation of my skill and ability. The class seemed to enjoy mine as well, and a majority of the comments were positive, with the only criticism being that I could have used more color. However, when the grading rubrics were returned, SEE ME was scrawled in red pen across the top next to a bold C+, an unheard of grade for me.

I stopped by Mr. Grant's office at the end of the day, with both my painting and the grading sheet in my hand. He was an older man of an indistinguishable age, gray and seemingly both senile and sharp as a pin. He was a tough teacher, incredibly opinionated and bold, who wasn't afraid to tell students their shortcomings. He had told a boy in our class the first week in the semester that he "didn't have what it takes to make it," which caused said boy to go through a mild crisis and switch majors. When told about the boy's fate from a student in the class, Mr. Grant looked pensive for a moment and said, "I guess I was right." Needless to say, I was worried.

I placed both the painting and the grading sheet on his desk and looked up at him, ready for an explanation. He ran his fingers through his thinning gray hair and smiled, though not unkindly. "You're probably wondering why you got this grade, aren't you, Gabe?"

"Yes. I don't usually get Cs. I'm a bit confused. I thought this was a good painting."

Mr. Grant nodded and started typing on his computer. After a moment I spoke up again, emboldened by his silence.

"I thought it was one of the better still life paintings in the class, if I'm being honest."

He looked up at me. "It was."

"Then why—"

He spun the screen of his desktop toward me. On it was the electronic portfolio I had submitted when applying to the program. The moody, dark baroque-styled portraits and still lifes I had painted scrolled across the screen. I looked back at him in confusion.

"Your technique is very strong," he said, "but you're not painterly. There's nothing expressive anywhere. Everything you do is one-note. It's heavy. Dark. You're the only student in your year who hasn't changed the way you've looked at art, at the world, since the first day of my class."

I shrugged. "This isn't my first formal painting class. I've been doing this for longer than a lot of the other people in my year. Not all of them, but many. I already have my own style. I have the technique to back it up."

"But you don't paint what's there," he said. "It's always just a dark representation. There's no artistic distortion, no creativity. You need to really *see*, and then paint that. *Feel*, and then paint that. That's what you're missing if you want to be successful."

"I guess I paint the world the way I see it."

He looked at me for a moment, his piercing blue eyes scanning mine. "Maybe so. I believe in you, Gabe. I think you can do better, that you can wake up. You're a strong painter, but you can achieve more. I think you have the ability to see the world in a different way. However, the grade still stands. Have a nice weekend, and good luck with your self-portrait project. I'll see you in class Monday."

I numbly stood up, grabbed my painting, and mumbled a quick goodbye. I made my way back to the studio, where a few students were working, Edgar and Amy among the group. Being freshmen, we didn't have any classes with the sophomores, but we shared workspaces. I went over to the easel where I had set out my in-progress self-portrait. Violet sketched quietly nearby. I picked up my brush and then glanced over at Edgar.

He was painting, a look of frustration on his face and his canvas facing away from the rest of the room. He bit his lip and pressed his free hand to his temple. His clothes were baggy and splattered with paint and layered on his slim frame. I watched him work, presumably on his self-portrait.

In the beginning of each academic year, every grade painted a self-portrait that would be displayed in the art department's first gallery event. I glanced toward my own portrait, moody and precise and incredibly typical for me. I decided to boost the color a bit and was in the middle of working a tiny bit of purplish-gray into my shadows when I heard Edgar sigh in frustration.

I turned around. Amy had made her way to him and was standing behind him, looking at his canvas. "It's horrible," Edgar said in a defeated voice, shaking his head and pressing his palms to his eyes. Amy shook her head and put her hand on his shoulder.

"Edgar. Don't be so hard on yourself. It's good. *Really* good." He shook his head again and stood up, wiping his eyes. He took a last look at the painting before bolting out of the room. Amy sighed and followed after him, leaving his work alone. It didn't look like they were coming back anytime soon, so I walked over to his canvas. Violet, who had also witnessed the ordeal, followed me.

"Holy shit!" she said, and all I could do was nod. His portrait was unbelievable, incredibly painterly and expressionistic, yet still remarkably sophisticated and well rendered. His use of color was outstanding; blues, reds, greens, purples, every color of the rainbow and more combining perfectly to create the soft and delicate fleshy planes of his face. He had a haunted and sad expression in the image, something so like to the real Edgar that it made the resemblance uncanny, and held so much weight and power it nearly took my breath away. The portrait was beautiful, expressive, and better than anything I could paint, probably would ever paint.

Without saying a word, I walked back and stared at my own self-portrait. It was good, the technique on point. The resemblance was there as well, the skill of the painter evident. However, that's all it was. Skill. Technique. No substance. I blinked, seeing my work for what it was for probably the first time. An uneasy feeling gnawed at me, and I packed up and went home.

The first department-wide art event, the portrait series, happened a month into the semester. Everyone's portraits were displayed side by side, lined up in the gallery on campus. We all dressed up in nice(ish) clothing and mingled with each other and the faculty as we viewed the art. My portrait seemed a little lighter, a little more colorful than usual, but I knew the change wasn't as significant as Mr. Grant had wanted. Yet my classmates still praised me on it, and I accepted the compliments graciously, not letting my feelings of failure show.

While it was exciting to see the rest of the students' work, the after-party was what everyone was waiting for. I was more than ready to get out of the gallery. As the crowd dwindled, I made my way over to Erica, who sat looking at Edgar's portrait. It had improved tremendously from the day I had seen it in the studio, which I wouldn't have believed possible. It was truly magnificent. I could stare at it for hours.

"Erica, do you want to head to the after-party together?"

She tore her eyes away from Edgar's painting and nodded. We went to the coat room to grab our belongings, and then made our way outside into the cool early October air. The party was at a house a few blocks off campus, and we walked in comfortable silence for a while. I could tell she was thinking about something, and when she finally did speak up, it wasn't really something I wanted to hear.

"I wasn't sure I was going to say anything, but Gabe, are you ever going to talk to Matthew?"

"About… that one party?"

She nodded, which shook her choppy blonde hair. "Yeah. He thinks you were leading him on. I'm not saying you were, but… you were pretty flirty until Edgar came along."

"You noticed that?"

She snorted. "It was really obvious. From the moment you saw Edgar, you didn't take your eyes off him. You still don't. Do you like him *that* much?"

I glanced up at the dark sky, the stars totally concealed by low-hanging clouds. "Do you believe in love at first sight?" I asked after a moment.

Her eyes went wide. "You don't actually—"

"No, no, not love. I don't think so. Just... from the first time I looked at him, I knew that I wanted to be with him. I can't explain it. And flirting with Matthew was fun, but not serious. I do feel pretty bad about it, but I just don't feel for him what I do for Edgar."

Erica considered this for a moment, and we spent the rest of the walk trudging along in pensive silence. Every so often I glanced at her, but she was deep in thought. We made it to the porch before she grabbed my arm and stopped me.

"If you really feel like that, go after Edgar. Just... make things right with Matthew. Okay?"

I nodded, and we walked into the house together. The air was smoky and heavy with the heat of bodies, and loud music pulsed through the room. The room was wild and alive with seemingly dozens of students laughing and dancing. It had a warm and thick atmosphere and smelled stale with booze. I lost Erica almost the moment I walked through the door. I rode the sea of people for a minute, in the general direction of the house bar. Once I grabbed whatever mixed drink they were serving, I spun around and began to look for Matthew.

He wasn't too hard to find; he and Violet were practically inseparable, and once you found one you found both. After looking around a bit, I noticed them leaning on a counter in the kitchen, watching the party unfold. When he saw me his eyes widened, and Violet nudged him. When they saw I was coming toward them, Violet whispered something in his ear and, with a fleeting backward glance, scurried away.

"Hey, Matthew, can I talk to you for a second?"

He nodded and nervously began to twist one of his many bracelets.

"I just wanted to say that I'm sorry if I gave you the wrong idea... if I led you on. I just want us to be friends, and I'm sorry that I messed up, that I—"

He cut me off with a smile and a shake of the head. "Gabe, it's fine. Really. I guess I was a little upset at first, but I get it, really. I'm not mad at you, and I'd really like for us to be friends. *Just* friends."

I smiled back at him, and we hugged each other. It felt amazing to be on good terms with him again. He really was a great guy; we were much better suited being *just* friends.

"Besides," he said, leaning in, "I think you should go for Edgar. You guys would be a cute couple." I looked at him and blinked, and then we both laughed. "I think he's actually here somewhere," Matthew continued. "You should go find him!"

"Maybe I will. Thanks, Matthew, see you later!"

I waved and stepped back into the crowd of the house party. Scanning the main room where people were dancing and mingling, I didn't see him. I stepped toward the back of the house, where the entrance to the basement was. I was just about to step down the stairs when I saw Amy, Ronny, and Edgar making their way up with mixed drinks in their hands.

"Hey, guys! How's your night going?" I asked as they reached the top of the staircase.

"Pretty good!" Ronny said. "There are a lot of hot guys here!"

I laughed and nodded and saw that Edgar was peeking at me and quickly turned away.

"Edgar, I loved your portrait. It was really beautiful," I said, looking right at him.

He ducked his head, and though it was hard to tell in the dim lighting, I think he blushed. "Uh…. Thanks, Gabe. I really liked yours too."

I smiled and thanked him, and noticed Amy and Ronny craning their heads toward the direction of the main room and the music.

"We'll see you both soon," Amy said, grabbing Ronny's hand and pulling him toward the main room. "We'll be on the dance floor!"

I turned back to Edgar to see that he was staring at me. "Did you actually like my portrait?" he asked, cocking his head.

"I honestly think it was the best one there," I said, nodding fiercely. "You're such an incredible painter. I think you captured so much in it. It was truly a work of art. It's obvious that you see the world in such an incredible way, you're just… really special."

He smiled and shook his head. "Thanks. I'm not sure I agree, but I appreciate it. It was a struggle. I think I'm just really hard on myself sometimes. I'm glad you liked it, though."

When he looked up at me and smiled, I could feel something lurch in my chest. I hadn't noticed before that his eyes were a beautiful mossy green, and his smile was so sweet and pure. What I felt for him may not have exactly been love at first sight, but it was *something*.

"Are you having a good night?" I asked him, gesturing to his drink and then to the party.

He shrugged and tugged at the collar of the slim black turtleneck he wore. "I think it's just really loud up here. It was a lot more quiet in the basement."

"Do you want to go down there? Oh, or you probably want to catch back up with your friends. I'm sorry I've kept you."

He shook his head rapidly. "We can go to the basement," he said shyly, and then quickly grabbed my hand to lead me downstairs.

His touch was unexpected, and the feeling of his cold hand slipping into mine was one of the most exciting things to ever happen to me. We parked ourselves on a ratty old couch in the corner of the basement, and he let go of my hand with a smile. I immediately missed the sensation. We both took sips of our drinks and shuddered at the taste and then laughed at our reactions.

"It's pretty strong, isn't it?" he said, taking another sip, grimacing, and then placing his cup on the floor.

"Definitely," I said, following suit and doing the exact same. "So, Edgar, where are you from?"

It seemed as if we talked for hours. The more we talked, the more he seemed to open up, get animated. I had never met a boy like Edgar, someone who saw the world through such an expressive lens, someone who saw how both good and bad life could be. He was incredibly intelligent and surprisingly wonderful to talk to. I don't think I had ever been so free with another person, so soon into talking with them. He was special.

As we talked, I could feel us getting closer and closer to each other, the air becoming more electric with every second. Casual touches turned to meaningful ones, he leaned on my shoulder, and I wrapped my arms around him. Suddenly it seemed as if we were eye to eye, nose to nose, almost mouth to mouth. I looked down at his smooth pink lips, his dark lashes that framed two deep mossy green ponds. I leaned forward, slowly and deliberately, to kiss him. However, he put his fingers to my lips and pulled away.

"I'm so sorry, Edgar, I shouldn't—"

"No, no, it's not you. It's just that... I'm... I'm not like you."

I looked at him questioningly, unsure of what he was getting at. "Why do you think that?"

He bit his lip and looked away. "I'm trans, Gabe."

My eyes widened, and I leaned back, trying to process it. "You... you're going to start to transition to live as a woman?"

He sighed and shook his head. "No... the opposite. I wasn't... born Edgar. I... I have a—"

"Oh."

He nodded and looked across the room. I could feel Edgar pulling away, retreating back into himself, and I was desperate for that not to happen. I didn't want to lose the connection I'd made with the wonderful boy I had laid eyes on and hadn't forgotten from the moment I saw him.

"That doesn't make me want to kiss you any less."

He looked at me and blinked, and then put his hand on my jaw. I nodded, and he slowly leaned closer and closer to me until our lips brushed by, just barely touching. He seemed nervous at first, unsure of what to do. However, the more we kissed, the more he grabbed my shirt and pulled me closer.

I moaned, and though I had been kissed dozens of times in the past, this felt like the first time I really understood. Inside me, it felt like there had been a small bird in my chest flapping wildly, desperate to get free, and his kiss had opened the cage. It felt electric, and I was hyperaware of the room around me, the world around me. I opened my eyes, and when I saw him, I saw everything anew.

It was like there was a vibrance to the earth, new colors and textures and sounds that swirled around me. The green of his eyes, the creamy color of his skin, the colored lights of the party, everything danced in front of me in perfect harmony. In that moment I truly understood what Mr. Grant had meant about *seeing, feeling*.

I looked at the world, alive and electric, spinning and dancing and swirling. I looked back at Edgar, the sweet boy who had captured my attention from the first second I laid eyes on him, and I knew my attention would never waver. The who both set a fire inside me and would ground me. I smiled at him and leaned in, whispering in his ear, "Thank you, Edgar. Thank you for helping me to see."

A longtime storyteller, NICK ANTHONY loves to explore different mediums of communicating his thoughts and beliefs on what's going on around him. He enjoys writing about many different types of people, although he is especially fascinated by telling the stories of those who are just on the brink of finding out something extraordinary, whether it be about themselves or about the world around them. Not only a writer, Nick is a costume designer as well, and is based on the East Coast. He's incredibly excited not only to get more of his writing out in the world, but that he also has a fantastic group of friends and family who support him. If he could give a piece of advice to anyone, it would be "Love as you are loved."

Twitter: @NikkiGoons
Email: NickAnthony369@gmail.com

Of College and Lost Dogs
by Mattye Johnson

CAEL IS beginning to think that all those overload classes had been a mistake. At the time, the perks were numerous: financial aid from the state, more challenging classes in subject areas she actually cared about, and graduating high school a year early. Now, that last item is seeming a lot less enticing once she's actually stepped foot onto campus in preparation for her first day of college. *College.* She misses the days when that word seemed inconsequential; far enough in the future not to be dwelled upon for years to come. It happened so fast. One day she was entering her first day of junior high and swearing she would never grow up enough to go to high school, and now she's in *college*, not just to look around the campus or to chat with advisors that are always looking over her instead of at her, but to go to classes and join clubs and meet professors.

Thankfully it's a community college, and she lives close enough to drive to campus every day, because she *knows* she can't handle a roommate or living in an unfamiliar place for so long. She glances at the brick building standing in front of her once more to ensure that it is, in fact, the site for her Introduction to Sociology class, and when she assures herself that it is, she follows the steady trail of students through the door.

It's not at all like her high school—where there were desks, there are now long tables that seat eight or nine people, and where there were chairs there are stools that look like they swivel in circles. For a moment Cael entertains the thought of spinning on one of them and has to quickly remind herself that this is college, and people would stare, and she'd possibly never make any friends for the duration of her two years here. That thought firmly in mind, she slips into a seat at the table in the back corner of the room, inhabited only by a boy who is furiously taking notes on the first page of what appears to be a brand-new notebook. He doesn't look up when she sits down or acknowledge her hesitant greeting, so she falls into silence and hopes that no one else sits down at the table.

As usual, fate betrays her, and two other people slide into seats on either side of the boy. Cael's ready to be annoyed, to cover herself even more and hide in her hoodie, when she gets a good look at the girl and is struck by how beautiful she is.

She greets the newcomers, hoping to grab the attention of the girl, but the only response she receives is a short wave from the boy who just sat down. The girl ignores her, as the other boy had, and Cael is starting to wonder if she is simply that undesirable to speak to.

The girl playfully taps the boy on the shoulder, causing him to look up and his pencil to clatter onto the table beside the half-filled page of his notebook. He grins when he sees her and hastily makes a sort of salute, thumb tucked into his palm. It's kind of strange, but this is college, and Cael reminds herself that strange things happen at college; that's the majority of the appeal. The girl repeats the motion back, her grin just as obvious, and Cael finds that she is aching to speak to her, despite the rude brush-off moments before.

"Hey," she tries again, this time looking directly at the girl, and is met with a look of annoyance from the boy who arrived with the girl and sat down next to her.

"My friends can't hear you," he says, exasperation clear in his tone. "Can't you see them signing?"

Signing? It takes a moment for her brain to catch on to the words, to connect a schema to them that makes sense in context. Now she sees them moving their hands in animated gestures, accompanied by the occasional lip movement, but absolutely no sound is uttered by either of them.

"They're deaf?" she asks, just to be sure, and the boy nods back.

"I'm Milo," he says after a moment, and taps the girl on the shoulder before signing something quickly that Cael has no hope of understanding.

The girl turns with a bright smile and signs something, deliberate pauses between the hand shapes. Cael thinks one of them sort of looks like an *I*, and one resembles an *L*, but other than that she is completely lost.

"That's Haile," Milo translates, eyes softening when he looks at her.

Cael wonders if they're together, or if they're just good friends. Up to that moment Milo had seemed awfully brash, especially compared to this new expression. Haile signs something else, her smile seemingly permanent. Cael looks to Milo for help, and he scowls but speaks again.

"That's her sign name."

He signs something to Haile, ending with a gesture to the other boy, who she immediately turns to tap on the shoulder, as he had already gone back to scribbling notes. She signs to him, prompting him to smile and repeat the modified salute, and then make gestures similar to the ones Haile had when she was conveying her name.

"Glenn. That's his sign name."

Cael nods, no longer knowing what to say. She wants to speak to Haile, more than anything, but she doesn't know a single word in American Sign Language, and if she were to attempt it, she's afraid that she would look like a depraved pantomime. It opens a hole in her chest, seeing them sign, and memories of her grandmother flood back and saturate her brain. Her grandmother was profoundly deaf, she was born that way, and when she was young Cael always wished she could learn sign to speak to her. Unfortunately, she never picked it up, and her grandmother passed away when Cael was six, so she never got the chance. Even now, she regrets it. When her grandmother was alive, they had spoken in their own language, a combination of miming, pointing at assorted objects, and writing things down, but they were never able to have a conversation, at least not really, not the way Cael sees it.

"Are you fluent?" she settles on asking Milo, trying to think of something, *anything*, that could help her have a conversation with Haile, who has gone back to looking over Glenn's shoulder at his notes. Milo shrugs, clearly not excited to continue the conversation, but it seems he's resigned himself to the fact that Cael isn't leaving.

"Pretty much. I translate for Haile and Glenn in class, and since my mom is deaf, I'm fairly fluent."

Cael spends a moment wondering how he takes notes if he's translating, but she seems to recall someone saying something about most lectures being recorded, depending on the professor, so she supposes that's an option. Before Cael can think of another question, Haile looks up and signs something to Milo with excitement. Her hands move so quickly Cael is astounded that Milo can follow, and her facial expressions follow each sign, changing as the sentiment of the sentence changes. Milo signs something back, hands moving more robotically than hers do and not quite as quickly. Still, it's obvious that he is extremely familiar with the language.

The professor begins to speak, something about how she knows none of them will read and abide by the syllabus, and that she is more than prepared to direct them to it when they have questions that could be answered with a glance over it. Haile glances at Cael, motioning from her back to herself, and signs something else, face contorted into a question expression, head cocked and eyebrows furrowed. Milo sighs and nods, turning back to Cael.

"She wants to know if you'll join us for lunch later. We're going to this new place that Glenn found. It's supposed to have good muffins."

Even without the muffins, Cael is sold. She says as much, though too quickly and stumbling over her words. With a shake of his head, Milo signs something to Haile, who grins and shoots Cael a bright smile.

Cael wishes, more than anything else, that she could tell her how beautiful her smile is.

AT LUNCH, Cael learns how to spell her own name. And Haile's, and Glenn's, but not Milo's, because he maintains that he is only there to translate and to have other people buy him food, not to be involved in the festivities. This new knowledge came out of ten minutes of painful silence where the other three spoke among themselves, using only sign, and Cael sat and watched them, not knowing a thing that was going on. Finally, Haile had proposed to Milo that they all teach her how to fingerspell, and he begrudgingly participated in vocalizing each letter as Haile or Glenn signed it.

She learns the sign for "name" as well—the first two fingers of her right hand tapping against a solid base of the first two fingers of her left hand. Haile looks ecstatic when Cael successfully explains in sign what her name is. Numbers, when they finally get to them, are much easier, and Cael learns in less than five minutes that Haile is eighteen, Glenn is nineteen, and that Milo is nearly nineteen and a half, emphasis on the half. For her part, Cael tells them she is seventeen.

"I'd love to be able to learn more, to talk to you without Milo," Cael says once they've all finished eating and teaching her to fingerspell most of the letters semicompetently. Milo shoots her an offended glance but relays the information to Haile, who smiles and taps Glenn on the shoulder. After a brief exchange, he hands her a piece of notebook paper and a pen, and she hastily scribbles down something on it and slides it across the table.

It's a number, presumably Haile's, with the words "text me! let's meet again tomorrow, does my dorm work for you? dorm B, room 11."

"That's perfect," Cael says, attempting to convey her answer with an awkward thumbs-up and a grin. Milo rolls his eyes at her feeble attempt, but when he goes to inform Haile of her answer, Haile playfully grabs his hands out of midair and shakes her head.

"Apparently your awful attempt at communication worked," Milo says, but he has that softness again, the one that only appears when Haile engages him in conversation or Glenn sends him a smirk across the table.

Whenever Glenn gets close enough to touch him, he does, often a gentle brush on the shoulder or brief contact between their hands. It's enough to make Cael wonder if there's something she's missing.

The whole drive home, all her mind is willing to entertain is that she has the number of the most beautiful girl on campus, she can fingerspell and sign said girl's name, and she's going to hang out in said girl's dorm tomorrow.

Suddenly, college doesn't seem as intimidating.

"YOU'RE HOME late" are the first words out of her mother's mouth. They're enough to make Cael miss the relative silence of lunch, so many words conveyed with so little sound. She can't get Haile out of her head, and the giddy feeling is still there, deep in the pit of her stomach, so she simply smiles at her mother and throws her backpack onto the couch.

"Yep, sorry. I went to lunch with some people I met today. I figured it would be okay."

It's a constant struggle—her mother wants her to go out, to meet people, to be social, and yet she has professed on numerous different occasions that she doesn't want her to grow up too fast, doesn't want her to stay out too late with the wrong people. When her mother talks about who the wrong people are exactly, they're always "them," faceless people shrouded in secrecy that Cael cannot help but imagine in oversized black hoodies.

"I suppose that's fine," her mother says, still appearing marginally concerned for her daughter. "I'm glad that you made friends so quickly."

"They're not friends yet," Cael corrects, because the last thing she needs is her mother inviting them over and seeing how Cael looks at Haile when she isn't looking, or the rosy blush that coats her cheeks when Haile laughs at a joke from Cael that Milo has translated. Plus, if her mother saw them signing and mentioned Cael's grandmother, she might have a breakdown on the spot, the last thing she wants to do in front of her new almost-friends.

"Will they be?"

Cael wants them to be, truly. She wants it so much that she aches, so she finds herself nodding.

"I hope so, Mom."

Too honest, it reveals more than Cael is comfortable with, but her brain is sluggish from the excitement of the day, and the words slip from her mouth without much consultation with her. Her mother hugs her from behind, arms wrapped around her shoulder in a quick embrace.

"I'm glad, honey. I was so worried that college would be overwhelming. I'm happy that you found your tribe."

Cael makes a face and pulls away.

"Tribe sounds so stupid," she says, not for the first time, not for the tenth time, but it's what her mother insists on calling the people who she will meet in college that are unlike the kids who went to her high school, people she has more than a location in common with.

"Maybe one day I'll listen," her mom teases, moving back to where she was working on compiling a stack of papers.

"We can only hope," Cael teases back, planting a quick kiss on her mother's cheek. "Want help with dinner?"

Her mother shakes her head absently, already focused on the papers yet again.

"No thanks, honey, I'm sure you've got homework. I've got soup on. It should be done in an hour or so."

Cael grabs her backpack, thankfully void of any such homework and instead filled with folded-up syllabuses, and goes downstairs to her room. All she can think of is Haile, and how much she would love to say something to her without Milo being intimately privy to it, as he is when he translates. It's not five minutes later when she has her computer open and Google pulled up, trying to think of the best way to ask the internet for phrases in American Sign Language.

It takes nearly an hour and an intense session of trial and error, but finally she compiles a set of signs that make her feel prepared. Like perhaps she can gain some sort of relevancy in Haile's life, perhaps even friendship.

She doesn't think about how it feels, just a bit, like making up for never learning to speak with her grandmother.

She doesn't even let herself hope for what she dreams of. It's not like she's been in a relationship since middle school, not like Lucas Relan really counted at all.

As IT turns out, mentally rehearsing the few signs she memorized the night before is a stressful activity in itself. Mentally rehearsing them while attempting to find a beautiful girl's dorm room, a girl she gets butterflies from even looking at, is significantly more stressful. She's armed with a notebook this time, and more pens than probably necessary, because she's not sure she could cope with another awkward silence.

Dorm B isn't hard to find. There are only dorms labeled A-C, understandable as the majority of students live at home. There are only three or four people in the hallway, all sitting in a circle at the end and bent over a collection of books and binders. Cael's eyes skirt the edge of their circle, avoiding eye contact as much as she possibly can. Haile's room is only a few rooms up the hall, just enough time for Cael to be gripped with the sudden panic about if Haile has a roommate or not. Will they be nice? Will they even be there?

Too late now. Cael reaches the door and knocks on it before she can stop herself with another unfounded anxiety. A moment passes, and then the door opens, but instead of Haile at the other side, it's a German shepherd with unusually long fur and furiously wagging tail. Haile is right behind the dog, her usual smile present.

"Who's this?" Cael asks, and then she bites her tongue, because of course Haile can't hear her, how dumb is she. With fumbling fingers, she pulls the notebook from her pocket, flips to the first blank page she sees, and quickly writes down her question. She presents it to Haile, who holds out her hand to take it and the pen. She gestures for Cael to come in and closes the door behind them, her dog returning to a small dog bed next to the bed Haile leads Cael to. She must have a roommate, because there is another one on the other side of the room, substantially messier than hers, the blanket lumped up into a mound on top of it.

Come to think of it, there's a shock of messy black hair peeking out from under it, the indication of the presence of a person. Cael is about to ask, before she remembers she needs the notepad for that, so she looks back to Haile, who has just finished writing. Haile hands her the notebook, which offers an explanation for the dog.

"that's anna, she's my service dog that hears things for me :). like when you knocked, she went to the door. i normally take her to class but she was a little sick yesterday."

Cael is quick to scribble down her response. "Is the person in the other bed your roommate? Is Anna doing better than yesterday?"

It's clunky and time-consuming, but talking to Haile is worth it. Haile reads the note and looks up with a smile and a nod. She points to Anna and nods, and then points to the other bed and signs "*Glenn*."

That's new, and Cael doesn't quite know how to process it. Normally a boy and a girl living together only means one thing, and they didn't *seem* like it yesterday. It seemed like Glenn was into Milo, but appearances can be deceiving.

"Are you and Glenn together?" she writes, trying not to hope for anything but an affirmative answer.

Haile reads the note, eyebrows scrunching up. She brings her first three fingers together in a decisive action, a beat between the action and the moment she seems to realize that Cael doesn't know what she means. Instead, she opts for shaking her head aggressively, a twinkle in her eyes that suggests humor.

"No!" she writes, pen digging in a bit more than usual. "we're just friends. he's sleeping right now, milo kept him up late last night studying. he'll never notice we're here until he wakes up. do you want to learn some words in sign?"

This is her opportunity to display what she learned in an attempt to impress Haile. Cael takes a breath, allowing a moment for it to pass through her body, sucking some jitters with it, and then smiles and begins to sign.

"*You're beautiful, I wanted to tell you.*"

She stumbles over a couple of the signs, but not horribly, and not enough that they don't invoke a rosy blush over Haile's cheeks and cause her smile to grow ever larger, hands moving in the air for a bit in excitement before returning to the notepad. She takes longer to respond, pen stuttering after every few words, causing Cael to bite her lip and hope she wasn't too forward. She thought this was acceptable in college, that the games of high school were over, but now she's not sure, and the delayed response kills her slowly until Haile hands the notebook back.

"you too, cael," she has written. "it was so cool of you to learn some sign for me! wow. i was thinking i'd teach you basic greetings today, if that sounds all right."

It reads like a stream of consciousness, endearing in the best way. Cael finds she doesn't even care that Haile didn't address the romantic implications of the statement, just basks in her approval.

Haile claps her hands together in excitement and gestures to the paper. Cael has a feeling that it means something to the effect of "Let's begin!"

As it turns out, the odd salute-like gesture means "hello," and the universally accepted wave means "goodbye." She learns "nice to meet you" as well, along with several other phrases that Haile deems important. She also learns that Haile loves art and math, two seemingly opposite disciplines, and that she can do equations Cael cannot even comprehend. She paints as well, although that is evident from the canvases spread throughout the room with paint caking the frames. Glenn somehow sleeps through it all, soft snores traveling across the room and a brief snuffling from time to time. All that's ever visible of the boy is his messy clump of hair, and it seems to become curlier in his sleep.

"He must have been really tired," Cael attempts to convey, the notebook now covered in scribbled descriptions of greetings and abstract words. She starts with Glenn's name, one of the signs she remembers clearly, and then creates a mix of charades and gestures to convey sleep. Haile nods as if she understands and signs Milo's name with a knowing smirk. She flattens her left palm and uses her right to move her splayed fingertips resting on the palm, hand slowly closing until it reaches her forehead and all of the fingers of her right hand touch. After, she points at books and mouths "learn," which Cael is fairly proud to figure out after only a few seconds of staring.

Anna has been sleeping as well, nose pointed toward the door but nonetheless a picture of rest. She's like a magnet. Cael can't help but look at her, and she feels a content expression dawn over her features at the sight of the large dog.

For a moment she visualizes Haile and herself, studying on her bed, Anna curled up behind them, head resting on the pillow. It's a nice picture, one so domestic that Cael doesn't know whether to laugh or cry, and yet it doesn't sound so taxing if she gets to spend more time with Haile.

Haile hands her the notebook again, having somehow found a blank page.

"want to come to lunch with Glenn and milo and i tomorrow? we're going to some new coffee-bar thing, and we could teach you some more. it would probably be easier with milo there to translate, anyway."

No notebook is needed to translate Cael's energetic nod. She wants to inform Haile that she likes it when it's just them, that Milo wouldn't make it easier, but that's for another time, because now she's just been invited out by the prettiest girl she's ever seen, even if her friends are going to be there. And besides, her friends aren't too bad. She's nearly grown fond of Glenn, entirely through his snoring and hair, which she supposes says something.

Either way, things are looking up.

"How can you not like bagels?" Milo appears positively scandalized, his whole body tilted away from Cael in faux disgust. "Bagels are the food of the gods for lowly, struggling college students like us."

Glenn snorts, signing something quickly, which Haile laughs at. Milo flips him off and then remembers Cael's existence and translates.

"He informed me that we are exactly three days into the semester and it's too early to be struggling. A completely biased and unfair assessment, if I do say so myself. It's never too early to struggle. It's college."

"Completely unfair," Cael agrees. "College is designed for struggle. But I still don't like bagels."

"I was following you there for a second," Milo says, voice drawling and monotone as usual. "But then you lost me when you disgraced the only acceptable breakfast food."

It's fascinating, watching his hands move in a language she cannot begin to understand. She can tell that the emphasis on the signs are different from the emphasis on the speech directly preceding it, and she wonders, not for the first time, how he manages to keep it all straight.

Haile signs something in return. The only words that Cael recognizes are "good" and "bagel"; since bagels had been the highlight of their discussion for the past five minutes, she picked up the sign.

"Apparently they're good with butter," Milo says, gesturing to Haile when he speaks. Glenn contributes something with a grin.

"And Glenn likes them with jam," Milo says, none of the fondness fading from his voice. "Strawberry jam," he corrects quickly at another insistent sign from Glenn.

"Did anyone actually understand the math from today?" Cael asks, because Analytic Geometry is the one class they're all in excepting Sociology, which means that they have classes together Mondays, Wednesdays, Thursdays, and Fridays. Five minutes into the lecture, she was already horribly lost and trying to decide if she even knows how to add or multiply, much less anything presented in the class.

Haile nods, a smile breaking out over her features. She signs something that causes Glenn to groan and Milo to make a face.

"Haile's wrong," he announces to the table at large. "That was *not* easy, and certainly not enjoyable."

Glenn is already signing, face twisted into a look of disgust that morphs into confusion. Milo nods in agreement before translating.

"It seems that Haile is the only one here who retained anything from the lecture. Which also means that it's her job to teach us the rest of the year." At Cael's questioning glance, he elaborates. "Every semester we all get together on Saturdays, and whoever's good at a subject teaches the rest. So Haile's usually in charge of math, I've got psychology and philosophy, and Glenn is our savior in history and science."

He turns to Glenn and signs something. Glenn makes another face and replies. Haile nods along to whatever point he's making, eyebrows furrowed and hair fluttering with the movements of her head.

"It's hard to keep up with the professor in Geometry," Milo says as Glenn signs. "It—there's a lot of motion, a lot of chaos, and Milo can't interpret fast enough a lot of the time because—the professor never stops fucking talking."

Haile's signing yes as Glenn speaks, Cael remembers that motion, and then Milo takes over speaking for her when Glenn is done.

"Yes, in Microbiology the professor doesn't make a lot of sense, and he's always turned away from us, so I can't even try to figure out what Milo misses. That man is an asshole." Milo speaks for himself in the last sentence, scowling at the apparent thought of their microbiology professor.

"Are you all in all of the same classes?" Cael asks curiously, because that seems odd considering the different tracks they're all on. Milo nods, though.

"It's easier for me to just interpret for them right now, and it's mostly general classes anyway, so it works out for all of us. The college doesn't really know what to do with Glenn or Haile, so when they found out I learned to sign because my mom is deaf, they stuck us all together. It's also why they let Haile and Glenn room together, even though the dorm isn't co-ed by room."

Glenn taps the table to gain their attention, frustration evident on his face. Milo nods and speaks when Glenn begins to sign.

"It's like they see us as without sex—not capable of intimacy or something. Just because our ears don't work doesn't mean the rest of us doesn't." It's apparently a sore subject for Glenn, as his features become a picture of controlled anger.

Haile places a hand on his shoulder and signs something, and he responds. Milo translates with a laugh.

"I know we're both gay, but still. It's the principle." Milo falls silent and signs something back, probably somewhat of an inside joke because both Haile and Glenn laugh. Cael doesn't inquire into it. She does, however, latch on to the declaration that Haile is, in fact, interested in girls, which is suddenly the best news she's heard all year. It's too perfect, really—a beautiful girl with an adorable dog and great friends, *and* she likes girls.

"Do you want to study with us on Saturday?" Milo asks, in a brief moment where he has lost his usual smugness. Cael jumps at the chance.

"Yeah, that would be great. Where should I meet you?"

Milo reaches down to feed Anna a bit of toast, earning himself a playful slap from Haile and a firm reprimand.

"Their dorm is good. You any good at English?"

THERE'S SOMETHING to be said for setting your ringtone as different from your alarm sound, especially when the phone rings in the middle of the night.

Cael would have ignored it and written it off as a telemarketer, except the contact name reads "Haile" and Cael jolts into a sitting position and answers it, praying that something bad didn't happen that would cause someone to call her on Haile's phone.

"Hello?" she responds, not sure who will answer, but all she receives is silence and then the ominous click that signals the end of a call. She's already a split second away from clicking Callback when her phone chimes with a text.

> *Haile* ♥
> *sorry i woke you! it was the only way i was sure you would notice my text and i need your help. anna is gone and milo isn't picking up, and neither is glenn, and he isn't in the room. can you come and help me find anna??*

Cael scrambles to type back that she'll be there as soon as she can. Thank God her mother sleeps like the dead, and thank God she finally got her own car a short month before. It's laughably easy to exit the house: the floor doesn't squeak and the door doesn't slam, not like in all those movies she watched about teenagers sneaking out to go to parties while she sat at home on the couch with her mom. At the time she envied them, but now she's not so sure, because it's raining and seems to be getting darker by the second, and driving seems like an especially perilous pastime. Still, she can't even dream of not showing up on campus for Haile, so she turns onto the road, rain beating down on her car and headlights seeming far too bright in contrast with the darkness seeping over her.

The campus is less than a half hour away, a bit more with how overly cautious Cael is being due to the rain. She *wants* to careen to the campus as quickly as possible, and her fear of crashing is the only thing holding her back. A few cars pass her, and her immediate reaction is to wonder what in the hell they're doing out at three in the morning, disregarding that she too is out at three. She wonders if they question why she is out like she questions why they are.

God, she's worried. *Anna.* What if something happened, what if they don't find her? It's a chilling thought, one that grips her with fear and refuses to let go, even when she pulls into the parking lot in front of Haile's residence hall. The parking lot is full, as it should be; it's the middle of the *night*, and *fuck*, Cael doesn't know what to do. She can't enter the dorm, not without a key card that she doesn't have, so she texts Haile a short message informing her of her arrival.

It's only a moment later when Haile bursts through the doors, makeup smeared but composure mostly intact. She looks utterly drained, and yet her eyes are wide and looking around the parking lot.

Cael's phone dings.

> *Haile* ♥
> *she was gone an hour ago, and she's not anywhere in the building. can you call her? i think maybe she escaped and she's on the grounds somewhere. walk around with me?*

"Of course," Cael says aloud, nodding to accent her point. She calls for the dog, and when no dog arrives, she walks after Haile, who has motioned for her to follow. The rain hasn't let up at all. She's already soaked, her hair sticking to her scalp and the back of her neck. Grass concedes to puddles of water as they walk on it, and she's beginning to hope that Anna is lost on the path somewhere and not back in the woods behind the campus, not the area Haile keeps nervously eyeing as if she doesn't want to mention it. At least the path is lit by failing excuses for streetlights; the woods are completely shrouded in darkness, and the trees seem nearly menacing.

"Anna!" Cael calls for what seems like the hundredth time, hoping the dog will come running to them, tongue hanging out and somehow looking smug even though she's a dog.

No such luck.

She taps Haile's shoulder and signs Glenn's name, accenting it with a questioning expression. She hopes it makes sense that she's asking if Haile ever found Glenn. Haile shakes her head, and for the first time Cael notices small tear tracks that originate from her eyes. She's shaking too, shivering in the cold and looking around for her dog that doesn't seem to be anywhere to be found. The forest seems more and more like a distinct possibility, and yet it's the last thing Cael wants to consider.

"Anna! Anna, come here!" Cael calls again. Only this time, a sound emanates from beside them, from inside the brick that comprises Dorm C.

The bark of a dog.

"Haile!" Cael says, tapping her shoulder with a sense of urgency she wasn't sure she was capable of mere seconds ago. Haile whips around to face her, expression twisted into a mix between questioning and hope.

Cael gestures toward the building, fingerspelling to Haile. A-N-N-A. Haile brightens, pointing at the building and then repeating Cael's spelling, this time considerably faster and without the noticeable pauses as Cael tried to think of the correct handshape.

They speed up, moving toward the building that is completely silent except for the bark that Cael had heard. It's dark as well, understandable at three thirty in the morning on a Thursday. Haile flashes her card, which evidently works for all the dorms, unless she has one for when she visits Milo, and they push the doors open. Cael calls for Anna again, hoping no one wakes up and asks why she's there. The dog barks again, just a few rooms down the hall, and she moves toward it in a modified walking-running motion that carries her until she stops in front of the door the dog is evidently behind.

"*Milo*," Haile signs, staring at the door. She looks hurt and a bit surprised, which is enough for Cael to infer that this dorm room houses none other than one Milo Smite.

Haile yanks open the door and reaches out to flip on the lights, hands falling to rest on her hips as she takes in the sight in front of her. Milo is asleep in the bed on the right side of the room, and in his bed, covered in what appears to be rainbow food coloring, is Anna, who has perked up to look at them. Her tail wags, conveying her excitement, and although Cael knows she doesn't do it on purpose, it's a *little* funny when it hits Milo square in the face.

"What the fuck," he mutters, eyes opening to find out what woke him. Haile stalks over to the bed, eyes fiery as they set sights on Milo. She signs something, motions sharp and concise, gestures painfully precise. The boy sits up, eyes still cloudy with sleep. He responds, his gestures sluggish and large, as though he hasn't woken up enough to care.

"Hey, what the fuck is going on? Why did you take Anna?" Cael finally asks, fed up with whatever excuses Milo is sure to be using. He shoots her an annoyed look but switches to English, voice just as subdued as his signs.

"We were *trying* to get Haile's party ready. She wasn't supposed to notice until Glenn got back to bring her to it."

"Why is the dog rainbow?" Because *honestly*, that seems like a pertinent question right now.

"For the party," Milo says, as if they are both so incredibly stupid he cannot understand it. Haile is staring at him, lost, because he hasn't bothered to translate any of his words for her.

"The dog is rainbow for Haile's coming-out party. She came out to all of us this time last year, and Glenn and I thought we would throw her a party. To remember it. Except you weren't supposed to find out at *three in the fucking morning*."

Haile has given up trying to follow the conversation and instead elected to sit on the bed with Anna and run her shaky hands through her fur. Cael doesn't quite know what to say. She doesn't know Milo well enough to truly yell at him, but at the same time, she can't believe he took Haile's dog without even *asking*.

"Where's Glenn?" she asks instead. Milo sighs, ignoring Haile's signed question, which seems like a complete dick move.

"He's getting shit for the party. He should be back by now; he might have gone to his room."

Haile shoots Milo one last dirty look and slides off the bed, Anna jumping off after her. She approaches Cael, and before she can even question what is happening, Haile presses a soft kiss to her lips. After she pulls away, she signs something, and Cael desperately looks to Milo for a translation, which he grudgingly gives.

"She said thank you."

WITH A text to her mother, Cael stays in Haile's room that night. She doesn't have any of her clothes or her textbooks, but Haile lends her shorts and a tank top to sleep in, and when it is discovered that Glenn is back and sound asleep in his bed, Haile elects to lecture him in the morning.

When Cael is preparing to find a place to sleep on the floor, perhaps with a stolen blanket or two, Haile shakes her head and pats the bed. For a moment Cael isn't certain that she is actually being invited to sleep in the other girl's bed, but when the patting becomes more insistent she carefully crawls into it. It's a strange feeling, because she hasn't slept in someone else's bed since she was seven, at a sleepover with four other people. She thinks normally she would be nervous, but the toll of waking up in the middle of the night, driving to campus, and looking for Anna was enough to diminish that. Anna sleeps with them, Haile's hand never breaking contact with her fur the entire night. Anna wakes them as well; evidently she's trained to recognize Haile's alarm clock and wake up her and Glenn, and it's somewhat of a pleasant surprise to wait up to a dog's cheerful face and a sound of a new alarm rather than the normal alarm Cael sets that she's learned to despise.

Haile is unnaturally cheerful in the morning, all smiles and floating motions. Glenn has to be woken three times to even consider getting out of bed, and even then he takes a solid half an hour to wake up enough to put on different clothes. It's odd, waking up and getting ready for the day with two other people in complete silence, and yet a whole conversation's going on that she doesn't understand any of, except for the occasional mention of Milo or a common sign like "yes" or "no." When she recognizes one, even if it is just a simple affirmative, Cael can't help but feel a little proud, like maybe, someday, she might be able to hold a conversation with Haile in her language. For now she settles on taking the clothes Haile offers her and then sitting on the bed, writing in her notebook, and trying to remember what she learned in class last Tuesday. Plus, there's the supposed party Milo and Glenn were planning, even if that whole encounter and the search for Anna feels more like a fever dream than an event that actually occurred. She's not sure how to bring up the kiss, so she doesn't, and focuses on forgetting it, because there's no way it will happen again.

Just before they are about to leave for class, conveniently sharing their first class period, Milo arrives at the door with an apologetic grimace and a box of doughnuts. Haile glances at Glenn, seemingly remembering that she never gave him that lecture, but lets Milo in anyway, even though Cael is fairly certain it has more to do with the doughnuts than any desire to converse with him. He signs something to her, and while she remains looking unimpressed with what he's saying, she takes a doughnut and hands the box to Glenn.

"Would you just follow me? Fuck class, I promise this is worth it," Milo finally settles on saying, this time translating it into English as well for Cael's benefit. And, well, she knows there's something bad about following men with doughnuts and vague promises, but Haile already is, and Glenn is trailing behind them, smirking like he distinctly had something to do with this. The dog is still rainbow, which either adds to the hilarity of the situation or derails it more. Cael can't decide.

They trek across campus, Cael only feeling one stab of guilt for missing class, especially her first week of college. She reminds herself that she'd rather be with Haile and Glenn and Milo, and that she has to see this party they set up, because it's bound to be something entertaining at worst.

It's right at the edge of the woods, far enough away from the center of campus that the buildings are hardly visible, but not deep enough in the woods for there to be a chance of a bear attack. It's a sight. There are rainbow balloons hanging from at least three trees and a large banner strung across two of them that reads "Congrats! You're gay!" with the "gay" above a word that has been completely scribbled out in black

Sharpie. There's a table too, one of those small camping ones that's used for drinks, that contains a plate of cupcakes and a stack of cups but no apparent liquid to put in the cups. Even so, it's obvious that effort was put into setting it up, and Cael's anger at Milo for taking Anna lessens, just a bit.

Glenn pecks Milo on the lips, and Cael just catches it when she turns from looking at the spectacle in front of them. Glenn blushes when he sees she's noticed, but Milo doesn't, just stands there, infuriatingly calm as always.

"When did that happen?" Cael asks, mimicking Haile's questioning gaze.

Milo shrugs, pulling Glenn even closer.

"When we were setting up the party. Nothing like a pitch-black forest and freezing rain to bring about romance."

Haile signs something that looks suspiciously akin to something like "finally," and Glenn snorts.

"When are you going to get on with it and ask Cael out?" Milo asks, eyebrows raised as he signs to Haile and speaks aloud as if it's an afterthought.

Haile rolls her eyes at him, but she doesn't address how frozen Cael suddenly gets at the prospect, the utterly amazing and *thrilling* prospect of Haile being her girlfriend or even liking her, and seriously *when did that happen?* Instead she grabs the notebook and scribbles down a sentence, which she shows to Cael.

"it'd be cool if we went out."

And Cael signs yes, because she knows how, and because it's enough, and she hopes it accurately conveys her excitement. She tries to think of something else, *anything* Haile has taught her, but she can't, so instead she presses her lips to Haile's and hopes it's clear enough.

It is.

MATTYE JOHNSON writes of places where she wishes she could go and people who she wishes she could meet. She likes animals—and has too many to count at this point—but they include a miniature horse named Amber, who seems to be made out of solid gold, and a rooster that she has slowly won over. Her sense of humor includes taking pictures next to road signs in various cities that contain the word "Broadway" and immediately joking that it's the closest she'll ever get, due to being trapped in a small town in Idaho. She's, to quote a tweet by Andy Mientus, "sad and scary and bi and young and furious and fabulous." She's still working on the "fabulous" part, but she's getting there.

2:00 A.M.
by Sonali Gattani

[iMESSAGE]
[THU, DEC 1, 8:19 AM]
    New phone who did
    FUCK
    ***dis

    Oh my god stop spamming me, it was one typo

    You're literally the worst
    Posner heard my phone vibrating because of your spam
    I swear if I get detention because of you…

    But you are also on your phone in class
    Hypocrisy much??

    [Thu, Dec 1, 8:44 AM]

    I don't deserve to be attacked like this

    I'M TURNING MY PHONE OFF
    KARA USES SPAM. IT HAS NO EFFECT.

    BYE I'LL SEE YOU IN HELL

[MON, DEC 12, 4:14 PM]
    Listen

    No, shut up
    You didn't have a frickin freshman flirting with you all throughout lunch
    She put her HAND on my THIGH

    I AM GAY, HOW DO YOU NOT SEE THE PROBLEM?

    I come to you in this, my most vulnerable moment, and you TEASE me

Worst best friend ever istg
I'm revoking your best friend privileges

That's right
You have to make your own popcorn tonight
No mooching off me, I don't care how badly you burn yours

Sorry pal I don't make the rules
Talk shit get hit
Metaphorically hit, because I am weak, but hit nonetheless

Are you trying to flatter your way back into my good books?
Because if so
Flattery will get you everywhere

You know, I could get used to this "O Benevolent Majesty" thing

[WED, DEC 21, 2:31 PM]
FREEDOM

Okay but you're a nerd, so your opinion doesn't count

We both know you're already thinking about how many chapters you wanna get ahead for calc over break
For some absurd reason, the sight of an integral doesn't fill you with inexplicable terror

Math is the devil's handiwork, you'll never convince me otherwise

[Wed, Dec 21, 3:15 PM]

ANYWAY
Enough talk about the unspeakable horrors of calculus
You're still coming over on Christmas Eve, right?

Just making sure
It would be awkward if I set out an extra plate and everything and
you just
Didn't come

AW YISS
IT'S GONNA BE LIT

[Wed, Dec 21, 4:55 PM]

Oh btw
You aren't allowed to bring your calc textbook with you
Or I won't let you into my house

Watch me
I'll go through your whole backpack I don't give a fuck

You know you love me
Deep down in your cold cold heart, you love me

[MON, DEC 26, 11:16 AM]

I have not stopped playing with this fidget cube all day tysm omg
Best Christmas present ever

[MON, JAN 9, 1:30 AM]

Yeah, what's up?

Nah, I was just rewatching Sailor Moon, nothing important

Shit, that's awful
I'm so sorry Kara. You shouldn't have to go through this.
I hate that they say all this stuff to you that's blatantly not true
And I hate that it makes you doubt yourself like this
You're not stupid for getting a B on one single test

You're not a freak for being ace
They're your family. They shouldn't be calling you names.

Of course you're gonna be okay
You're so close to graduating! And then after that you'll be out of their reach and you'll have your whole life ahead of you and no one will be able to tell you what to do!
You're really strong, you know? You didn't think you'd survive all these years, but you did. You found a way to keep going. And if you could make it through the past 18 years, you can make it through these last 5 months. I know you can.

Things may seem scary rn but
You're gonna be okay

[Mon, Jan 9, 2:48 AM]

If it counts for anything at all…
I believe in you
A lot
And we both know I'm never wrong

So if you don't believe in yourself
Believe in the me that believes in you

[THU, JAN 26, 7:35 PM]
Hey, sorry for going MIA, rehearsal ended super late

It's going pretty well
At this point we're just drilling lines and polishing choreography
It's basically the "practice" part of "practice makes perfect"

Of course we're gonna be perfect
WAIT OH MY GOD YOU MADE ME JINX IT

You know, as a member of the cast, I get a free ticket to the Saturday matinee
And I was GOING to give it to you
But I guess now I'll just have to give it to someone else

Because SOMEONE decided it would be funny to jinx 8 weeks of grueling hard work

Well
Maybe I could be persuaded otherwise
If you helped me out with something

WTF, why did you say no, I didn't even say what it was yet
Why are you so mean to meee

Okay, fine, you're right, I'm totally gonna ask you for calc help
Please please pleaaaase
I'm looking at the first problem and I can't even tell what derivative I'm supposed to be taking
And I still have a lit essay and history readings to finish tonight; I can't afford to spend like 3 hours on calc hw

[Thu, Jan 26, 10:04 PM]

YOU ARE AN ANGEL
The matinee ticket is yours
Anyone else who wants it will have to pry it from my cold, dead hands
After which they will have to face your wrath, as you avenge both my death and the insult to your good name
ANY POTENTIAL THIEF IS A DEAD (WO)MAN, I SWEAR IT BY THE OLD GODS AND THE NEW

Honestly what else did you expect from a theater kid though?

[WED, FEB 15, 1:16 AM]
We should make a pact
If we're both still single in like, idk, 15 years, we should get married

To each other, obviously

Okay but hear me out: tax benefits
Also it's kinda bullshit that society values romantic relationships as the epitome of relationships

Two best friends should be able to live together and adopt a dog and make each other lunch without turning heads
Imagine how great it would be to live together
I could make you food so you wouldn't starve
And you could wake me up in the mornings so I would actually get to work on time
And if we can get tax benefits out of it, why not?

Yeah, you're right
I'm being a little ridiculous
Sorry
It must be all the Valentine's Day hype getting to me

We're still making a discount chocolate run later, right?

K
Good night!

[Wed, Feb 22, 10:51 AM]
You picked the perfect time to get sick
We had a test in history AND calc
I think I did okay in history? You're definitely gonna ace it, it was a lot of memorization and a couple analysis questions, and I know you've been hitting the flashcards pretty hard
That calc test though
YIKES
Although you'll probably enjoy it, considering you actually think math is FUN

Anyway, I have all your homework. I'll stop by after tutoring to drop it off
I hope you're sleeping and staying warm
If you're not in bed when I come over I'll steal your phone and replace all your contact names with Harry Potter characters

[Sat, Mar 11, 1:47 AM]

I'm so warm in bed though
Don't wanna open my window, it'll let in a draft

What do you mean you're HERE? Why are you in my backyard??
Did you sneak out? Do your parents know?

Oh

They're not going to kill you
Murder is illegal
Although they shouldn't be hurting you at all, no matter how upset
they are.
What they did isn't right. You know that, right?

Hold on, I'm coming right back, I just need to grab the first aid kit
Try to focus on your breathing
Do you want to call someone? Or file a report? I can help you find
resources if you want
We'll figure this out. You'll be okay.

[SAT, MAR 18, 3:33 PM]
WASN'T IT AMAZING

I KNOW OH MY GOD
Totally worth all the extra hours and late rehearsals

I can't believe we're already halfway done
Just two more shows!
I haven't stopped being in awe tbh
I'm really glad you came!

I can't, sorry
The leads are holding an after-party
Hey, wanna see if I can sneak you in? I'm sure no one would mind
I know parties aren't really your thing but it could be fun!
Are you sure?

K
I'll see you Monday then!

[FRI, MAR 24, 3:35 PM]
    YOU'LL NEVER BELIEVE WHAT HAPPENED
    BLAKE ASHBURN JUST ASKED ME OUT
    We're getting coffee tomorrow
    Oh my god what do I wear what do I say what do I do how much cologne do I use PLEASE SEND HELP

[SAT, MAR 25, 6:15 PM]
    Lmk whenever you're free?
    I've got so much to share

[MON, MAR 27, 7:49 AM]
    Heyyyy where were you this morning?
    I waited in the cafeteria for so long I was almost late to class
    Did you get sick again? I thought we agreed to limit how many sick days we took so we could ditch class together after finals

    Crap, calc is starting and Posner's getting ready to take up hw
    Which I forgot to do
    Because I went on a date with Blake Ashburn
    Which I still need to tell you about btw
    RIP my calc grade

    SAVED BY THE INTERCOM
    Bauman just called an assembly
    Posner's gonna have to take up hw tomorrow

    [Mon, Mar 27, 10:12 AM]
    Bauman just told us
    I… I can't bring myself to believe it

[THU, MAR 30, 1:59 AM]
    Why?
    Help me understand, Kara

[FRI, APR 7, 7:48 AM]
So
Um
I actually did my math hw last night
You should be proud of me

[Fri, Apr 7, 8:56 AM]
Can you believe Posner didn't think I could do it?
I could tell when he was grading mine because he side-eyed me the whole time
It was surreal
I might not be a massive nerd like you but that doesn't mean I can't do my own math hw from time to time
I didn't get this far in life with just my dashing good looks and boyish charm

[SUN, APR 30, 10:35 PM]
Blake broke up with me today
He said I was "too much" for him
That I had too much baggage
I don't really know what he was expecting though?
As if he's more important to me than you are
I'm not going to stop talking about you just because he kissed me a few times
You were my best friend way before he was my boyfriend

Anyway
It's not like Blake Ashburn is the only other gay guy in the world
There'll be others, especially once I finally leave this ass-backwards town

[SAT, MAY 20, 1:14 AM]
What did I do to make you think you couldn't talk to me?
I told you we would figure it out
What did I do to make you not believe me?

I trust you with my life, you know
Always have
Always will

Wish you'd felt the same

[MON, MAY 22, 11:16 PM]
Did you see me walk across the stage??
I don't even remember it lmao
Everything from being called onstage to sitting back down is just
a massive blur

You know what's ridiculous? I didn't cry when I got my diploma
but I did when they called your name
Niagara Falls relocated to my face for a whole five minutes
You would have given me so much shit if you'd seen me

[TUE, MAY 23, 1:48 AM]
I can't believe it's all over
This is it
This is the end of high school
We're all going our separate ways after this, how crazy is that?
We're gonna be freshmen again in August. God, that's trippy

It's so stupid
I've been looking forward to today for so long but
Now that it's here…

I don't want to say goodbye

It won't be goodbye, will it?

[MON, JUN 12, 11:54 AM]
I have so many blankets

At least 7

Why do I have so many blankets?

More importantly, what do I DO with so many blankets?

I'm gonna make a blanket fort

You would have liked blanket forts, I think

They make you feel like the outside world doesn't exist

[THU, JUL 6, 9:15 AM]

Happy birthday!

I'm gonna visit you later today

So much has happened that I wanna tell you about but I haven't really had a chance to text

It'll sound better in person anyway

[SAT, AUG 26, 2:30 PM]

The first thing my roommate said when he walked in was, and I quote, "Don't have sex on my bed and don't eat my food"

After which he plugged in his headphones, started playing CSGO, and completely ignored me for the following 2 hours

College is wild

Can you imagine what things would be like if we were roommates?

Remember that one time we talked about it?

Well, I talked about it. You told me I was being stupid.

I guess you were right

I know I shouldn't be thinking about "what-ifs"

Still, this would be more fun if you were here

We could have made a blanket fort tomorrow night before classes start and told each other stupid jokes and Facebook-stalked random people on the freshmen Facebook page

Instead I'm going to eat your favorite ice cream and watch Sailor Moon on rabb.it and pretend you're on the other end of the connection

[WED, OCT 18, 8:36 PM]
    Can't believe calc is still ruining my life
    I can't even copy your hw anymore
    How am I supposed to pass this class? By actually learning calc?

    Not a chance in hell
    Satan himself couldn't make me

[TUE, OCT 31, 5:42 PM]
    A new development: I've started copying someone else's calc hw

    His name is Ryan
    He's really cute
    I think he might be smarter than you
    I think I might ask him out

    Wish me luck?

[WED, NOV 22, 2:00 AM]
    Was I not important enough for you?
    Did you think I didn't need you? Did you think I didn't care about you?

    I can't stop thinking about you
    About how much better everything would be if you were here
    And how lost I am without you here to keep me grounded

    Why did you leave me alone?
    Why do I have to figure out how to keep going without you? I didn't ask for this. I didn't want this.
    It's so selfish of you, to force me to deal with the aftermath while you got off scot free

    Fuck you
    For thinking what you did was okay

For hurting me like this

For acting likc our friendship didn't mean anything, like it didn't matter

Why couldn't I make you see that you mattered?

[Sun, Mar 25, 2:01 AM]

Somehow it's already been a year

I visited your grave earlier
It didn't look like anyone else had been there since I came over the summer
Not even your parents, can you imagine?
It made me angry, that no one cared enough to remember you. That no one felt the need to recognize that you had existed, at one point.

But then I thought... you wouldn't have wanted that from us, would you?
You wouldn't have wanted us to get hung up on who you were, who you used to be
You were never one to dwell on memories

You always said life goes on
Ironic, in the end, but true
You're not a part of my life anymore, no matter how much I want you to be, and I can't change that
But I can accept it, and figure out how to keep going. That's what you'd tell me to do, anyway

Life goes on
And I can't bring you back to life via text log
So maybe...
Maybe it's time for me to move on too.

SONALI GATTANI is a writer, artist, musician, and aspiring caffeine addict from Tulsa, Oklahoma. She holds a bachelor's degree in Cognitive Neuroscience, though she doesn't make a habit of writing about brains. Instead, she dabbles in both urban fantasy and contemporary fiction and often draws inspiration from her own life and experiences. For instance, she wrote her story "2:00 A.M." at two in the morning after receiving no responses to the texts she had sent, because her friends, like most normal humans, were all asleep.

She is currently happily adrift in the sea of life and is waiting to see where she ends up. She hopes you'll accompany her on her journey.

143
by Chloe Smith

As I walked toward the small iron gate of the cemetery, the sun beating down on my back and the wind rustling in the nearby trees, my mind wandered, and I remembered the day he told me about her just as the gate creaked open, cool against my hand.

I'd just received the news that I'd gotten into university, after getting the grades I needed. He was happy for me and insisted on us celebrating, even going so far as to buying us a cheap bottle of champagne, as long as I only had one *small* glass.

"To you!" He smiled, awkwardly lifting his champagne flute in the air and spilling a little of his drink on his jeans in the process. It wasn't like my dad at all—to be this caring, let alone so goofy and awkward with it.

Some would blame it on my mom dying when I was young. Apparently it's common for some single parents to become distant when they lose a spouse. After all, they probably had a longer and closer relationship with them than they did with you. Or maybe that's just something some people say—to help me feel better, or cope, or whatever. I don't know. But I don't really believe it, because while my mom's presence in his life definitely made him a pretty good dad and functional human being, there were times I'd see him while she was still around, when I'd come downstairs for a glass of water or milk in the middle of the night, sitting on the sofa nursing a glass of scotch with trails of tears glinting on his pale cheeks, like a secret in invisible ink.

Whenever I saw him the next day he'd wiped them away, and I couldn't bring myself to ask him about it. Because even then, at around seven, I would remember how sad and little he looked in that moment, hidden away downstairs so no one would see him cry. And since I never found the words to ask my mom either, not before she died three years later, it remained a secret.

Her death was a blow to our family that couldn't be patched up, not even with time, the "greatest healer." It was eight years since she left us, and I still felt her loss in my chest, like a wound that never quite recovered.

Compared to my dad, though, I'd done just fine—he'd started drinking more to cope, leaving a string of nannies to help me find my feet and my place in the world. It hurt at first when I'd find him in his chair, eyes distant and far away, tears flowing freely, and no matter how many times I tried to speak to him, he never responded.

Once I was so upset by this I wailed loudly for a good few minutes, begging him just to *Say something, Dad, please*—but a nanny quickly ran in and scooped me up, soothing me gently as she took me away. She tried to explain that Daddy was in a lot of pain since Mommy left, and he just needed time to get fixed up.

I was too young to understand, but I tried. I made him crayon drawings, crude little family portraits of me and him holding hands and smiling brightly in sickeningly bright yellows and blues, to try to show him that no matter what, we were still a family, that I'd never leave him, and that I'd be around when he got fixed up. I'd leave them on his chair or lap with no reply or even recognition. I'd kiss him on the cheek and skulk away to my room. My friend in second grade, Emily, always had *her* drawings pinned up on the fridge. I saw them whenever I went over to her house. I'd often sit by myself during lunch at school, stewing in anger and confusion. Although that might have also been because I couldn't stop thinking about how pretty Emily's hair was, all golden and shiny in the sunlight while she kicked a soccer ball around—but that was a whole other thing, I later realized.

Thankfully, one of the ridiculous sayings that were parroted to me by well-wishers did come true eventually, after a whole string of nannies came and went as I grew up—time did heal the gaping wound that kept me and my dad apart, but it took a lot longer than I think anyone expected. In fact, even when Dad was able to get out of bed and smile and look after me again, there was still this distance between us. Like someone had bent a photo of us in half, leaving that indent right down the middle and separating us even more than we already were. While he was there physically, I never felt he was there for me, not really—like there was something always stopping him from being present with me, even years after Mom left us. So that didn't help me at all when I realized I was gay and needed someone to talk to, but thankfully I had friends who were there for me in that regard. There's just something about not being able to be honest with your own family, with your own dad, though, that cut deep for a long time in my early teens.

But if he wasn't going to be honest and present with me, then how could he expect me to? I could only follow his example, which left our relationship one of distance, coldness, and nontruths for a very long time.

EXCEPT FOR that night—that night was different, and one where he actually opened up to me. Kind of. It was the night he drank most of the champagne because I insisted I didn't want to drink, and slept noisily on his chair in the corner of the room, snoring his head off. With his head lolling to the side, he looked like a small child, if it wasn't for all the wrinkles. I don't think I'd ever realized how old my dad really was, but I saw his skin was graying like his hair, the ghost of past happiness that seemed a lifetime ago now. I could still hear our joyous laughter mingling as he pushed me on the swings at the park, with Mom watching and smiling, blurring every so often as he pushed me into the air like I was going to actually fly away, the relief when I fell back into his arms. But that was over a decade ago, and I felt a twinge of sadness that I couldn't remember the last time I'd seen him really smile. He was fading away in front of me and I hadn't really noticed.

I was about to get up and leave the room until I heard him speak.

"Brighton," he said quietly.

My eyes snapped to his face again, but his eyes were still closed. I thought for a moment he was just mumbling gibberish, until I realized he was actually saying something interesting.

"Brighton… that's where she is. That's where she is. Brighton."

"Dad!" I said, loudly and quickly, to wake him up.

His eyes snapped open and he groaned quietly, reaching for his head. "Hm? Don't shout, please… my head… hurts…."

"Who's 'she'?" I asked, too curious to feel much sympathy.

"Who's who?"

"You—you were talking in your sleep just now, and you mentioned a 'she,' and you kept saying she's in Brighton. Who were you talking about? What do you mean?"

He sighed, and his eyes shone with such sadness that I felt my heart lurch. I'd not seen him look so *broken* in a long time.

"Well, Pen, I suppose… I suppose… it's time I that I tell you about your aunt."

"Aunt? But I don't have an aunt!" I spluttered, wondering if he was so drunk he didn't know what he was saying.

"Yes, you do," he said, his eyes weary. He sighed and motioned for me to move closer to him. I sat on the arm of the sofa, my heart pounding so strongly, it was a wonder he couldn't hear it in the silence of the room. "And I'm sorry. I'm so sorry I—I kept her from you for so long, but just let me explain…."

He told me all about Catherine North, his older sister by five years, who I hadn't known existed for the entire eighteen years of my life. She was pretty, even when she cut her hair short and made their mother upset, he said, and she liked to sing and had a beautiful voice. She had trouble with her hands, so he helped her with her sewing when it got too difficult for her.

"She was always there for me. She always looked after me, and would sing to help me get to sleep when I had nightmares. I was lucky, because some of the boys in my class at school had horrible siblings who would terrorize them and make their lives a misery. But not Catherine. No, she lit up my life, made it brighter, better. She was the best big sister I could ever have… until…." He stopped talking and started to sob quietly. I stayed stock-still, unsure of what to do.

I placed my hand on his shoulder in an attempt to comfort him, and when I did, he blinked and looked up at me in that lost way, and I felt like a kid again, when I saw him crying secretly in the middle of the night. But this time I wouldn't leave—not until I understood why.

He blinked again, and when he started to speak, his voice was quiet at first, still wet and croaky with tears, but got stronger as he continued.

"One day, Catherine… she… told our parents that she was a lesbian, and was in a relationship with a girl who lived on our street—Heather."

A smile spread on my face as my universe shifted just a little at this news. I had to grip the sofa while I tried to digest it.

My dad, not understanding, reached out and gave my hand a squeeze. "I know it's a bit of a shock." He had no idea—the fact that there was someone out there, in my very own family, just like me, meant more than I could ever say. So I didn't and instead offered a small smile, hoping that by "shock" he didn't mean anything negative.

"No, no—not in a bad way," he added quickly. "It's just that we had no idea, and apparently it had been going on for a while. I always felt bad that I never realized, or she never trusted me enough to tell me. I was her brother… but I guess she was right to hide part of herself away like that, even from me, even though I thought we were close. After all… I didn't stop them."

"Stop who, Dad?"

"My parents. When they found out, they disowned her, and I didn't do anything. I mean, I was just a kid… but I should have stopped them… I should have…." He trailed off again. "But that's not the worst thing," he whispered through the tears that dripped down his face.

"What is?" I asked gently.

"I realized that she was never really herself with us, not properly. Not honestly. She couldn't be, because she knew how they would react. And when she was so, so brave and came out, they threw her out. Out of this damn house too. That's why I ended up inheriting it when they died, and not her. Because they hated her and pretended she didn't even exist. And I never truly got to know my sister because of my own family… I never even spoke to her again before she died. And it kills me. It kills me," he said, before wiping his wet eyes and getting up and moving into the kitchen. I held my breath, waiting for the familiar clink of the bottle meeting the glass as he poured, but found myself breathing a sigh of relief when I heard the kettle boiling and the sound of him making a cup of tea instead.

THAT NIGHT, lying in bed, my mind too busy to sleep, I managed to find the *real* her. Well, her real digital self—thanks to social media.

Her Twitter profile was a part of her, her life, laid out in pictures, and I devoured every single word she sent out into the world like I was starving. And I was—starving to know her, to reach in and pull her out, but reading each tweet over and over again would have to do.

Not that she tweeted much or very often, only sporadically over the past two years, but for me it was more than enough, especially as it was better than nothing.

@catherineishere: @hettieisthere 143
Liked by @hettieisthere
@hettieisthere replied: 143
@catherineishere: All You Need Is Love, Love Is All You Need
Liked by @hettieisthere
@catherineishere: Family might let you down. But it's the family you find, and who finds you, that's the truest and most loving.
Liked by @hettieisthere
@catherineishere: Blackbirds make the sweetest sounds! Beautiful, my favorite sound and my favorite bird.
Liked by @hettieisthere
@catherineishere: While I love to sing, I never could do so as well as the King. I wonder if I can dig out those old LPs…
Liked by @hettieisthere
@hettieisthere replied: I'll help you look, and then we can see if our old bones are still up to the job of dancing the night away. Save me the first one, though?
Liked by @catherineishere

@catherineishere replied: Always. 143
Liked by @hettieisthere
@hettieisthere replied: 143
@catherineishere: A wonderful day was had today. I hope the same can be said for you, Twitter. I hope if you haven't today, you have a genuine reason to smile very soon.
Liked by @hettieisthere
@catherineishere: Roses are the most beautiful flower is the entire world. They're so beautiful they almost surpass @hettieisthere in terms of beauty.
Liked by @hettieisthere
@hettieisthere replied: <3 You are my reason to smile <3
Liked by @catherineishere
@catherineishere replied to @hettieisthere: As are you, love. How do you make those heart things, by the way?
@catherineishere: @hettieisthere 143
Liked by @hettieisthere
@hettieisthere replied: 143

There it was again, that "143," repeated each time to the same person, who gave her name as Hettie on her profile and who would always tweet it right back. A message in a secret code, over and over again—but it was getting too late to decode it then, so I decided to shelve it, with a mental note to figure out its meaning as soon as I could.

I also found something else during my search—a tweet near the beginning of Catherine's timeline that seemed to be part of a thread, though the earlier tweets looked to have been deleted—that piqued my interest just as much as the code did.

@catherineishere: That said, despite everything that happened, he once randomly left me a letter telling me he was sorry that he abandoned me and told me that he loved me. I always appreciated that.
Liked by @hettieisthere
@hettieisthere replied: I'm sure he knows you did, love.
Liked by @catherineishere

"He?" Who could "he" be? My mind instantly thought of my dad, mumbling about his sister in his sleep, the tears that fell silently down his face as he tried his hardest to hide them from me. To hide it all from

me.... But it was late, and my brain was too tired to successfully put these puzzle pieces together.

So instead of using up the dwindling brainpower I had left, I scrolled through her Twitter profile, focusing on her obvious love for Hettie—who, I assumed, was Heather. (I couldn't be sure because, unlike my aunt, her Twitter profile was quite bare apart from tweets from Catherine, a link to a YouTube video of someone doing tricks on a skateboard, and an impressive sketch of what looked like someone sitting, head bowed, beneath a tree. To top it off, she didn't even have a profile picture.) However, Aunt Catherine expressed her opinions very openly on her profile, including her love of the Beatles, Elvis Presley, and Vera Lynch, not to mention art.

As I kept scrolling, my eyes grew heavier and heavier. In the end I had to give in, replaying the video of a blackbird singing, chirpy and joyful, to lull me off to sleep. And when I woke up, I had a smile on my face for the first time in a very long time.

I BLINKED at the bright blue sky above me, as it took me a second to remember I was in the cemetery, caught in the memories that played in my head like the "Previously on..." segment before your favorite show starts. I shook my head slightly and made my way carefully down the path to what I guessed was my aunt's eternal resting place. My legs were stiff and aching slightly, from all the standing around, but it was fine. I could manage, work through it. I just had to find her....

The trees rustled gently as I walked past them, as if they were willing me on in quiet applause. In one tree, quite far back near the gate, sat a bird. Small and black, it stood out from the green leaves surrounding it like a carefully sculpted piece of onyx perched precariously on a branch. It regarded me for a moment and then looked away, as if judging me okay to be there, or at least not dangerous enough to try to scare away with its song or by flying straight at me. I nodded at it, a silent sign of my thanks, and kept on walking. A thought in the back of my mind niggled at me, almost as if I recognized that bird from somewhere, but it soon disappeared as I concentrated on the tombstones until I finally discovered hers.

It was quite grand, all things considered. I mean, I wasn't quite sure what I expected, but when I first saw it, I was kind of surprised that it was so... elegant. I didn't know that tombstones could look like that. It was a slab of shining black, engraved with a faded gold that made it seem almost timeless. On it was written in an elegant, swirling font:

Catherine North
1950—2017

I sighed, releasing my anxiety about not finding her or Dad being wrong about where her grave was located, and admired the place where she was laid to rest. It was nice—quiet and quaint. It reminded me of the countryside, with its few trees and its large patch of lush green grass. The sun was so high in the sky that its rays landed perfectly on her tombstone, so it shone beautifully. When I looked around, no longer entirely absorbed in her, I realized that her neighbor, just to her right, was a woman named Heather.

Heather! It had to be her. The times of birth and death correlated. Even the stone itself was similar. The same dark, shiny black, engraved with the same dull gold. Even the font mirrored my aunt's.

Heather "Hettie" Abbott
1950—2017

The fact that they remained together in death warmed my heart. I realized that on my first glance, I'd missed the small verses that were inscribed on their gravestones, Catherine's first, and then Heather's.

One day, my love, we will find Four wheels and travel together to someplace and stay there awhile. Three days, a few weeks, who knows or cares; as long as we're together, I'll stay forever. Yours…

With you, One year feels like days, Four weeks a second, Three days a moment. Eternally we stay. I stay. Yours…

My eyes filled with tears as I let what I read sink in. It was a beautiful promise, even if I could sense that there was a meaning behind it I didn't quite understand. Because there it was again, that One-Four-Three repeated over and over, this message they were determined to convey as eternally as their names on their tombstones.

Quickly, I fished my phone out of my jacket pocket and finally asked the internet—*What does 143 mean?*

I love you replied the internet, in pixilated ink on the softly glowing screen.

If I wasn't on the verge of crying before, I definitely was now. The tears built up, and I just let them fall, watering the bunch of roses I held in my hands and the blades of grass below me as they dripped off my cheeks, because I wasn't even bothering to wipe them away. The mixture of emotions swirling through me at that moment was enough to sweep me away completely. *Surprise, admiration, love,* but mainly and mostly—*pride.* I felt indescribable pride as I stood there opposite the everlasting declarations of love two women had made to each other.

The fact that I finally understood the code made me feel proud of myself, but that wasn't it. It was that my own aunt, someone living before me in a much more difficult time, so unabashedly and proudly loved another woman. There was nothing, I decided at that moment, like the feeling that you weren't alone in the world, and that someone else was just like you. Something about seeing them both there, and seeing it spelled out in their own words, made it so much more powerful and so much more real.

My aunt Catherine had loved women, just like me—and she found a woman she loved for the rest of her life. And that woman loved her too, and that love was so strong that they made sure it existed beyond their deaths, in a way that was meaningful to them.

Just witnessing and realizing all that, on that cold, quiet day, was enough to make another emotion unfurl within me, stronger than the others before—*hope.*

Before that moment, I'd never really considered my own future, not really, not beyond university, and certainly not marriage, and a house, and kids. It was too scary and so far away—but now, seeing that someone just like me, a member of my own family, no less, had beaten the odds and found such a true, everlasting love in a time when she was ostracized, meant that no matter what, I had this hope that I could one day find the same love, someplace, somewhere.

Sniffing and finally wiping away the tears, I carefully placed the bunch of roses on the ground. I hadn't thought to bring two, because I didn't realize Heather was here with her. So instead of splitting the flowers up, I simply placed the bunch between them so they could share in the love the bunch showcased. I hope if they were watching from wherever they were, they understood the gesture, as silly as it was. Resolving to bring two bunches next time, I stood up straight, my back twinging with the pain of moving a little too quickly, and I became even more aware of the dull ache in my legs, stronger now because I'd been standing so long. Dammit. I really should've brought my cane. Never mind, you live and learn. And anyway, it was more than worth it.

I checked the time and realized I'd be late for class if I didn't leave soon, but before I left, I traced her name with my finger—*Catherine North*—feeling the cool faded gold, almost amber now.

I wondered if she had been a hugger, or what her smile looked like. I wondered if she had a particular scent, maybe a perfume she liked. But I didn't have any memories like that, nothing that could evoke some deep-seated sensory signals to remind me of her. I guess the cool sensation of her name engraved in stone on my skin was one, and the smell of fresh roses was another. I realized that though I'd never met her, I missed her. I missed her presence in my life and what she could have changed about me or helped me with. My homework, visits on the holidays, coming out to her first, confiding in her, advice about girls… all of that gone and never existing in the first place, all at once—and I felt the loss deep down in the depth of my heart.

But, I thought as I turned away, at least I had now. At least I knew her at all, and I could visit her whenever I liked. And whether she was here or not, she still made a difference in my life, because even if I couldn't see her, I knew that no matter what, I wasn't alone anymore. She had come before me and fought battles I could only have nightmares about or read about in history books, and for that, I'll always be thankful—and I'll always have her near, because she shaped the way for me to even be.

When I closed the gate as I left, I heard the bird from earlier chirp at me, a short cheerful tune. I recognized it instantly as the song from the video I was listening to last night—a blackbird. And I wondered if, maybe, that could be Catherine, wishing me well. But despite another sensory trigger to remind me of her, it would've been nice to actually speak to her, all the same.

As I checked my phone on my way to class, I saw a very interesting advert pop up in the "suggested posts" of my Facebook feed. I read it eagerly, only slightly worried that whatever algorithm was running behind this site could somehow read my mind now and wasn't just basing ads on sites I'd visited or things I'd searched.

Tonight only: Visit Felicity Mort, medium, in a rare live show! Want to join the audience and get tickets? Click here.

A medium, huh? Just the idea of hearing from Aunt Catherine was enough to dispel any doubts I had about it being some kind of hack. After all, there was nothing about her this Felicity could somehow get from me—considering that I knew next to nothing about her! And she'd have no chance to ask me anything either. Plus, there'd be a packed audience, based on the number of comments from people saying they'd be there. After a quick Google search of her name and reading a few very positive reviews about her and her shows, I didn't take me long to be completely sold on the idea. Within seconds I'd tapped my screen a few times and secured my ticket. After all—what did I have to lose?

When I got home, Dad sat in the living room watching one of his favorite comedians performing stand-up, and laughing so genuinely that I was caught off guard for a moment. When he asked where I was that afternoon, I felt that telling him the truth would dampen his good mood, so I lied.

"I was just visiting a friend," I said quickly.

"Oh really? That's nice, sweetheart," he said, still looking at the TV.

"Yeah," I replied, "and I think I'm going to go and see them again later. But I'll be back tonight. That okay?"

"Sure thing. Just call me if you need me, okay?" he said, and I nodded, thanking him before retreating to my room to make preparations for who I was hoping to meet tonight—if I was lucky.

THE ROOM itself was hot and sticky, thanks to the crowded audience and my heart pumping blood so fast that I felt ill. I hated to admit I was nervous—but I was. What if Aunt Catherine didn't "speak" to me? What if she did and I didn't really want to hear what she had to say? My breath quickened as the medium scanned the crowd, looking for an audience member and trying to match them up with the relative she'd gotten through to. My heart stopped as her eyes landed on me and her gaze lingered for a moment. She opened her mouth to speak, and I thought I might actually faint, only for her to start talking to someone whose grandma had a message for them.

I breathed a shaky sigh of relief as the man being spoken to behind me burst into loud sobs, and I tried to think of what I would ask her, if I actually had the chance.

What made Nan and Gramps so mad at you? Are you upset with your family for what they did? Do you regret not being closer with my dad? Or not meeting me? When did you and Heather meet? Where did you meet? Were you happy? When did you realize you liked girls? Did you know I do too?

Dozens of questions flew around my head, making me feel even more nauseated than before. I tried to block the feeling by focusing on what was happening around me, as the medium had finished delivering her previous message. The man behind me, the recipient, thanked her, choked up and happy. Suddenly, despite not focusing on what I'd ask Aunt Catherine, a single question popped into my head.

Are you proud of me?

I started to wonder what prompted that question to appear like that, out of thin air, before the medium spoke a name that made me actually jump out of my seat. *Her name.*

"Catherine North," she said, looking around for a reaction, seemingly missing my momentary flight from my seat. "Do we have a relative of a Catherine North here?"

"Yes. Me," I said, raising my hand, my voice shaking a little. "I'm her niece."

"Ah yes. Penelope," she replied, but it wasn't a question. She already knew my name.

"How do you—" I asked, shocked.

Even from where I was sitting, I could see a smile spread on her face.

"She speaks very highly of you. She says you have great Twitter posts that make her smile, although she still doesn't get some of the memes. Thanks for liking a few of her tweets, she says—and she so wishes she could have met you before she passed, because she wants nothing more than to give you a big hug. She and Heather love the roses, though—and they both say thank you. Thank you very much."

A smattering of confused laughter broke out around me, but I remained frozen in my seat, stunned. If I had any doubts about whether this woman was a fraud or was genuinely able to talk to the dead, I was absolutely sold on the latter. How else would she know that I'd liked a few of Catherine's tweets when I was scrolling through her profile the other night? And that I'd brought roses to her grave? There was no way this woman could have found that out before I arrived, as she had no idea I'd even be in the audience. I felt a chill run through me and tears sprang to my eyes as I imagined my aunt and her kind blue eyes and red-lipsticked smile big on her face, no longer a profile image on a screen, but real and speaking real words to the medium. I wiped the hot tears away quickly, not wanting to embarrass myself, before the medium commanded silence again and continued to speak.

"She tells me that she would love to stay and answer all your questions, but she doesn't have the time—however, to answer a few of them, we were friends in our teens and met when she moved into a house on the street where I lived. And yes, we were very happy, no matter what. We still are."

I held on tightly to the scratchy armrests on my stiff theater seat as the universe seemed to shift around me again for a second. I nodded and opened my mouth to give her a quick thank-you, and to tell Aunty that despite our distance, I loved her very much. But the medium spoke first.

"Hold on, she's not done yet. Before she goes, she wants to tell you that she loves you very much."

"T-thank you. Please tell her I love her too," I managed to say, unable to stop the tears falling down my face. Or not caring.

"And to answer one last question, Penelope…," she says, and even through my tears, I could see the face of the medium smiling kindly up at me.

"Yes, she is. More than you know."

WHEN I got home, I told my dad everything. Where I'd been, what I heard, and more importantly, what I felt. I couldn't help it—it all rushed out before I could even think about stopping it. He listened carefully, not saying a word at first, and when I cried, my tears preventing from speaking coherently, he sat me down and held my hand, soothing me for the first time in years.

"I'm sorry," he said when I finally stopped. "I'm so sorry, Penelope. I should have—I—"

"It's okay. I understand."

He shook his head, frustrated. "No, you shouldn't have to understand. I'm your dad. It's my job to look after you, to protect you—and I—I let you down. I'm sorry. I'm so sorry." He pulled me into a quick hug and started to cry too. I realized the hug was a way to try to hide his tears. I pulled back and wiped them away carefully with the long sleeve of my shirt, and he sniffed. "No, don't—"

"Shush," I said, continuing to wipe the tears from his face. He laughed lightly.

"You're just like your mother. You know, when you'd see me upset during the night, she'd come downstairs and wipe my tears like that and try to soothe me." He sat up a little, looking at my shocked expression. "Yes, I'd always hear you come down the stairs, despite your efforts to be quiet and pretend you didn't see me, but I always did. I just never wanted to let you know I saw you because…." His mouth turned down, and a sadness lit up his eyes that made my chest heave. "I had a lot of pain, Penelope, locked up inside me, from way before I met your mother. And I let that fester and eat me up, just like I did the pain I harbored when your mom died, and I let that eat away at our relationship and your upbringing instead, when it all got too much to hold inside. I'm so sorry, and I don't ever expect you to forgive me for that. In fact, I understand if you hate me—"

"No," I said, shaking my head. "I used to, a little, when I was younger. But not anymore." I reached over to grab his hand again. "I think I understand now what it's like to hold secrets inside you so much they hurt, and then when you find pain on top of that—I can't imagine…."

"Wait—what do you mean?" he asked, confused.

"I mean I have my own secrets, and for a while, some of them were so heavy, it hurt. I get that. It was about your sister, wasn't it?"

"Yes, Catherine. There was more to that story than I first explained. You see, our parents—when they found out, they—" He blinked back tears before he continued, his voice shaking with emotion. "They yelled, and yelled, and yelled, and told her to get out. They said as far as they were concerned, they didn't have a daughter—and that she was… that she was dead to them. And then that was it, she was dead as far as they were concerned, because they never spoke of her again. And I never saw her or heard from her again—until…."

"Until?"

"One day, a long time ago now, I traveled to Brighton for work," he explained quietly. "Just the usual work day, but then the boss said we could enjoy ourselves, take in the nightlife before we traveled home the next day if we wanted to… so I decided to try out a few bars, and after a while, I found myself in one, and—and—"

"And what, Dad?" I prompted gently.

"I saw her there."

He shook with the emotion of admitting the secret that had pained him for so long. "I saw her that night, in one of the bars. She was singing—I think she performed there every night. Maybe she was employed there or something. But I ordered my drink, and I heard her voice. I knew as soon as I heard that beautiful light sound, it was unmistakably her. Then I turned, and there she was—like an angel or an apparition of some sort. I felt so shocked it was like I was in a trance," he continued. "I'll always regret not speaking to her that night. Not going up to her and telling her that I loved her, and no matter what I was told by them, I always loved her, because she was my big sister—she was Catherine, no matter what, and she had the strength to be who she was, no matter the cost. I was so proud of her, and I loved her—and I should have told her. I should have told her to her face. I mean, I wrote her a quick note that night, on a napkin, no less—telling her that I was sorry for abandoning her, but that I loved her and always would. But I left as soon as I asked the barman to give it to her, too chicken to stay until her set was over. They probably thought it was my number or trash or something, and threw it away. She probably never even got it."

"I'm sure she knew, Dad," I said, too caught up in the moment to really think and desperate to comfort him.

"Yes—but... what if she didn't? What if she thought I hated her because she was a lesbian?"

"Well, did you?" I said quickly, trying to rationalize his anxieties.

"No, of course not!" he said, his voice shaking with passion. "Despite what my parents thought, I never thought it right to hate anyone for who they are."

"Good," I said, nodding and making a decision in that moment.

"Good?" he asked, thrown slightly off guard—maybe it was the determination that was probably clear on my face.

"Yeah. Because... and I should have told you a long time ago, but you had your stuff to deal with. And so did I, I guess. But now we're okay, I feel like I can tell you. Dad... I'm a lesbian."

In the beat of silence that followed my admission, I swear I felt my heart stop. I scanned his face desperately for a reaction while my mind went through every possible scenario in a millisecond, but my dad reacted in a way that even I couldn't guess.

He suddenly reached out and pulled me into a tight, loving hug. I hugged back tightly and started to cry. I felt his heart thudding dully under his sweatshirt and realized when he spoke that he was crying too. "Oh, Pen... I love you so much."

"I love you too," I said, though it was muffled slightly by my sobs.

"And I want you to know that I'm proud of you for telling me, and thank you, because I know it's hard, especially because things have been difficult for us, and for me—especially because I made it so, in the past. But I, I want you to know that nothing will change. Well, not for the bad, anyway. Things will definitely start changing for the good now. Because

I don't ever, ever want you to change." He broke away to look at me, tears shining on his face. "Ever, you hear me?"

"Okay," I said, smiling up at him as he nodded and resumed the hug.

"Good. Because you're perfect, okay? Just as you are. Honestly, some days I can't believe I had a part in making someone as amazing as you. But—while you're amazing, I'm not. And this is a promise to you that I'm going to work so hard to do better for the both of us, and eventually I might catch up to be as great as you."

I sniffed, and he continued talking softly. "Don't cry, love. I'm sorry I keep talking. I should let you talk. Go on—"

"No, I—I'm just so grateful for you and for Aunt Catherine…."

"Me too, sweetheart. You're the best thing that ever happened to me, and you know what? Catherine would be so, so proud of you. So… how long have you known? Do you have a girlfriend? Have you tried Tinder yet?"

I laughed into his shoulder, quiet and so damn happy, and released him to answer his questions. "Since I was about thirteen, no, and no—although I wouldn't rule it out. Maybe in a few years, if I haven't met anyone yet."

What followed were a few hours of love, laughter, and genuine conversation. It felt, for the first time, that I had my dad back. I watched his face light up with happiness as he talked with me and listened to me relate tales of my gay awakening and growing up and discovery and accepting and embracing who I was. And I felt free, finally able to be truly me in my own home, finally able to embrace who I was with one of the most important people in my life. It was incredible. A night that I would remember with a smile and a glowing positivity in my chest for the rest of my life. For forever.

"Maybe this is the right time to finish this bottle. To celebrate," Dad said after a while, fishing out the champagne from the other day, half of it still swirling around in the olive-colored bottle. He passed me a glass before I could object. "Only a few sips, mind you."

I smiled as he poured a tiny bit into my glass and then put the bottle away before filling his glass with water. After handing my glass to me, he held his aloft and said proudly, "I've never actually made a toast before… how about—to you, to bravery, to love, to family, to Catherine, to Heather—"

"To new beginnings?" I added.

He smiled lovingly before gently clicking his glass against mine. "Yes, to all that, and to new beginnings."

LATER THAT night, buzzing slightly with a happiness I hadn't felt in years, a happiness that made me feel like I was floating, almost like I'd drank an entire bottle of that champagne and not a few sips, I collapsed onto my bed and grabbed my phone. It didn't take me long to find her profile again—my fingers seemed to search it out on autopilot, and before I knew it, I sent out a tweet addressed to her.

@catherineishere Hey, Aunty. I'm sorry I never got the chance to meet you, but I just wanted to say thank you, thank you for being you, for living and choosing love even when it cost you your family. You're incredible. 143—P

I must have drifted off to sleep as soon as I sent it, as I don't remember anything else but pressing Send. When I woke, my phone screen was digging awkwardly into my cheek, leaving a soft pink mark. As I glanced at it quickly in the mirror before I went downstairs, I grazed my fingers across it, wondering how the feeling of it didn't wake me up in the night. It was right on the cheek, a small outline of the top corner of the rectangle, like the imprint of a quick kiss.

The mere idea of that made me lighter somehow and made the slow descent down the stairs thanks to my stair lift much more bearable then I thought it would be after last night's events.

WHEN I made it into the kitchen, Dad had made me breakfast. He whistled happily as he bustled around the room, and when he opened the fridge to grab the milk, I saw that the champagne bottle was still there, which meant he hadn't touched a drop, since it had the same amount of liquid sitting in it as it did when I went to bed last night. As I digested this information, the next thing I noticed was that all my old drawings from when I was a kid were stuck up on the fridge door, a little faded now but still there, in pride of place. I felt a weight in my chest dissipate, and I almost started crying right there in the middle of the kitchen.

"I kept them all," he said, cupping a steaming mug of tea in his hand, before placing it on the table and motioning for me to sit down.

"Thank you," I said, pulling up a chair and blowing on the tea gently, watching the white steam swirl up to the ceiling, dancing.

"Oh, and I've got this for you," he said, turning to retrieve a photo frame, yellows and reds and purples and blues striped all along the side of the wooden sides in a bright neon rainbow. Inside was an old photo, yellowing with age. I looked at it in awe, as a girl around my age smiled up at another girl happily, her arm around her. And the other girl was smiling too, bright and joyous, right back at her. It was a moment of pure happiness captured candidly on film.

"Is that—?" I asked, the rest of the question getting stuck in my throat as it attempted to leave, I was so choked up.

"That's a photo of Catherine and Heather together one night, when they were babysitting me. I think Mom and Dad had gone to the cinema— anyway, I was fooling around with Dad's old camera and snapped this photo of them. I forgot about all the snaps I took until after Catherine left, and I decided to get the roll developed. Most of the photos were garbage, but I couldn't bring myself to get rid of this one. I thought you might like it," he said. "And I wanted to talk to you about our local Pride parade next month… I was wondering whether you wanted to go, because I'd be happy to drive and go with you…," he said, smiling sincerely and looking years younger with it.

The image in front of me started to blur as tears filled my eyes, and I sniffed, hoping that could convey the mixture of emotions that were swirling inside me right now. "Thanks, Dad. It means a lot."

He nodded, still smiling, and reached down to give my shoulder an affectionate squeeze.

"You don't have to thank me. You're my daughter and I love you, silly." He said, choked up now, too.

"Love you too, Dad." I said, and we laughed as we both sat there in the kitchen, crying over a photo. But it was more than that and we both knew it, and we laughed with the exuberance of it, of a million past mistakes just fading away and being rewritten with love.

"She'd be really proud of you, you know," he said, the smile on his face obvious even though I couldn't see it. "Your aunt Catherine. She really would."

"Yeah, I know," I said, smiling up at him and watching the shock spread over his features as I went into more detail about what the medium told me that night. It was my turn to laugh then, but he soon joined in and promised that he would go and apologize to Catherine, face-to-face, finally.

"I think I'll go and place some flowers at her graveside too. Make it a regular thing, those visits. After my AA meetings," he said, later on, when we went out for some food. "Would you like to come too, Pen? You could meet me at the cemetery gates if you have class."

"Yes," I said quickly, lowering the forkful of food I'd just lifted to my mouth to speak, and never meaning something I'd said more in my whole entire life. "We can go this weekend, if you like. But make sure we bring roses—she loves roses. And some for Heather too."

"Yeah, she does—wait, how do you know that?" he said as I smiled at the shocked expression that lit up his face.

"I have my ways," I said before grinning at him and asking him to please pass the ketchup. I would never get over that look on his face when I explained that I'd found her Twitter account and showed him her profile, finally remembering the one tweet I realized now, after his admission, that she must have addressed to him in the hope that he would see it. That look—the gentle shock and then the grin, forming even slower on his face but making him practically glow with happiness as he laughed out of pure joy that she forgave him, after all those years, and loved him still.... There was nothing better than that moment and seeing him so happy. He leaned over as he passed the ketchup to me and kissed my head gently, gratefully conveying love without words, and suddenly there it was, that deep feeling of me being content again. I wondered if feeling so happy would now become a regular occurrence, and I smiled at the possibility that yes, it just might. I also realized that I'd never stop being grateful to her, for so many reasons—my wonderful, incredible, outstanding aunt, and for all that she'd done for us, and for me.

LATER THAT weekend, after his first successful meeting, we placed two large bunches of roses at her graveside and two more at Heather's. Then my dad reached for my hand and squeezed it tightly, and we stayed there opposite the gravestones for a while in the most comfortable silence I'd ever experienced in my life. The sun shone brightly above us, making the back of my neck burn a little, and if I listened close enough, I swore I could hear two blackbirds singing happily, a beautiful wordless duet. I imagined them soaring above us, gliding in a glorious flight, a sign sent from her, from them, together and happy forever, and I smiled.

CHLOE SMITH is a disabled writer and poet from the United Kingdom. She is a Foyle Young Poet of the Year 2015 and her poetry has been published in a few different anthologies, including the *Great British Write off: Whispering Words* anthology. Her flash fiction has been published in *Ellipsis Zine* and the *Ginger Collect*. Her first ever short story, "Plenty of Fish," was published by Harmony Ink Press in the *Harmonious Hearts 2016* anthology.

She's always wanted to be a writer ever since she knew books existed, especially when she found out that writing those books could be an actual job. She's still working on getting that status of "published author and poet" with her own books and poetry collections on the shelves, but thinks as long as there are people out there who will read her work (and occasionally even like it!), then she's most of the way there already.

Chloe lives in England with her family, who she loves very much. If she's not writing, then she's probably thinking up a new story idea, rewatching episodes of *Doctor Who*, or drinking tea (as long as it's decaf).

Twitter: @ch1oewrites
Website: chloesmithwrites.wordpress.com

Dev's Law
by A. Aduma

I.

I WAS seated on the back door steps of our house enjoying the sun and going through my WhatsApp when the neighbor's door opened and slammed shut.

Law stepped out carrying his telescope and looking like a man on a mission.

I frowned and looked Law over. He looked different with his hat off. I wasn't used to him with his hat off. I didn't even realize it could come off.

"Stop staring." He glowered as he unboxed his telescope.

I blinked and looked away, back to my phone. I was awaiting a message from Juno, a guy I'd met online. We'd met face-to-face recently after a month of texting. I didn't think he enjoyed the date as much as I did. He was online and my message was read, but he hadn't replied yet.

I turned back to Law, unable to help it. He looked so different… like a model or something, which was weird because I'd never have thought it was possible. It was Law! The kid who chewed on his pencils until they looked like brooms at the ends. The kid who spent too much time outside looking at stars. I'd sneak in the back door after a night of partying, wasted and drunk, only to jump nearly out of my skin when my eyes happened upon his silhouette—his hat on, I might add.

I didn't get the significance. The hat was faded denim with a colorful Batman print on it.

I'd always meant to ask, but I'd never gotten round to it. Now didn't seem like a bad time. "Where's your hat?"

"In the wash," he said and proceeded to set up his telescope. It wasn't night yet, and the sun was still shining overhead. It didn't make sense. Or maybe they now made cheap telescopes that could see stars during the day.

"Isn't it too early to set up?" I stood and walked over to his side. We shared a yard and lived three steps apart. Mum didn't like it much because Law's dad constantly filled it with junk where Mum wanted a small vegetable patch to grow tomatoes.

"I know," he mumbled, still setting up his telescope.

On nearing, I noticed his shaking hands, which wouldn't have been a big deal except I'd seen him do this before and he was always so meticulous, so careful with his telescope. I tried to catch his eye to see what was up, only to realize Law had been crying. His eyes were red and his lower eyelids and eyelashes wet.

My palms moistened in panic, and I passed my tongue over my drying lips. I didn't know how to deal with other people's emotions. Mine were hard enough.

But Law had been crying, and pretty hard too.

I imagined bailing but thought better of it. Law looked like he needed a hug. I was good at hugs. I loved hugs. And not just simple bro hugs or the ones girls gave as greetings. I liked going all in, body pulled close and tight, arms nice and snug around the partner. Would Law appreciate that or freak out? He'd probably find it peculiar. Still, I had to do something.

"Hey, Law, what's up?" I asked, in what I hoped came out as a kind voice, but the slight panic made it come out weird, like I was being choked.

He stopped setting up his telescope and inhaled sharply. "Don't use that tone on me."

"What tone?" I knew what tone. I hated that tone. The laced-with-pity tone. Like when I came second in the last 200-meter race I ran, just behind by a second. A second! After, there'd been all these pitiful voices that made me want to pull out my hair.

I asked because if he could rant about that—the pity tone, he'd feel better. At least I had.

He looked up and glared before darting his cloudy eyes away. "You know what tone."

"Why have you been crying?"

"None of your business." He choked before the tears started to stream. He ducked his head, peeked his eye through the standing telescope, and cursed. "I can't fucking see."

He huffed and pulled back, narrowed angry eyes fixed on the telescope like it was its fault. How dare the telescope!

"Yeah. It's dayti—" Before I could finish, Law lunged at the telescope, gripped it like he planned to do foul damage. I shrieked, blocked his arm, and grabbed the telescope from his hands before he could crash the thing on the ground.

Law had explained how important it was, something about being having a good resolution. I'd nodded my head. Law was smart, ridiculously so. He'd even gotten a scholarship to some fancy school with British architectural designs—I think he'd called them Victorian.

"Whoa, bro!" I backed away, telescope in hand, and put it a good distance from Law's reach. When I turned back to Law, he really did look worse for wear, as if he'd fall apart any moment now and like he desperately needed a hug to pull himself together. "Come here." I pulled him to me by his shoulders, and he practically collapsed on me and began sobbing.

My arms went round his waist, and I just held him.

He smelled like coconut oil and a washing detergent we used too. He also felt so small in my arms. Smaller than I'd ever imagined, like maybe he didn't eat enough. This made me imagine feeding him. Lasagna, maybe. I really enjoyed making lasagna.

I had to focus, though, on what was important.

Law was still sniffling quietly on my shoulder, and he needed someone; in this case, me.

"Let's go to my place," I offered. "I could make you chicken mushroom soup or a sundae and you can talk or we can play Minecraft."

Law sniffed and mumbled, "Sundae sounds good."

"Sundae it is." I hoped he'd pull back and we'd start moving, but he held on tightly, and my arms remained around his waist. "I could carry you," I offered.

"Huh?"

"If you don't want to walk," I added.

"Oh, right." He drew back and I let go. His eyes remained fixed on the ground, and he fervently chewed on his lower lip.

He was embarrassed, which made a lot of sense. Showing your sad emotions, your truest emotions, did that to you. I couldn't let him feel that way because to me he was being brave. Whenever I got sad or pissed, I'd run to calm myself.

"Come on, then." I closed my hand over his and pulled him toward the door. I then stopped abruptly. "Your telescope."

And instead of dropping his hand, I walked with him to get it. We then made our way up the narrow stairs and through the door into the small kitchen. Mum, my older sister Roni, and I had painted it red a week ago, my favorite color, which beat the washed out yellow before.

"It's…." Law paused and looked around. "Red. Everywhere!"

I grinned and admired it. From the walls to the cabinets, it was a matte red, leaving only brown for the countertops. Dad didn't like it, thought it was too "extra."

"Yeah. This way I can concentrate better on my cooking." I turned to him. "So, a sundae?"

"Will it take long?"

"I'll have to slice up some fruits; which would you like?"

He grimaced. "Maybe we can skip that and just eat ice cream?" He huffed. "Can we watch something?"

"Sure."

I gave his hand a squeeze before letting go. I grabbed the ice cream carton and spoons, then led him to my room. We didn't have a TV in the living room, not since my cousin Chale broke it. I had my own TV, though, one I'd bought to facilitate my love for movies and occasional video games. Mum didn't like it, but Roni, when she came home for the holidays, would sneak into my room and use it to watch YouTube videos.

At the entrance to my bedroom, Law paused, looking torn. He'd been here once before, but he hadn't stayed long.

It was funny. Law lived next door but avoided coming over, like our house had the plague or something. I tried not to take it personally.

It was a small rectangle of a room, and my twin bed ran from one end to the next against one wall, facing another wall where I'd put up the TV and a desk with the Mac I'd slaved two jobs for, cleaning pools and working at a drive-thru. The room was the same brilliant red as the kitchen, and the furniture was mismatched—whatever was cheap or free. Dad and I had upcycled some stuff, like my shelf and bed.

The room smelled kind of stale and was too untidy, with shoes and socks everywhere, but it was my safe haven.

Here I got to be me for a few minutes, even if Mum barged in every ten seconds whenever she was home to ask what I was up to. Not drugs, Mum! Not drugs.

We settled on the bed, resting our backs on large pillows Roni had gifted me, sitting closer than two bros would, but I felt Law needed it. The movie I chose was *The Shape of Water*. I thought Law would probably like it because it was sci-fi and Law was definitely a science guy. Instead he started sobbing twenty-five minutes into the movie.

I put my arm around him, and he laid his head on my chest. "Please tell me he gets a happy ending?" Law sniffed and burrowed deeper, his coconut scent overpowering my olfactory cells.

"Who?" I wasn't paying attention. How could I? I was a boy of seventeen, with hormones raging and a cute boy really close to me.

"Charles? The neighbor."

He was talking about the movie, Charles who was gay and a neighbor to Eliza, the main character. I tried to recall the ending. "I don't think so, but his hair grew." Charles wore a toupee because he was embarrassed of his bald head.

"How?"

"Amphibian Man, but that will come later."

"So he doesn't get a boyfriend?"

I frowned. "No, he doesn't."

Law pulled back, and his wet eyes met mine. He looked so vulnerable my heart ached. If he was my boyfriend, I'd have cuddled him in bed under the sheets and tried to make him sleep or forget, even if for a second. But he wasn't.

"I'm gay, Dev," Law announced, determination clear in his voice.

"Ooh," I said. I hadn't known that, but I'd tried to figure it out. The first time I'd seen Law, he'd had his eyes on a big textbook, chewing on his lips while he waited for the school bus. I'd never gotten an accurate pin on his sexuality, and trust me, I thought about it, maybe too much. Law was a little bit weird in a nerdy and geeky kind of way, and it made it hard to tell. It always served to remind me he was out of my league.

"My dad found out." Law looked away, and the tears started up. "He's… he's disgusted. He stormed out the house and hasn't been back in two days."

I pulled him back quickly. I could picture his pain, not entirely, but I knew something close to that. Roni, bless her, had pressured me to come out and gone ahead to hold my hand through it. Man, I loved her. Mum had burst into tears, and Dad had remained entirely too quiet.

I'd started to freak out, but Roni had been there still holding my hand while her other hand rested on my thigh, gripping it tightly. Those few seconds while I waited for a reply, I'd thought for sure I'd end up with my ass on the pavement.

"But why?" Mum had asked.

"I don't know," I muttered, wondering if I had my way whether I'd have been gay or not, thinking maybe I could retract my words and try to date girls with curvy, fleshy bodies and flowery scents.

Roni glared at Mum, but Mum started wailing again. She stood and hugged me. I had still been seated stiffly on the sofa holding on to Roni while Mum bent awkwardly to pull me into a hug. "I expected Roni to be the gay one," she'd said.

"Really?" Roni asked in a sarcastic tone. Roni dressed like Aaliyah and Missy Elliot, including the baggy sweats and girl boxers.

Mum pulled back and looked at my dad who sat quietly on his La-Z-Boy armchair we got for a steal at a garage sale. "Whadya think, Francis?"

Dad shrugged, and I held my breath. I'd been afraid of him the most. "I guess he needs another sex talk."

I exhaled in relief and nearly cried with joy. It was acceptance, of sort.

Dad, though, he never got round to giving me the sex talk, but he warned me not to get AIDS. Was that homophobic? I couldn't tell for sure. Mum asked if I had a boyfriend, I said no, and she said, "Good, because you're not allowed one until you are eighteen."

The topic never came up again. I felt that Mum's and Dad's coping mechanism was to pretend it never happened. It sucked, a lot, but I kept reminding myself it could have gone worse.

Or better, another part of me thought—the angry side. The part angry that I had to "come out." That it was a rite of passage when someone was queer. That it was a big deal. That someone's sexual orientation described everything someone was. Skin color too, I thought, remembering Juno's reaction the first time he saw me. We hadn't traded pics. I hated trading pics. Just having my picture floating in some dude's gallery, it didn't feel right. He'd been irritated to see me, probably wondering "Who is this person?" Then I'd introduced myself and he'd blatantly said, "I didn't know you were black."

I hadn't known I had to come out as black too.

The date had progressed, and apart from that I figured it was nice, but Juno didn't seem much into it, looking back. We had stuff to talk about, he'd laughed some, and I laughed some… now he was ignoring me.

But this wasn't about me. Poor Law, his family was falling apart. He was falling apart. "I'm so sorry." I rubbed his back in slow, sensual strokes like Mum used to whenever I got tonsillitis. It didn't help with the tonsillitis, though, just my mental state.

Law hiccupped. "I wish I didn't like boys."

"No, don't say that. You're who you are, and that's important. You're who you were meant to be, nothing you can do about it apart from embracing it."

Law didn't say anything for a while. He remained firmly on my chest. I could feel his rapidly beating heart, and I thought if I could take him to a star to make him feel better, I would have. No questions.

"My dad, he said to keep away from you."

My heart stung; it wasn't easy hearing you were not wanted. His dad and I didn't even see each other often. "Oh." It was all I could manage.

"He thought I'd get gay cooties from you."

I laughed. That shit was hilarious. People were so ignorant. I thought back to Socrates, who chose death over ignorance. I'd be Socrates, given a chance. "He wouldn't be the first." Or the last, I could bet comfortably.

"I'm sorry," Law said.

I dug my fingers through his curls—oily, soft, and tender—pushing them back so I had access to his eyes. He didn't look up like I expected, but I got to see his beautiful long lashes from a whole new vantage point. "It's not your fault, Law. Don't apologize."

My fingers went through his hair again, grazing his skull, and he sighed. I did it again.

"What's your mum saying?"

"Mum, she knew before and didn't mind. She made me swear not to tell my dad, though, at least not before college. She's been real supportive, but I feel like I've ruined her marriage."

"How'd he find out?"

Law paused a while before he looked up, his red eyes meeting mine dead-on. I felt my gut knot. "I was jerking off to gay porn."

"Oh." I swallowed a lump lodged in my throat while my brain, without my permission, tried to formulate images of Law in his room waxing his Buick and then his dad accidentally barging in. That hit the wall when I realized I'd never been to Law's house the six months we'd lived as neighbors. Now I knew why.

"That has to be the worst way, right?" Law chewed on his lip. He did that a lot.

"I don't think so. You know T?"

Law nodded. T was my best bud.

"He got found with a dick up his ass."

Law gasped. "No way."

"Way."

"Then what?"

I shrugged. "He got a beating from his dad and mum, got kicked out. Then his aunt, she's a counselor, took him in."

"Shit." Law grimaced.

I nodded.

"What if Dad comes back and kicks me out?" Law's eyes got panicky, and I could bet I looked like that during that long pause when I came out and waited for my mum and dad's reaction.

"I'll take you in," I offered. We weren't rich or anything, but we'd manage. I had a job and some savings I didn't need as much since I'd gotten a full scholarship. Dad would probably get irritated—he didn't like strangers much—Mum would be happy to have extra people in the house, and Roni would suggest to Law he sue his parents for negligence or something.

"You'd do that?"

"Of course. We're friends, right?"

Law smiled a sad smile. "Yeah. Let's watch the movie."

"You're sure?"

"Yes."

I pressed Play and we got back to the '60s, when Eliza and Amphibian Man were falling for each other. And looking at it, I thought it was pretty cool just loving someone the way they are. Who cares if they were a different species?

Law was sniffling when the credits rolled, not that I could blame him. First time I watched the movie, my chest became real tight and my eyes stung like I'd cry any minute.

"Fuck, that was terrible." Law moaned and sniffed some more. "Why'd you make me watch that?"

I smiled and shrugged. "It's a favorite of mine."

"I'd never have guessed."

"There's much you don't know," I said.

"Sadly," Law murmured. "Oh crap, we forgot about the ice cream." He reached over me to grab the carton of ice cream, squeezing my gut in the process. He opened it, and inside was liquid chocolate floating about.

"How about we grab cups and drink it?"

Law chuckled. "Are you serious?"

"Maybe. It depends—how daring are you?"

Law blinked a couple of times and frowned at the carton. "Not much, but let's do it."

"Awesome."

We trudged down the stairs just as Mum was coming in through the back door. Her eyes went wide as she glanced between Law and me. "Hey, Mum."

"Hi." She looked to Law, who had his eyes firmly fixed on his feet. "Hey, Law, what a surprise."

"Hey, Mrs. Dylan."

Mum closed the door and stepped into the kitchen while I got us cups. "What are you doing?"

"We want to drink the melted ice cream." I pointed to the carton still in Law's grip.

Mum gave me a look. "Seriously?"

"Yeah. Want some?"

"No. I'm going to shower and probably nap. Your dad arrive yet?"

"Not yet." I'd have known. Dad usually sighed really loudly when he got home after a day at work. Then he'd proceed to make a racket in the kitchen just pouring himself a glass of water; it was his way of saying he was home.

Mum gave us a final glance and left the kitchen.

I poured the ice cream and handed one cup over to Law.

"It's going to be disgusting," Law remarked.

I didn't doubt it. "First one to finish gets to dare or ask the other person anything they want."

"Oh. Okay." He looked unsure.

"No pressure."

"Just how crazy will the dares be?"

I grinned. He wasn't ready for what T and I got into, including sending nudes to random contacts on our phone. I shivered, remembering sending one to my aunt Fay. She'd even gone ahead to announce it in church. Mum went ballistic and ruined a loaf of perfectly good French bread, hitting me with it, and Dad didn't say anything. "Up to you. The dare can be as small as knocking on your neighbor's door and running away or licking the underside of a shoe."

Law made a face. "That's not small."

"Okay, hugging random big strangers on the street."

"What kind of stuff do you get up to, Dev?"

I shrugged. "Thank boredom and T."

"Are you and T together or something?" Law asked.

I chuckled. "No. T would throw up if he heard you say that. T likes pretty much anyone but me, and T's definitely not my type."

"Oh."

"Mm-hm. Now, you in? 'Cause it's getting warmer."

"I am."

"So you know, I can be competitive." I gave him a hard look.

He grinned wide. I'd not seen him grin so widely in a while. He had a nice grin. "You clearly have never seen me in a math decathlon."

"In three."

I began the countdown to three. My gaze on his as we stared each other down, it was kind of hot. Pretty much all eye contact to someone you were attracted to was hot, making my gut twist and my mind go fuzzy for a couple of milliseconds, so that I hesitated before saying three.

I won, of course. T and I were always competing to eat disgusting stuff, the most memorable being hot chili. Somehow it got up in my nose and I ended up snorting hot chili. I didn't know noses could feel so violated until that day.

"So truth or dare?" Law asked, looking shy. He'd probably never done a crazy dare before.

"Truth."

"Ooh. Okay."

"How'd you know you liked guys?"

He chucked nervously. "That's not bad." He chewed his lip. "When I was eleven a boy kissed me and I thought it was nicer than when a girl had, but I didn't think much of it." He sighed and went on, "Last year a boy asked me out and I freaked out. I wanted to say yes so badly but didn't. It got me thinking."

I nodded my head.

"What about you?"

I smiled. "I got a crush on Roni's male classmate when I was nine, and I told my cousin. He said that was gay, and when I looked up the definition, I thought for sure I was gay. I didn't come out until I was fourteen, though."

Law looked sad like he'd cry, so I went to him and pulled him in for a hug.

"I don't cry this often, so you know."

"It's admirable I was taught not to cry. I think my tears probably dried up."

"I wish that was me. I just hope things turn out okay."

I rubbed his back. "They might. If they don't, I'll be here for you. That's for sure."

"Thanks… for being there."

"No problem."

We stood in the ridiculously red kitchen, holding each other for so long I thought for sure my legs had cramped up.

"I better go." Law pulled back, and I released him. "Thanks."

"Sure. Be strong and don't apologize for being yourself." It's what Roni had told me that day of my coming out.

It didn't make sense then, in that moment of slight panic. Later I'd realized being gay was no less different than the color of my skin or the structure of my DNA. I was born this way; there was no apologizing for that. There was no changing that. I was only left with embracing it.

Law nodded and exhaled deeply. He grabbed his telescope, which I'd left on the kitchen trolley, and started for the door.

"I hope you come again," I said, walking him out.

"I will."

I watched him walk the short steps to his back door. At his door, he gave me a small wave, braced himself, and then disappeared into the house.

I hoped things turned out okay, sooner than later. Law was a good person. Being gay was probably eating him, which sucked because he'd done nothing wrong. He was just himself.

Mum was in the kitchen going through the fridge when I got back in. It meant she hadn't slept, and maybe she'd sat on the stairs listening in. My gut churned, feeling angry and a bit violated. She was my mum, yeah, but boundaries, dammit!

"It's nice what you're doing."

"Mum, don't tell me you were eavesdropping."

"I didn't mean to. I came down for a glass of juice and heard what was happening."

I frowned at her.

"Okay, I'm sorry, but he looked so guilty I wondered if y'all were up to no good."

"You could have asked," I pointed out.

"I'm sorry." Mum sipped her juice. "I wish parents didn't have to be dramatic about sexuality."

I looked at her with disbelieving eyes. "Mum, you cried!"

"Of course I cried! That same week Dante of Mama Lee's got beat up by dumb hoodlums after he was caught with a dick down his throat. I could see you in his place all beaten up, and let me tell you, there are some things mums can't do without worrying about."

I swallowed thickly. I remembered. Dante recovered physically. I couldn't tell for his mental state, being I hadn't seen him in forever.

"So you know, it doesn't matter to me, but I worry about the rest of the world." She pulled me into a hug, squeezed me, and let go. Mum was a hugger. I guess I got it from her. "So what exactly is up with Law?"

"His dad found out he's gay and hasn't been home in a two days. His mum's okay, though."

"Well." Mum huffed.

I nodded solemnly.

"I'm going to guess his dad is caught between religion and his son. Islam is pretty strict," Mum commented.

"Weren't you?" Mum was a devout Christian who never missed church and whose music playlist consisted one hundred and two percent of gospel music.

Mum shrugged. "God is love. Now, if Law needs anything, we're here to help, okay?"

I grinned at that. "I'll let him know."

"Now make supper. I'm thinking mashed potatoes."

"We don't have potatoes." I'd used the last making maru bhajias for Roni last week. They were her favorite.

"Okay, make whatever. I've gone to nap."

I gave her a look.

"For real this time."

When she left I dived into my pocket for my phone. It had been buzzing for a while. I found six chats with new messages, one of them being T with a tirade of messages. He was in Tobago with his cousins for the holiday, lucky bastard. Of course he'd bombard me with photos of him having fun. I missed him.

I replied to the texts, mostly from group chats, and scrolled farther down to Juno. No new message, and he was still online! I thought of sending another message but decided against it. It wasn't meant to be, I guessed, which sucked because he got my obsession with indie films and musicals.

I typed a message back to T.

Die!!

I checked my Snapchat, which was just more T, and then scrolled through IG. On IG I came across Law's story. On a blue background were the words, "Man was born free, yet everywhere he is in chains."

On a second pink background were the words, "Society is dependent upon a criticism of its own traditions."

I chewed on it and decided to send a reply after liking the posts.

Doing good?

I waited all of three minutes before I realized I had dinner to prepare, my favorite house chore, my worst being washing the dishes. We didn't have a dishwasher, so I had to scrub the pots and pans with a brush. It sucked.

I decided some lamb stew and yams would do. It was something I'd cooked over a dozen times and only took an hour, and finished just as Dad walked through the door. He looked tired and exhausted with life, as usual.

He grunted a hello.

"Hey, Dad."

"That lamb stew?" he asked, heading for the pan.

"It is."

"Good. Make me a plate while I shower." He thundered up the stairs, and a moment later I heard Mum's laughter.

Right on cue, I thought.

Dad and I weren't best buds, just two awkward people with the same blood. It was just always weird between us. Never with Mum, though. I think for sure they loved each other.

I made Dad a plate and placed it next to his La-Z-Boy. I made my own plate too, carried it up the stairs to my room, set it on the bedside table, fell on the bed, and logged on to IG.

Law's reply was waiting for me.

Trying.... Can't stop thinking about The Shape of Water.

Yeah?

Like she seriously fell in love with a fish!! Isn't that bestiality?

Love conquers all? Also I'm guessing you haven't checked out yaoi or slash—you see creepy things over there. Chill lemme send a meme.

I sent a meme comparing *Game of Thrones'* incest scene of Jon Snow and Daenerys Targaryen to a boy being fucked by a serpent monster—the monster all scales and tentacles. The caption: "This is nothing" over the *Game of Thrones* photo.

Too late I realized the pic was probably too nasty. Like, Law was the most innocent person I knew, and I felt a need to protect that. He was precious.

Holy Cow!! Are you for real??

Welcome to yaoi.

That's like GROSS!!

And then he sent a gif of someone throwing up.

That's actually tame.

Do I want to know how you know? what kind of stuff are you into, Dev!!

I sent a mouth-sealed emoji.

It felt like he was flirting and me flirting back. I loved flirting. It always felt empowering, even if it was just for fun. This felt different in a way, making my skin crawl and my whole body feel on edge, like I was about to fall into a frozen pool. I could see it happening but didn't know how to stop it. It didn't make sense.

Now I'm curious.

If I tell you, you'll have to give me something in return.

Like....

I answer this, I ask you a question, you answer then ask me, I answer....

Cool.

So I told him; I told him I loved yaoi and all its weirdness. I promised to send a link to some of my favorites. In turn I asked him to name a guilty pleasure—listening to country. At which I laughed so hard Mum barged into the room to see what was up.

After that we pretty much exchanged embarrassing tidbits about ourselves, which was refreshing. Normally our online relationship involved me sending him memes and him replying with laughing emojis, or he'd send the memes and I'd reply with laughing emojis.

I liked this better.

It made me happy. I had a stupid grin plastered on my face every time I received a message from Law. I just hoped he had a matching stupid grin while texting me.

At twelve he said good night, and I tried to sleep but couldn't. I ended up going over our texts, smiling like a fool.

At about one in the morning, I got a text, thinking it was Law with a case of insomnia. It wasn't—it was T.

What you doing up late? Who's the lucky bitch?

Your mum.

He sent back a string of middle fingers followed by a text message.

Dude, I was gonna loan you my Savage jersey ... forget it.

First of all, the jersey is loaned to you.

Ass. I go away one week and you get more sass than Rihanna.

If you hadn't left ....

I didn't like that he'd left me all alone with no best friend to share in my silliness.

Hahahaha, still clingy I see. Seriously, though, who's he?

Who he?

Bruh, I've read your story. Rolling eyes emoji.

I went back and looked over my story, cringing at how obvious it was. "Feeling feelings." Shit. I quickly looked at my views and sighed in relief when I didn't see Law's name, but Juno had viewed it—why, though? I deleted the post.

Okay, like it's no biggie... don't go crazy or something, I began.

Okay ....

Or jump into any conclusion. I sent a second text. *I'm serious! Don't go crazy!*

He sent me a gif with "Get on with it" captioned against the video.

I'm texting Law. Or was—meh.

T's reply was immediate and long.

Your neighbor? The kid with the denim cap? The geeky one? The one with the baggy clothes? The one you tripped over first time you saw him? The one who didn't know who Nas was? The one who laughed so hard he snorted on a poor old lady at the bus stop? The one who smiles like he's six and still believes in unicorns? Is it that one?

I fucking hate you. Angry face emoji.

He sent a meme of a kid smiling innocently.

So .... How'd you and Law happen?

There's no 'we' the way you think 'we'. He and I spent the day together.

Do I get more details?

That's it.

T sent a meme of a girl rolling her eyes.

Dude, like what's this? I was hoping for some sexed up shit.

Like what?

Anything but this! I can't. Anyway, so what happens next?

I don't know, he has shit he's dealing with.

T sent the blinking man gif. The bastard had a meme for every occasion.

You diva. I'm out.

You know I like you (somehow) but dude you're like a coward or something. You've liked Law for six months now and you've not done anything about it. If he's dealing with shit then be there for him, dammit, and show him what he can get and more if he chooses to be with you. Leave the decision for him, TELL him. If he says no fuck him, now you know, you move forward. If he says yes you've gained something, but don't do nothing!!

Damn. I looked over the text again and again, my gut knotting up. I felt nervous and slightly excited by T's suggestion. So nervous I started to sweat in my armpits, back, and spine.

And there was just a short second of me imagining telling Law what I felt, him saying yes, and me being there for him in a "proper" manner. Somehow this made me remember the feel of him in my arms and how vulnerable he looked. Phantom feelings from earlier when we'd hugged came out so strong, I could feel him so vividly I felt my dick grow hard.

Shit. T didn't mean this.

Cool, T. I'll try.

You better.

I got to sleep.

A'ight but I'm checking in tomorrow.

I slid the phone under my pillow and settled into a comfortable sleeping position, a fetal position facing the wall. I closed my eyes and tried calling on sleep.

II.

I DIDN'T sleep right. My mind kept wandering to Law. Was he all right? Would he be all right? My heart beat so loudly and fast I barely got a chance to breathe.

I finally got to sleep in the wee hours when Mum and Dad were waking up to go to work. I woke up a few hours after that, earlier than I was accustomed, to a dead phone and a quiet house.

I put the phone in the charger, grabbed my running shoes, and went for my morning run. I needed to burn the nervous energy and probably get some sleep after.

The thing I liked about running was I didn't have a chance to think. I was always too busy battling my thoughts with my body, wondering if I'd be able to complete the next mile, considering how much my legs were hurting.

But somehow, even with my battles of will, Law slithered into my thoughts, hatched eggs, and he became all I could think about.

It wasn't fair what his dad was doing, making Law feel unwanted like that. Making him feel wrong for this world.

I found myself cutting through a street I didn't run on to get back home quickly, find Law, and see how he was doing. Despite T's meaningful words, I decided against speaking of my feelings. Law had enough shit on his plate.

To my utter dismay, Law's dad was in the backyard surrounded by a cloud of white smoke smelling of tobacco. He turned my way and I froze. Law's dad was a scary-looking guy. He was ridiculously tall and stiff, with frown lines so deep they had to be imprinted on his bones. He had dark eyebrows that were always furrowed, a forehead with deep creases, and hard eyes that didn't seem to blink.

Those hard eyes found mine, and I could swear his entire body tightened. So did mine, with nerves and fear. Law's dad looked like a lion ready to pounce.

He blew out smoke, and it clouded his face, shrouding him with doom—which I could have sworn was impossible in broad daylight with the sun shining overhead.

"Devon, is it?" Law's dad had a deep Somali accent that doused the fire in his words.

"Yes." I stood at attention with my eyes on his, bracing myself for the worst. If he called me out, I'd call him out right back.

He paused and took a puff, giving me a chance to blink. It clicked then. Muslims weren't supposed to smoke; Law's dad was smoking. And how was Law? How was he? I feared asking, imagining I'd probably be pouring oil on flames.

He nodded as if contemplating something. "You're homosexual too?"

"Yes," I said.

He nodded again. "So's my son."

I tried reading into his voice, but it was unchanging in pitch and lacked expression.

I bit my lip and grappled with something to say. "So?" Which meant, was it a problem?

He threw his cigarette on the ground and stepped on it. "Nothing." He glared and disappeared into his house. What did that mean?

I dashed into my house, ran up the stairs, and grabbed my phone off the charger. I found Law's number and dialed it. The phone rang seven times and he still didn't pick up. That got me worried. It was Saturday, and Law had weekends off. Was he fine? Why was he not picking up?

I spent the next hour trying to gather courage to go next door and see if Law was okay. That's when it hit; I was a fucking coward. T was right. *But why?* I asked myself. There was nothing to fear, nothing serious… except maybe making shit worse for Law if they were bad already. Then again, Law could be in a worse place and needed my help while I was too chickenshit to do something about it.

"I am going over," I said out loud. I needed a plan, one that didn't seem too obvious and wouldn't put Law in trouble. But what to do? I wasn't particularly smart or intelligent.

Finally I decided fuck it; it would come on the way.

I grabbed my phone and shot T a text.

I've gone to Law's—if I don't make it back in an hour call the police. It'll most likely be the dad's fault!!

Okay, maybe I was a bit dramatic.

I pocketed my phone and walked next door, my knees weak and my guts all twisted up. I thought for sure I was going to vomit. I rubbed my hands and knocked.

Law's dad opened the door. "What?"

"Uh…. Is Law in?" I blurted.

"Why?"

"He helped fix my laptop, but it's acting up again." I mentally clapped myself on the back. That seemed legit and didn't imply much. "He's not picking up."

"He's not in, he went with his mother."

My heart leaped to my throat. "What!" Like forever? Holy shit! I swallowed a lump and asked, "Uh, will he be back?"

"He lives here, no?"

That was good, right? I hoped it was. "Do you know what time?"

"In the evening."

"Okay, thanks."

Law's dad grunted assent, and I walked back to my house, feeling his eyes burrowing into my back.

I sat down on the sofa and stilled myself. I was shaking all over and sweating profusely.

T's text was waiting for me but nothing from Law. Dammit, he'd better be all right. He'd better come back. I'd hug him so tight his ribs would hurt. Law's dad better not have been lying.

Do I want to know?

Probably not.

Did you tell him?

Not yet, he's unreachable.

He's ghosting you already? Lmfao. Laughing emojis.

Holy fuck, I hadn't even considered that. What if his dad told him to keep away and Law went with it? *Not funny.*

It was so not funny. It was all I could think of for the next few hours. Dammit, T. Why were we even friends? Because I admired how true T was to himself. He didn't hide his thoughts, his feelings, his weaknesses and strengths. He wore it all like armor, and proudly too.

Still, he distorted my state of mind. In an effort to dispel the bad mood I cleaned my room and the rest of the house, then embarked on baking a fruitcake, or tried to. I was shit at baking. Things were made worse when I peeked in the oven every ten minutes to check the progress.

The cake came out squishy and far too spongy. It didn't taste bad, if you didn't think about it too much. I didn't.

At six, just when I thought I'd never see Law again, the doorbell rang and there he was with that cap of his worn backward, wearing a baggy shirt over baggy shorts.

Without waiting I pulled him into a hug and squeezed him tight until he squeaked.

"Man, I was so fucking worried." I pulled back and looked him over. He had bugged eyes, but otherwise he looked fine. No scars or anything.

"Twenty missed calls. I didn't carry my phone."

"How's that possible?" My phone was my lifeline.

"My aunt Muna went into labor, and Mum was too excited. She asked me to drive her because Dad was too tired. Aunt Muna is forty-one, it's her first child. The doctors said she couldn't get pregnant, but I guess Allah blessed her."

I pulled him close again by his shoulders. I liked him close. "Your dad came back."

Law grimaced and swallowed. "I know."

"How'd that go?"

Law sighed. "We spoke, during morning prayers, of all times. He said he'll take it a step at a time and apologized for leaving the way he did."

I hugged him again. That sounded good. I felt relieved.

"I made it clear I wouldn't hide who I was or try to change it. I wanted him to know that."

I felt a swell of pride; Law saying that to his scary-looking dad had to have taken not two but three balls. "And?"

"He said okay and went on to mention he hoped I remained a good student." Law squeezed me and huffed. "I was fucking terrified, so scared. I mean, it could have gone to shit."

I squeezed him back. "You were brave."

"I'm not usually brave."

"There's a first time for everything."

"I felt like I was soaring when I said that." He sounded excited. "Like I could do anything, I just had to set my mind to it. I want to be brave more often. It's a high on its own."

I chuckled at his words. I didn't know Law got high. It was something I would have liked to see. "What else do you want to be brave at?"

"Everything!"

And out of nowhere his lips were pressed on mine. I froze, my mind slamming to a halt.

Just as quick as his lips had landed on mine, he pulled back, his eyes wide and disbelieving. "Whoa!" he said and tried to extract himself from my hug. That seemed to be the kick my mind needed to start functioning again.

I tightened my hold; if he thought he was getting away after that, he was joking.

"I didn't mean to!" Law explained.

I frowned. "What?"

"I'm sorry." Law couldn't meet my eyes.

I decided I might as well speak my mind if being brave was the theme of the day. Just get it on with, and if Law had been carried away by the moment, I'd make sure that happened often. "I have to tell you something."

"Oh." He glanced at me, his eyes focusing on mine, then my lips, before looking away at the cake I'd made.

How did someone confess their feelings? I'd never done it before. I'd done stuff with guys but never confessing feelings; there'd never been feelings before. "I don't want to take advantage of you," I began.

"What?" Law looked up.

"You know, you are coming out. It's difficult, and I don't want to take advantage of that."

Law frowned and looked back at the cake.

I exhaled and went on with it. "ButIlikeyou." I stumbled through the words in a rush, my heart thumping like an *Isukuti* drum. I could bet Law heard it. My tongue didn't even feel like mine.

"Huh?" Law looked up, his eyes confused.

Ah shit. I had to say it again. "I like you… a lot." I held my breath and watched Law take in my words.

He looked me dead in the eye, a soft smile on his lips. "Really? Me?"

I exhaled and smiled back. "Yes."

"Me too," Law said.

My heart wanted to explode with joy. "Really?"

He nodded. "I don't know if you know, but you're the reason I use the bus," Law said shyly.

"What?"

"I like talking to you and Johnny in the morning. It's weird, right?"

Not at all, I liked those conversations with Johnny too. Johnny was a DJ who bagged groceries, talked too much, and served as a bridge between Law and me on those bus rides in the morning while we both went to school.

"I like it." I pulled him close until I felt his erection pressing against me. Law made a noise that was the opposite of weird.

"Can I kiss you?" Law asked bashfully.

"Anytime."

I was the one to lean in, closing the gap between us. Law's lips were soft, delicate, and wet. His mouth tasted like vanilla and all that's right in the universe.

When our tongues met, he moaned or I did. It was hard to tell with all the blood rushing south. I pulled him even tighter than was possible, and my hands went to his ass just about the same time I rutted against him, our dicks brushing together.

Law pulled away with a deep groan and initiated the second thrust. I thrust back, kissed his neck, and captured his mouth again with mine. Meanwhile, his hands migrated from my hair to under my shirt, caressing my back muscles.

Law kissed hard, pressing me painfully against the counter until it dug painfully into my ass. I was too hot to be bothered.

I loved it. It felt good. It felt right.

When I couldn't breathe again, I pulled back an inch and began sucking on his lower lip, all while we thrust frantically against each other.

I was so going to come, in my pants no less.

Just when I thought that, the door swung open, and there stood Mum holding a bag of groceries. Law and I jumped apart, but it was too late. She'd seen. Damn.

"Devon! What on earth!" Mum said. Mum didn't use my full name often. She didn't curse either—she was religious like that.

I felt so scared that my dick went from a hundred to zero real quick.

"Holy mother of Christ! How will I ever unsee this?" She glared at me, stepped into the kitchen, and gingerly placed the bag of groceries on the counter.

"I'll, uh, go," Law said in a choked up voice.

I couldn't even face him. I wanted to die of embarrassment. Him going sounded like a great idea, and I wished I could too. If he went he wouldn't witness Mum reading me the riot act, and I wouldn't have to go through it with my mind still disoriented.

"No way." Mum shook her head.

What? I was pretty sure she was infringing on some freedoms and rights by denying Law permission to leave. "Mum!"

"We're having the sex talk," she said in a sure and determined voice.

My eyes went real wide.

Kill me now. Dear Lord, send down lightning to strike me. "Mum!" I said again. Apparently my brain was faulty and incapable of stringing words together.

"In the living room. Let's go." She gave me eyes that didn't leave much room for discussion.

We ended up seated on the sofa, a good distance between Law and me, with Mum standing before us, two cucumbers and a box of condoms in hand.

"We're going to practice putting these condoms on, first and foremost." She handed us the cucumbers and gave us the box to pick condoms.

I gave her disbelieving eyes. "Mum, we weren't even doing much. Just kissing," I protested.

"But you're dating, right?" Mum asked.

Jeez, we hadn't even discussed that. I didn't want to say the wrong thing, though. Mum didn't like us dating while still in high school. She'd argued with Roni about that for a week when Roni announced she'd gotten a boyfriend. Mum hadn't been happy. I didn't want to make Mum unhappy. On the other hand, I wanted to be with Law, so if I said no I'd be lying to him. But I thought, what if I said yes and he wasn't ready?

I glanced over at him, and I swear, I could read my doubts written in his eyes. My emotions precisely in his eyes.

"Yes," I said. Law gave me a small smile, and I held on to that as Mum went on to explain the importance of a condom in oral and anal sex—kill me already—and the importance of getting periodically tested. She didn't even shy away from talking about anal sex, like the prepping and all that, importance of lube and enemas… at that point my mind shut down. Some things I didn't need my Mum telling me. Christ!

Finally, at the end of it all, Mum smiled and asked, "So are we now in the know?"

"Maybe even a bit too much," I mumbled.

"Good. Just remember, safe sex is great sex." She turned to Law, who looked shook. "You good?"

"Mm-hm." Law seemed unsure.

"Want to stay for dinner? Dev will be making us some mashed potatoes."

"Ah, next time? I'm making dinner too." Law wouldn't meet my mum's eyes.

"Okay, next time. I'd like to know you as Dev's boyfriend." She grabbed the cucumbers and condoms, then left.

Law turned to me, wide-eyed. He opened his mouth, but I placed my hand over it and pointed to my ear and back where Mum had gone. Most definitely she was eavesdropping.

"I'll walk you out," I offered.

"What the fuck was that!" Law hissed as soon as we stepped into our shared yard. He had a shocked expression on his face, mixed with amusement.

I grimaced. "That's my mum."

"OMG, like… whoa."

"I know."

"I won't look at your mum the same."

"I have to sit through dinner with her." That was so gonna be awkward.

Law grinned. "Did your sister get the same talk?"

I grimaced. "Roni's was worse. Mum even dragged her to a labor room to witness deliveries, just to emphasize the importance of a condom and contraceptives."

"Holy cow!"

I nodded.

We didn't say anything for a while. I thought about Roni; we hadn't talked in days, four I think. I'd call her today and check in.

"So we're dating?" Law asked, pulling me from my thoughts.

I smiled, reached for his hand, and clasped it in mine. "It's only fair after that ordeal."

"I was just thinking the same." He grinned back.

"Come here, boyfriend." I pulled him into a hug and planted a kiss on his forehead. Law kissed my neck in return.

"I'm really liking being brave."

"Me too. Too much awesome stuff." No wonder T lived such a happy life.

"Do you want to sneak out and look at the stars tonight? And that's a euphemism for kiss." Law looked at me through his long lashes, and I nearly wept. He was so gorgeous and he liked me back. *He liked me back!* Not forgetting he'd be all right.

He was going to be okay. I'd make sure of it.

I chuckled. "I'd love to look at stars with you."

A. ADUMA started school at the age of three, where she enjoyed relative calm, ate too many cakes, and spent her afternoons sleeping. She also stole building bricks and took them home with her even after a thorough search by the class teacher.

At the age of seven she was exposed to her first storybook, *The Little Mermaid*, which she didn't read but spent a good amount of time fawning over the pretty pictures of Ariel and her sisters while trying not to be scared off by skeletons that were apparently Satanic, if you asked her grandmother. *The Secret Garden* by Frances Hodgson Burnett and *Black Beauty* by Anna Sewell were the first books she recalls reading and completing because they brought to her eyes endless streams of tears that so far only Sandra Bullock and Hugh Grant in *Two Weeks Notice* had been able to unleash.

At the age of twelve she won best playwright in a school competition and had the pleasure of watching her play come to life during a graduation ceremony. In high school, she wrote corny poems about her crushes but had the good sense to not send the cringe-inducing poems their way. Currently Aduma is at the University of Nairobi doing a degree in economics, which unfortunately has more math than she expected.

Find A. Aduma on Twitter @MayHorizontal.

The Head That Wears a Crown
by Kat Freydl

HERE'S WHAT you need to know: Charlie is a boy, and he believes in ghosts.

The ghosts were easy to accept draping over the coffin at his mother's funeral, dripping onto the pavement outside the dance recital his father forgot to come to, curling themselves around the dresses hung starched and pressed in his closet. Dr. Pembrook always said that it's a coping mechanism, and sure, Charlie gets it. He took AP Psychology. You have a patient with a dead mom who sees ghosts, the ghosts are probably a coping mechanism, whatever. He *gets* it. He's bored of it. The ghosts are easy. The boyhood is the thing he chokes on.

The thing is, he thinks he's probably always known, but it doesn't quite hit until the mile run in his gym class.

His brother, Cal, would've hated this school, with its arbitrary four-year gym requirement and its thematic lunch menus. He's twenty and has his GED and spends his time underneath cars and behind shotguns in equal measure, so you do the math on that one, and it's just Charlie here, keeping his head down and his grades up, and here's a secret: Charlie wishes he was average, because maybe then he wouldn't feel so duty-bound to do something *better*, something *suitable for a lady*, or whatever his dad wants for him, because he hates school, he really does. Anyway, Charlie's here desperately trying to be as unathletic as possible, because *God* is he sick of being unsuccessfully recruited for women's basketball on account of his gangling legs, his sinewy arms, not sure if he's fooling anyone with his purposely dragging feet and carefully composed expression of exhaustion. Adam Smith, a soccer player with the lowest stamina Charlie has ever seen, is directly in his line of sight. In front of Adam is a ghost, but no one can see it except Charlie, which he is accustomed to. What he is not accustomed to is the way he finds himself clenching his teeth, because at this pace, he can feel every time his A cups painfully bounce (he *assumes* they're A cups—he's worn sports bras, easier to find at Walmart and less agonizing to buy when you're with your brother, for as long as he can remember), and the way his back is cramping makes him suspect he'll be starting his period soon, so that's fucking wonderful. And then the bell is ringing just as Charlie's shitty beat-up hand-me-down sneakers touch down on his final lap, and Adam gives him this companionable, sympathetic shoulder clap, and the ghost behind Adam stares at him with sad eyes, and Charlie's line of sight is right at Adam's pecs, his flat chest, and his eyes travel up to a jaw that he can tell will be chiseled and dotted with stubble one day, and he thinks *That's what I'm supposed to look like.*

So, shit, you know?

CHARLIE WAS thirteen when he first got sent to therapy. He sat on a beanbag chair with his legs drawn to his chest, twisting the fibers of the carpet under his fingers because it was something to do, and also because Dr. Pembrook was not an easy woman to look in the eye. The only word he could think of to describe her was *hawkish*, cheekbones jutting out beneath a pair of cat-eye glasses that did no favors for her sharp face, eyes sympathetic in a way that made Charlie's stomach hurt. She sat crisscross applesauce on a beanbag chair across from him, which he appreciated.

"We could sit here in silence some more," she said finally, "but I do charge sixty dollars per session, so you might as well talk about something. Whatever you want. I'm your captive listener."

Charlie paused in his carpet-twisting for a moment. His best pair of shoes cost six dollars at Goodwill, and his father once drove him and his brother around grocery stores after hours looking for thrown-out loaves of just-stale-enough bread, but sure, okay. Sixty dollars a session.

"Twenty-two percent of the world's population sees ghosts," he said, without entirely meaning to. "That's over a billion people. I'm not special."

He peered up at her, just for a second, and Dr. Pembrook gave him a little smile. "Not unique, perhaps, but special—"

"Oh God, no, please not that," Charlie blurted out. "I don't need to be told I'm special. Like, I'll pay you sixty dollars a session to *not* tell me I'm special. That's not what this is."

"Then what is it?"

Charlie scowled. "I know what you're trying to do. Can we just be upfront here? My dad called you because his thirteen-year-old kid has a dead mom, and that dead mom believed in ghosts, and now his kid says she's *seeing* ghosts, and for some reason *that's* the line for therapy, not, oh, I don't know, the fucking *grief* one experiences when their mom dies, and—" He exhaled sharply. "I don't need you to do the whole gentle listener thing, okay? Just… be upfront with me."

Dr. Pembrook was still meeting his gaze levelly.

"Okay," she said. "So, twenty-two percent of the population sees ghosts. You're right on that. Did you know that six percent of the world experiences a psychotic episode in their lifetime? Not quite as many, but still a significant amount."

Charlie's heart did something strange and unpleasant in his chest. "You think I'm having a psychotic episode?"

"There have been studies done. Psychotic episodes are quite possibly a coping mechanism for existential distress." She leaned forward on her beanbag chair, so fucking earnestly that Charlie ached with it. He felt himself softening against his will. "But no, Charlie. I don't think you're having a psychotic episode."

"Then what is this?"

That, maybe, was what she was waiting for, because she sat back and clicked her pen.

"That's what we're going to try to figure out."

HE USUALLY runs home, a five-mile jog that barely leaves him out of breath anymore, but today he walks, painfully aware of how he feels in his own body. His chest is wrong. His arms are wrong. His hips are wrong. Everything is too soft, too curvy, too tender. His hair—shit, his hair, which swings well past his waist when it's not in the tight coil at the back of his neck he perfected at age ten. He suddenly feels like he weighs a thousand pounds, and a cramp shoots through him, dull and aching and wrong wrong wrong. He starts to run.

See, when Mom was alive, she was the kind of mom who had snacks prepared when school let out, who asked about their days and put report cards on refrigerators and gave them kisses on the tops of their heads. Dad would get home whenever he got home, and she would ask him about *his* day, give him notes on his sermons, coax him into slipping off his suit coat and joining the family at the dinner table. Mom was the only person Charlie ever saw make Dad smile.

When she died, their dad never came home, really, not at first, didn't even notice that Cal stopped going to school. It got even worse when he decided to *take his sermons on the road*, as he put it, stopped being John Waters, Father Of Two, and became John Waters, Traveling Evangelist of Moderate Daytime Televangelism Fame. All that's on their refrigerator right now is a printout of Isaiah 11:4, *And with the breath of His lips He will slay the wicked.*

The point is, nobody's home when Charlie bursts through the front door, so the first thing he does is boot up the wheezing laptop that lives in their kitchen, a gigantic, hulking Dell that weighs at least ten pounds, shooing away the ghost that wisps out of the back of the monitor, drumming his fingers impatiently as it boots up, and brings up a search engine. He's not very good at research when he can't hold it in his hands, but he's learning.

folk tales gender swap
supernatural being wrong body
girl to boy mythology
monsters that cause wrong gender

Unsurprisingly, he doesn't find much. It's maybe a little sad that he was hoping this was something he could exorcise, could reason with through a Ouija board.

girl wants to be a boy more than anything in the world
my whole body hurts and my skin doesn't belong to me
how to get rid of breasts
why do i want to be a boy so much it hurts

He doesn't know how long he sits there, reading through pages and pages of articles about plastic surgery and women with breast cancer and people born with both ovaries and testes before he pushes away from the desk, breathing hard. His fucking stomach hurts. He wonders if this is like alien hand syndrome, where sometimes people's hands just stop listening to their brains and do whatever they want. He clears the browser history and slams the laptop shut. His body doesn't belong to him. He storms into his bedroom, trembling, and drags his backpack over to his bed, throws back the cover and crawls under them, dragging the hefty dictionary he keeps beside the bed onto his lap, and God, if he doesn't hate the way he compulsively checks the salt lines he keeps in front of his bedroom door first, gives one more cursory glance at the typically vague note his father left—*Unexpected trip for work, Cal has money for pizza*—checks the salt lines, checks the salt lines.

Girl (n). 1. A female child. Synonyms: female, child, daughter.

Boy (n). 1. A male child or young man. Synonyms: lad, schoolboy, male child, youth, young man, laddie, stripling; 2. Exclamation, informal. Used to express strong feelings, especially of excitement or admiration.

Charlie doesn't know what he was expecting.

He runs out of ideas then, and he's flipping through the *T*s for testosterone or testes or he doesn't fucking know, okay, he's just looking, and he comes across transgender.

Transgender (adj). 1. Denoting or relating to a person whose sense of personal identity and gender does not correspond with their birth sex. See entry for "dysphoria."

Well.

He feels like he's choking, like his lungs aren't working. He flips to the *D*s.

Dysphoria (n). 1. A state of unease or generalized dissatisfaction with life. See also: gender dysphoria (n): the condition of feeling one's emotional and psychological identity as male or female to be opposite to one's biological sex. Origin (Greek)—from dusphoros ('hard to bear').

Charlie thinks of skirts, of how they used to use to dress him up for church on Christmas, how Cal would tie his curly hair into braids so, so carefully, tongue caught between his teeth in concentration, thinks about how his favorite part was getting home and wriggling out of the skirt and into one of Cal's hand-me-down pairs of jeans that hung loose on his hips. He thinks about how he's too sinewy for the girls, too soft for the guys, how he cried and cried and cried when he started his period, scaring the shit out of Cal and their father and trying to explain through hitching sobs that no, he was fine, yes it hurt but no he wasn't dying, he just *wanted* to and he didn't understand *why*, and before he realizes it he's throwing the dictionary at the wall, doesn't feel any better when it slumps spine-first onto the filthy carpet, balls himself up as tightly as he can underneath the comforter, and resolutely does not cry.

THE THING is, it's not like Charlie existed in a vacuum. It's not like he didn't know that most people don't line their thresholds with salt to ward off evil spirits, that most people don't ask for Ouija boards and holy water for Christmas. It's not like he didn't know he was objectively crazy.

"Let's not say *crazy*," Dr. Pembrook said.

"Then what? *Alternately* sane? Don't bullshit me, Caroline." When they hit the year mark, Dr. Pembrook told Charlie he could call her by her first name. He did, sometimes, but in his head she was still Dr. Pembrook.

"Well, no." She took off her glasses, which Charlie had come to know meant business.

"Think of hypochondriacs, for example. I had a patient who began drinking hand sanitizer because she was convinced she had *C. diff.* Did you know that bacteria cells outnumber our body cells ten to one? I didn't either, until I met this patient. She was a functional, average person in her daily life, but she got fixated on the idea that the bacteria was taking over. She knew everything there was to know about bacteria and about every obscure bacterial infection you could imagine, but she was still a person. She *knew* when she was being irrational. She just couldn't stop it." She took a breath. "The point is, ghosts are your bacteria, Charlie. But I think it's different for you."

The thing is, Charlie's mother had a journal, a little leather-bound thing with a Celtic cross on the front. It was one of the gifts the church gave her when she first got diagnosed, and giving it to Charlie was the last thing she ever definitively did, and what was he going to do, not read it? Some passages:

A person with poor eyesight is susceptible to spiritual sight.

Charlie had 20/20 vision, but Dr. Pembrook with her glasses looked at him like she understood him.

To thwart evil spirits, line the threshold with salt.

Charlie did this. Every night.

Ghosts never touch the ground and you can never be too careful.

Charlie was still trying to figure that one out.

The ghost is with you.

This, Charlie didn't fully understand either, but he believed.

He apparently said some of this out loud, because Dr. Pembrook made a humming sound and said, "Yes, the journal," in that voice Charlie dreaded.

"Charlie, do you think it is at all possible that you cling to this belief as a way of connecting with your mom? It's the last thing she gave you."

"Of course I think it's possible," he said. Like he said before, it's not like Charlie existed in a vacuum. "But… but it's different. It's… hard to explain."

"Because you see them?"

"Well, no. I don't, even."

Dr. Pembrook looked up from her notepad. "What?"

"I mean…." Charlie stared up at the popcorn ceiling like it was going to tell him how to explain this, but it held no answers, just the same water stain that looked vaguely like a rabbit if he stared hard enough. "I believe in them. But I don't see them, necessarily. I just… know they're there."

"I see," Dr. Pembrook said. Charlie could hear the frown in her voice.

"God, no, okay, don't put on the therapist voice with me."

"I *am* literally your therapist," she said, which would probably have made Charlie laugh some other time, but he was starting to think he was on the verge of something here, and he bit his lip.

"No, okay, it's just that… it's just that I don't believe in them the way you believe in Santa Claus. I believe in them the way you believe in gravity. It's there, and I can't see it for sure, but it has an impact on my life anyway. It's… it's the way my dad believes in God, this nebulous *thing* that you can't describe even if you want to. And it's like… okay, with gravity, astronauts can't *see* it, but they float, right? And for all we know they float for some other, weirder reason, but no, we all believe in this thing called gravity, so that must be the explanation, but it doesn't make any difference. It could be gravity or it could be… God, I don't know, invisible rubber bands or something, and it wouldn't make any fucking difference. And my dad, he prays anyway, just in case this God he can't see is listening, and he has no reason to think anything that happens is the result of that prayer, but he believes hard enough that he goes around preaching about it anyway. God is real to him, and gravity is real to… to most people, I assume, and ghosts are real to me. I don't *have* to see them."

Dr. Pembrook was quiet for a long time, long enough for Charlie to grind out a desperate attempt at a joke—"*I* believe in gravity, by the way"—and finally she looked up at him.

"So all this time, when you've said you see them, you mean you *feel* them?"

Charlie thought about it. "Yeah. Yeah, I guess so."

Dr. Pembrook took a long breath. "When do you feel them, Charlie?"

He told her about feeling them at his mother's funeral. About the dance recital. About the dresses. About how they pooled in his chest in gym class, when he thought about his mother, when he dressed up for church on the rare occasion his father made him come to the sermons.

"Okay," Dr. Pembrook said finally. Her glasses, which she had put back on to scrawl some notes on her notepad, came off again. "Okay, I think we've been going about this all wrong."

BY THE time Cal gets home, mouth pinched in a way that says *headache* and eyes hard in a way that says *don't ask*, smelling like engine oil and tobacco, Charlie has tucked this all away where it belongs. He's at the little table in the middle of his room memorizing the Latin rite of exorcism.

Here is what you need to know about Cal: he does not believe in ghosts, but he believes that Charlie believes.

"Heya, Charlie," Cal says, smiling a little. He throws his leather jacket onto the floor the way Charlie hates, throws himself down on the chair next to him. A ghost whispers out of the jacket, hovers above the dictionary Charlie cast aside.

"Hey." He knows he's being too quiet, Cal's going to notice something's wrong, but he's hoping he can put it off to a headache, which is not so much a lie as it is a glaring omission.

"Head hurt?" Charlie's hair is loose around his shoulders, and he guesses he's not surprised that Cal's noticed—the back-of-the-neck knot is efficient but pulls too hard at his head sometimes, makes the headaches worse and the migraines unbearable.

He nods. "Yeah. It's fine, though. Livable." Cal puts his head on Charlie's shoulder, starts doing the one-handed braid he became a pro at when he was fourteen and Charlie was ten. Cal does this sometimes.

"Why are you all clingy?"

"I had a shit day. There was a girl, and she was pretty, and I'm the guy whose dad is a traveling evangelist...."

"Duuuuuude."

"I know, I know, it's all very exciting. How do we even talk to normal people?"

"How the fuck would I know? You're literally my only friend, Cal." It's as simple and immensely fucked up as that.

"I don't know, I just saw her and felt like I was *supposed* to talk to her, you know? It was okay at first, but my last name came up, and the inevitable 'Are you related to *that* John Waters?' conversation happened. I guess her grandma watches his sermons religiously, pun *fully* intended. Obviously she wasn't into it. Apparently John Waters isn't for everyone, which is fair."

Charlie pauses. "*Supposed* to talk to her. That's really weird, Cal."

"Read: how do we even talk to normal people?"

The thing is, Cal does not believe in ghosts, but if he spills salt he throws a little over his shoulder, and when they go hiking he avoids fairy rings like he'll die if he doesn't, and sometimes when he's not trying so hard to be whatever he *thinks* he's supposed to be, he throws around words like *fate*, like *destiny*.

Charlie has his ghosts, and Cal has fate.

Cal reads over his shoulder for a while, ties the braid neatly at the end (Cal always keeps hair ties on his wrist because he is a ridiculous man), lets it fall over Charlie's right shoulder, and Charlie wrenches himself up to go to the bathroom.

"Hey, I'm ordering pizza. You want?"

"Veggie?" Charlie bats his eyelashes.

"What the fuck ever, dude. That shit's the reason you're wasting away. I'm making it half meat lover's."

Charlie smiles a little and shuts the door.

The smile drops off his face as he stands in front of the mirror and palms his chest, *wrong wrong wrong*, and he feels something strange and horrible welling up in him, feels the ghost in his room juddering in alarm. He guesses nothing was going to keep this at bay for long, but he needs to change his pad (he was right about his period, fuck his fucking life), and he hastily wipes his stinging eyes because he doesn't have time for this. He takes a deep breath, clenching his teeth against another debilitating cramp, and does what he has to. The trash can in here is overflowing, so he rolls up the old one in its wrapper and brings it outside, chucks it in the tiny wastebasket next to the table.

"Ohhhhh," Cal says then, all fucking knowingly, and fuck him. Honestly, Charlie can't hide anything from him. "That explains it, grumpy. Heating pad?"

For some reason this, of all things, is what makes the tears spill over. Charlie clutches his stomach, curls up on his bed, and trembles with suppressed sobs.

"Shit. That bad? Okay, kid, okay, hold on," Cal is saying somewhere, distant and soft, and Charlie squeezes his eyes shut so, so tightly. His skin feels hot, like it should be melting right off him. He aches. Charlie is prone to the kinds of period cramps that have, on more than one occasion, induced vomiting or fainting, so this is not exactly unexpected, but once Cal gets a good look at him, it's all going to be over. "Okayokayokay," Cal is saying as he putters around. The fact that he knows exactly what to do almost makes this worse.

He hands him the heating pad. "Charlie. Talk to me. What hurts?"

Everything, he doesn't say. *Absolutely everything.*

"Hormones," he chokes out weakly. "I'm fine."

"Bullshit," Cal bites back, and then, more softly, "Why so sad, kiddo?"

Charlie can't look at him. He buries his face in his pillow, and there's this heavy, lingering silence, and then Cal is crawling beside him, shoes still on, and sprawls across the bed the way he sometimes does when he's drunk, and Charlie turns over and clutches at his shirt and weeps his fucking heart out.

"Just breathe, dude," Cal is saying, and Charlie fucking loves him for this. "Breathe. We can do the rest. This is totally fucking understandable, you know? Hurts like a bitch. You're totally allowed to cry." And God, Charlie loves the way Cal does this, turns the *you* into *us*, sounds wrung out like he's hurting too.

He breathes hard into Cal's chest for a while. They're curved together like a couple of parentheses in the way that really started freaking their father out when Charlie grew boobs, but seriously, John, he just wants his brother, you know? You can't travel around giving sermons, leave your kid to raise your other fucking kid, and then be mad when they cling a little. Cal palms the back of his head and says nonsense things, and Charlie sniffs with an air of finality and looks up at him, finally, through his bangs.

Cal is pale, and he looks slightly terrified. The first time Charlie had been laid low by period cramps, Cal insisted on being given a crash course on all things menstrual, and after reading a couple of blog posts about people with uteruses passing out or not going to the hospital for burst appendixes because they thought it had just been cramps, he sat down for a long time, left the house, and came back a few hours later with five different brands of pad, every period-related painkiller he could get his hands on, and two different heating pads. This does not mean that he did not freak the fuck out the time Charlie fainted from cramps while they were standing at the bus stop. This does not mean he is not freaking the fuck out now.

"I'm okay," Charlie says.

Cal doesn't look convinced but knows better than to push here. He sighs. "You're okay."

They lie like that for a while, and it's Cal who breaks the silence. It usually is.

"What were you working on when I came in?"

"The Latin rite of exorcism," he says. "Which is exactly what it sounds like, except I read somewhere that it can also, and I quote, 'protect against the power of the Evil One.'"

"Oh. Uh… neat."

Charlie stifles a laugh in Cal's shoulder. "You don't have to be so *supportive* all the time. It's objectively ridiculous."

Cal shrugs. "I mean, yeah, but you *know* it's objectively ridiculous. Dad took his crazy and made a living from it."

Charlie musters a grin, then lies back on the bed, rolling that word around in his head like a marble. *Crazy. Crazy. Crazy.*

He takes this thing that's been welling up in his chest and shoves it back down, tells himself he's overreacting, that it's a *coping mechanism*, that it doesn't matter. He's Charlotte Waters. He's Cal's sister. He's a girl. He won't even tell Cal about this, because it'll just be another *thing*, another thing he doesn't believe but believes that *Charlie* believes. And Charlie doesn't need that.

He can handle this on his own.

THE LAST session Charlie ever had with Dr. Pembrook, she had new glasses, and he doesn't think he'll ever forget that. They were round, and suddenly she wasn't hawkish at all. Soft brown eyes peered from behind the circular lenses, set in a face that was thin but not quite so sharp. Charlie didn't mention them.

"So, we talked last session about how you don't really see the ghosts. How they're more of a feeling. I want to talk more about that with you today."

Charlie looked at that popcorn ceiling, something that had become a habit, and looked for the rabbit-shaped water stain. It wasn't there. Someone had patched and painted over it. He looked down again.

"Charlie, I think you're deflecting, but deflecting *what*, I don't know. You're incredibly well-adjusted concerning your mother's death. It is not uncommon to hang on to stress-borne delusions well past the point of recovery, but if you know they're not there, if you're not physically seeing them, they're not *delusions*, per se. Has there been anything else on your mind? Anything bothering you, causing these emotional reactions? These ghosts? I have a feeling they won't go away until you face whatever prompts them."

Charlie bit his lip. "I mean. Uh, at the moment, I'm kind of pissed at my dad."

Dr. Pembrook's eyebrows lifted. "Oh?"

"Yeah, I mean…." He shrugged. "I mean, he's always, like, been a pastor. And that's cool. He was always Episcopal or something. Never forced it on me or Cal. Preached tolerance and love but with a side of Jesus."

Her lips quirked. "But now?"

"Now… ever since his televangelist shit started picking up, he's… changed. And maybe it's because Mom isn't there to keep him in check, but he's become downright fundamentalist. *Gays are going to hell*, the whole nine. I just think it's kind of shitty of him. My mom's sister has a partner, you know? A wife. Like, did you forget about that? And how can you think God cares about bullshit like that?"

She wrote something down. "You seem to be taking this quite personally."

"I mean… I'm not gay, if that's what you're getting at. But it would be nice to have the room to explore, if I wanted to, and yeah, I know how that sounds. I'm not closeted. I just…." Charlie shrugged. "We have one computer that the whole house shares, and I go to school in fucking Texas. It's not like I can access this information on my own. There's so much I don't even know." He forced himself to pause, to take a breath.

"Okay. There's some stuff to unpack there."

"There really isn't," Charlie said tiredly. "I promise not everything I say has hidden meaning. I just honestly can't think of anything that's, like, *causing these emotional reactions*, or however you put it. I just feel a little bit wrong all the time, like I'm not in the right body. Like I'm not living the right life. Like there's all these pieces I don't even have access to because I live with my brother and my dad might as well not be there and all I have are the same ten books I've read over and over and fucking dial-up internet. What am I supposed to do with that?"

Charlie was certain that he wasn't making any sense, but as always, Dr. Pembrook looked at him like she understood. She didn't say anything, though, and Charlie's mouth kept moving, unbidden. "Like… there's little ghosts all the time, but there's this one big ghost that's always with me, and I can't figure it out. I just can't fucking figure it out."

His stomach dropped to his feet. Mom's journal. *The ghost is with you.* If Dr. Pembrook saw his face pale, she didn't mention it.

"What about your brother? Can he help with this at all?"

Charlie's stomach twisted. "Cal… he's great, but I don't know. I guess I'm scared of what might happen. What if he's the same as my dad? And I don't want to start asking all these vague questions and have him overanalyze it. It's not his job. I don't know."

"It still may be worth trying to fight that discomfort. What's the worst that could happen?"

Charlie hated that question, because *so much* could happen. He didn't have an answer, really, but his mouth was moving again, whether he wanted it to or not.

"There's this story in the Bible," he said. "It's one of my dad's favorites. Moses is talking to God, and he says, 'Suppose I go to the Israelites and say to them, "The God of your fathers has sent me to you," and they ask me, "What is his name?" Then what shall I tell them?' And God, who is unsurprisingly cryptic about this whole thing, says, 'I am who I am.'" Charlie stared at the ceiling again, because there was no fucking way he could do this and look at her at the same time. "And there's always just been... something about that. Another translation says that it could also mean 'I will be who I will be.' And like... I want that, you know? Just... this self-defining thing. God is because he is and his name is irrelevant. He is because he is because he is."

The session ended with no substantial progress having been made, and Charlie left feeling the way he always felt after therapy—not better, not fixed, but more equipped to continue living as a semibroken person. He climbed into the battered old Chevy that was idling at the curb for him, startling as he realized it wasn't Cal but rather his father in the driver's seat, still dressed in his suit and tie.

"Uh. Hi, Dad. I didn't expect to see you—"

"Charlie, I looked up your therapist online."

Charlie's brow creased in confusion. His father had picked the therapist himself, presumably using the internet, and Charlie had been seeing her for three years now. It was a bit late to take an interest in her character.

"Uh. Okay?"

"We're done with her," he said simply, like he hadn't just dropped a bomb, no room for argument.

"*What?*"

His dad braked hard at a stop sign like it was an act of aggression. "Her website talks about her *partner*, Charlie," he said, words clipped with fury. "You don't need any 'counsel' she can give you. And think of what would happen if anyone found out my daughter was getting therapy from... from one of *those* people. I just can't risk it. Besides, don't you think you've got yourself sorted out by now?"

Charlie felt himself shrinking, felt something big and cavernous open in his chest, and he took a breath. Took a breath. Took a breath.

"Yes, sir."

CHARLIE WAKES from a nightmare, an indistinct one that leaves him feeling like he's drowning, feeling like he's bursting out of his own skin. He shakes and gasps for air, sweat cooling on his forehead, and before he can process any of it, Cal is bursting through the door, eyes wild, and above all clutching a lamp, inexplicably. "Charlie—!"

He sits up, arms shaking with the strain of holding him up. "Cal?"

"You *screamed.*" He lowers the lamp. "I... brought a lamp."

Charlie musters a watery grin. "You, what, thought I was being attacked, and you reached for the lamp? As much as it pains me, we have *guns* in this house, Cal."

Cal rolls his eyes, sits on the edge of Charlie's mattress. "God, you scared the shit out of me."

"I scared the shit out of me too." Charlie lies down, closing his eyes, breathing very deliberately. "It was, uh, just a nightmare."

"That's what you get for taking a nap like a five-year-old," Cal says, but he starts playing with Charlie's fingers the way he used to do when Charlie was getting flu shots and terrified, so…. "I held off on ordering the pizza, but it's only, like, nine. That's still within acceptable pizza-eating hours."

Charlie bites his lip. Cal would never pry directly, but he knows he's scaring him. "I don't remember what it was, really. I just woke up scared."

"You used to get those dreams when you were stressed," Cal says mildly, and Charlie just really fucking loves his brother. He feels *known*, and suddenly he doesn't know what he's so afraid of. He thinks of Dr. Pembrook, of just last week, her earnest voice telling him *the ghosts won't go away until you face what prompts them, have you tried talking to your brother?* Of course Cal will understand. Of course he will.

"Do you ever—?" Charlie starts, and his voice is all hoarse, and as it turns out, he can't do this and make eye contact at the same time, so he presses his face into Cal's chest and grinds out "—feellikeyoureinthewrongbody?"

He doesn't repeat himself. He doesn't need to. They've spoken each other's language for their entire lives.

"I... not really, no?" He's trying so hard to be supportive.

"Like…." Charlie bites down on his lip the way Cal hates, making one side of it swell up more than the other. "Like maybe you're supposed to be a girl?"

"Uh, no, I—Charlie?" He's started shaking, and Cal can feel it. He feels the breakdown of earlier welling up in him, the tears and the ache and the terror.

"I think… I think maybe I…." He cuts himself off with a frustrated noise, a few stray tears leaking out.

"Do I feel like I'm supposed to be a girl?" Cal forges ahead. "Nah, not really. That's kind of your area, y'know? The bitching, the makeup, your hugs *alone*, Jesus, that's the girliest shit, but you're my kid sister, you know? It's—"

And there are ghosts trembling all around him, ghosts that only Charlie can see, and Charlie is pulling himself back, and he's trembling, and Cal's face is this careful mask, and Charlie *knows*, Charlie *knows* that Cal's number one talent is making him talk, pulling him the fuck out of migraines and nonverbal panic attacks and sullen freaking silences, badgering him until he won't be able to hold it back anymore, but it fucking *hurts* and Charlie is *angry* and Charlie is *hurting* and Charlie is saying, "I'm not your fucking sister," and then before he can stop himself he's saying, "I hurt every fucking day ohgodCal it's so bad, my hair is wrong my hips are wrong everythingisfuckingwrong I hate it I hate it I want to be like you and Dad it hurts so fucking bad and when I think about myself I don't think *she* I think fucking *he he he he he*," and at some point he stands up and Cal is standing too and Charlie is conscious that he's almost at eye level with him now and Cal is so big and solid and *boy* and Charlie *isn't* and he's saying in his quietest fucking voice, "I don't want to be your sister."

Cal's face has been set in a carefully composed calm through all this, standing across from Charlie with his hands on his shoulders, but at this last part, Charlie sees a flash of hurt, no no Cal no don't hurt. Charlie hurries to correct himself. "I mean—shit, Cal. I don't want to be your sister because I want to be your *brother*."

Cal is quiet for what feels like a very long time, and when he finally speaks, it's not what Charlie was expecting.

"So you weren't crying over cramps, then."

"Ah… no. More like crying over a crippling existential dread and the sensation of wearing a shoe that's too small. But like… all the time."

"You're a sasquatch, your shoes are always too small."

"Screw you!"

"Do you want to tell Dad?"

"Oh. Um. Do I?"

"You got me, kid. He's probably going to want it to be something he can preach to, y'know? That's how he works. But… we kind of know how that ends, you know? He stopped you from going to fucking *therapy* because your therapist had a wife. This is not a man who is the pinnacle of reason."

Cal threw a fucking fit about the therapy thing, of course, but in the end he could only do so much. The hours he puts in at the auto shop only pull in so much money, and their father is not generous with the grocery stipends he leaves them. Cal spewed some bullshit about how *We'll make it work, Charlie, you let me worry about food*, but Charlie knows his brother, knows he'd work himself to death if he thought it would help Charlie. So he refused.

"Cal," he says, and nothing else. Fucking Cal.

"I know." He hugs him. "Can I say something really fucking self-indulgent?"

"Hi, I'm Charlie. Sometimes I cry for three hours without talking and then wake up screaming a few hours later because I love attention, nice to meet you."

"Okay, we get it, king of self-indulgence, but seriously, I just… this isn't exactly *news*, you know? Like you're my kid '*sister*'"—he puts extra emphasis on the air quotes, God, Charlie loves his brother—"but you're just this weird kid who loves reading shit and learning shit and refuses to be left behind, you know? Like I braid your hair and buy you pads, but we arm wrestle and I complain about girls and Dad's all '*stay in the car, Charlotte*' and asking all diligently about your homework and you just fucking do it, you know? Like you're there with your holy water and your exorcisms and it's a little creepy but I'm okay with it and you're beating me in races and kicking my ass when we spar and, shit, I thought maybe, I dunno, some girls are masculine, gender is a spectrum, but then I thought maybe you're into girls—are you, by the way? If so, this is going to be a fucking *excellent* discussion—and I was just kind of waiting for you to come to me, you know? You're just Charlie. Does that bother you? Are you changing it? Until then you're just fucking *Charlie*, you know? Baby sister. Baby brother. It's… semantics. It's not fucking… there's nothing astounding here. You're just. You are. You're immune to semantics."

"Your mom is immune to semantics," Charlie says, because he's starting to tear up again, and because yeah, okay, maybe he is also a ridiculous person. Maybe that's the only way to exist in their lives.

"Charlie, oh my *God*."

He stands up on his tiptoes—he's not quite there yet, but he's had this ache in his shins that means he's about to shoot the fuck up again, probably, and continue towering over girls and being unsuccessfully recruited for basketball every goddamn season until he graduates—and kisses his brother on the cheek.

"So. I'm going to order the fucking pizza. And then let's see what we can do about that hair."

IT'S A slow process. Charlie grips Cal's pant leg every now and then, makes him pause at every tier as his head gets lighter and lighter and lighter, years of confusion and shame and self-hatred sheared off with a pair of kitchen scissors, hair the same color as his mother's—midback. Shoulders. Chin. Just below the ears. He shivers each time he feels the cool metal on his scalp, hears the *shink* of the scissors freeing him strand by strand. Cal looks at him for a moment, tongue between his teeth in concentration. "You want sideburns?"

Charlie fucking *feels* his face light up, and Cal laughs hard and loud and honest, head thrown back, and pulls out his beard trimmer from underneath the sink. "Hold still, I've never done this on another person before."

He feels so fucking light, is the thing, and when Cal *finally* lets him look in the mirror, his face feels like it belongs to him. He runs his fingers over the short, spiky hair of the sideburns, over and over and over. *Sideburns*, he thinks, giddy. *I have sideburns.*

The doorbell rings while Cal's sweeping the hair off the bathroom floor, muttering disparaging remarks about how Charlie sheds like a dog. Charlie tips the pizza guy ten dollars, because God, everyone deserves to feel as good as he does right now.

"Thank y'all for the tip," the pizza guy drawls as Cal materializes at Charlie's elbow.

"Don't thank me," Cal says before Charlie can reply, smirking a little. "Thank my brother."

Charlie thinks sometimes there are moments like this, moments that feel like every other moment has been leading up to them. Here is the thing: the last time he ever saw his mother, she put her hand on his head and said, "My son, my baby boy." She'd been more and more forgetful toward the end, and he'd just kissed her on the forehead, thinking she thought he was Cal, but now he's not so sure. He thinks of the last journal entry his mother ever wrote—*the ghost is with you*—and for the first time it doesn't feel like a condemnation; it feels like a guide. Like maybe she *knew* through the tumor in her brain, through the fevers, through the shaking and the chapped lips and the hair she shook out of her pillowcase every morning. And for the first time he doesn't feel like this is a betrayal, doesn't think letting them go will be letting her go too. Every single ghost dissipates, especially the one sitting on Charlie's chest. He still has to tell their father. He's still in the wrong body, still aches all over and has a pair of A cups poking out accusingly from his chest, is still going to be called *she* and *her* and *Charlotte* by people he's never even met, but fuck.

Charlie can live on that for days.

KAT FREYDL is trans, queer, and shockingly bad at writing about themselves. When they're not writing, they're going on hours-long Wikipedia binges about whales, molecular biology, string theory, and the history of crime. They are currently studying anthropology and English, to the horror of their parents and distant relatives, and writing an awful lot of fan fiction.

Twitter: @schrod1ngerskat
Email: katfreydl@unc.edu

The Train Station
by B.K. Hayes

SHE WASN'T sure how she got there.

The concrete felt damp and cool beneath her bare feet. She curled her toes and took in a deep breath. How long would she have to wait?

She could smell the crisp saltiness of the ocean behind her; she could hear it chanting old secrets and hidden truths through the hollow reeds. She felt both at peace and foreign. It was as if she didn't belong there. Maybe she did once, in a dream long passed. But that was no longer her reality. The world was made of an energy that rejected her. Maybe not this place, though. Maybe she could finally find her true destination here.

Maybe. Maybe. Maybe.

The thick fog of the winter morning—or was it night?—concaved around her. Curling down her sweater. Running up the cuffs of her jeans. Chewing on her exposed neck. The wind rolled its fingers, almost knowingly, enticingly, over her cheeks.

The lamppost at the train station flickered in an uneven manner. When she looked up at it she saw tiny moths fluttering around it. The moths looked so delicate, yet they seemed unfazed by the bitter cold that surrounded them at the abandoned train station. As if they were living on an entirely different plane of existence.

There was nowhere to sit at the train station. There was hardly anywhere to stand. It felt like it was not even a train station, but rather a poorly cut slab of concrete placed in the middle of nowhere. It looked like it was floating on nothing and led to nothing.

She wasn't sure how long she looked out at the black abyss in front of her. It felt like a long time. The whole time she rubbed her thumb up and down the train ticket in her hand. That ticket held with it liberation and freedom, so she continually felt the need to reassure herself she hadn't lost it. She needed to know she still had one token left that was entirely in her control, and would lead to outcomes she had made for herself. That ticket would allow her to cut the strings glued to her head, hands, and feet. The strings that everyone else hooked their thoughts and opinions onto in an attempt to control where she went and who she became. The ticket in her hand was fully her own, though. She had decided to purchase it. She had decided to wait for the train. She had decided it all.

She felt a hand lightly touch her shoulder.

"Waiting for the train, are we?" a voice asked.

She hadn't even heard anyone else come onto the platform. She didn't turn around to look at them; she was worried her face would be covered in anguish and unpleasant to look at. She wasn't particularly in the mood to have other people looking at her. Keeping her head forward, she nodded.

"What led you to this station? It's not a very happy place, after all," the voice said. It was a soft voice, like a feathered pillow covered in sugar.

"It's just a train station," she replied. "It doesn't need to be happy. It just takes people where they want to go."

"And where would it be that you want to travel to?" the voice asked.

She stilled. An urge to turn and face the voice fell over her. She fought against it and continued to look forward. Where did she want to go? She couldn't remember. Maybe it was not one particular location. Or maybe it was. She wasn't sure. Maybe she just wanted to go away. She couldn't remember where she wanted to go, just that she wanted nothing more than to board the train and go away.

"I don't think I really want to go anywhere in particular."

"Ah," replied the voice. "Most people who come here say that."

They did? Curiously and against her better judgment, she turned around to face the voice.

The first thing she noticed was the woman's bright white eyes. They were completely empty, yet they seemed to be filled with something she could not explain. The woman's lips were covered in a deep bloodred lipstick. Her rich, silky brown skin glowed against the light of the lamppost. She wore a fitted tuxedo with a matching top hat and leather shoes.

Her eyes went wide. *"Aleja?"*

"Oh, Aleja, that's her name, is it? How beautiful, a very fitting name. I certainly don't mind going by it," she replied.

She got flashes of Aleja's smile in her mind. Broken and shattered images of hugs and tears and laughing on the rickety silver seats behind the school toilets rang through her mind. The faint and distant smell of strawberries curled around her neck. She could remember the touch of Aleja's knees against her own. Her heart started to hum in her chest the way it would back then. How long ago had it been since she had last seen Aleja? She couldn't remember. She just knew that if she left that train station she wouldn't be greeted by Aleja. She wouldn't be greeted by anyone.

"You know this woman, do you?" Aleja asked.

Did she know Aleja?

I think I loved her, she thought. Her heart felt heavy, like she had sandbags clipped to it, dragging it down past her feet and into the ground.

She couldn't reply. How was she supposed to? How was she supposed to articulate something she didn't fully understand or want to remember? She couldn't get the smell of those memories out of her heart.

"It's surprising," Aleja said. "Most people who come here wish to be greeted by someone they don't know. Do you want to tell me your name?"

She screwed her eyebrows together. Her name. Her name. What was her name? Did everyone have a name? Did she have a name? Surely not. "I don't think I've got a name," she mumbled, turning her head farther away from Aleja's.

"No name?" Aleja laughed. "Well, I guess I'll just have to call you that for the time being. If that's all right with you, Miss No-Name."

She didn't respond. She just curled her toes and continued to feel the cold ground beneath her. She didn't have time to remember the past and be around Aleja, or whoever she was. She just had to wait for the train. It would all be okay once she was able to board the train.

It would take her far away—it would fix everything.

She closed her eyes and focused on the texture and weight of the ticket in her hand. She rubbed her thumb up and down it. She tried to think of all the farmland and trees she would be able to look at while on the train. She thought of the long beaches and rolling hills. She thought of the sunrises and cloudy nights. She would be able to see it all.

"You sure have packed light, haven't you?" Aleja asked.

This Aleja was a very curious person, she thought. She didn't remember Aleja as an inquisitive person. She'd almost never asked about her, at least, she didn't think she had. She couldn't remember much of anything.

"I just mean," Aleja continued. "You can't be planning on traveling very far if you haven't packed anything. Is it a day trip you've planned? If so I would suggest leaving this train station. No day trips here."

What was she on about? She couldn't understand why this person cared so much about where she went. And she knew the woman really was just some person. She might look like Aleja, but she certainly wasn't her. No chance.

She kept her face forward and continued to wait for the train.

SHE KNEW she had made a mistake.

She knew she had ruined her shot at happiness. How else was she supposed to view it? She knew that was how everyone else saw it, and she couldn't argue with them. She had ruined everything. Of course she had. *Of course she had.*

She couldn't remember when her happiness had started to chip away from her. She couldn't remember when she had begun to give up on herself. Maybe it had been a long time ago. Maybe it had only started a couple of years ago. Everything had begun to blend and drip into each other, so it was hard for her to figure out what happened seven years ago and what happened seven months ago.

It felt as though she had been walking through life with a tiny hole at the back of her head, where her soul had begun to dribble and leak out of. By the time she realized it, she had already lost most of who she was.

Useless

Useless

Useless

She didn't know how she was supposed to be somebody when she had locked herself out of all her viable options. When she had nothing left of herself to give. How was she supposed to get out of her town? How was she supposed to feel included and integrated?

How was she ever supposed to find love?

It felt as if everything had already been decided for her. She knew that no matter how hard she tried she was destined to end up in the exact same spot each time.

She was not entirely surprised that things turned out the way they did, just hurt. A part of her had always known her heart and mind would give up one day. She knew, when she was younger and dreaming of what would one day be, that she was simply trying to calm her nerves with whimsical fables that would never be. Her life was constantly in a state of lagging, but she had become skilled at pushing away her thoughts of emotional destitution and otherness. It was inevitable that it would all eventually catch up with her. Truth was not something someone could run away from forever.

If she left her room and walked around her town, she would see those she had gone to school with, and they would be doing more than her.

They would be more than her. Though she probably wouldn't see some of them at all. Some of them had moved away to go to university. She was more afraid to run into those who had stayed to go to the local university. So she hardly left the house. She could not bear to have them all look at her and pick away at her heart, for they would see it was no longer strong enough to give strength and guidance to anyone, let alone herself.

Failure

Failure

Failure

Though many people might not have known her personally, she had created a reputation for herself as someone who was able to be a pillar for those around her. But she knew now that if anyone were to talk to her for more than five minutes, they would see nothing more than a mannequin made out of skin whose heart was only warm because it would stop beating if it became anything else. The mere thought of that happening sent her into a spiral that she couldn't imagine being able to handle for any long period of time.

She knew she had no one to blame other than herself. That made it worse, though. A burden like that was hard to carry. It was the kind of weight that would make your lungs collapse at night, forcing you awake. It was the kind of weight that would squeeze your heart and cause you to physically twitch and curve your body forward. It was a weight she felt she was incapable of escaping.

Disappointment

Disappointment

Disappointment

Her room was dark and musty, like someone had spilled a painter's dirty water over it, but she could still see the faint words on the book in front of her. She could still see the loose hairs falling over her eyes. Her eyes were moving over the words on the page, but she wasn't reading any of them. She wasn't concerned by it; it was the same as every other day. She liked to trick herself into thinking she was actually doing something and not just wasting all her days. She liked to try and trick herself into thinking she was somewhat similar to all those people she knew who had gone off to university, outside her town or otherwise. She didn't want to think about how everyone else was out there being somebody. It had become apparent to her that no matter who she constructed herself to be or where she took herself, she would never be somebody or anybody or anything. She would always be nobody.

She would always be nothing—to herself and everyone else.

SHE COULD still feel Aleja's eyes on her. They were heavy; it almost made her feel like her heels were being pushed down into the concrete of the platform.

"Why did you come to this station? Why this one?"

She shrugged.

"What emotions brought you here?"

She shrugged.

"Do you really want to stay here? Why can't you go back?"

She shrugged.

"Does anyone know you're here?"

She shrugged.

"Where do you plan on going to?"

She shrugged.

"I think you do know. Come on, please tell me," Aleja said. "You may not believe me, but I want to help you. I don't want you to be here, but you probably won't be able to leave until you talk to me."

She turned back to face the woman. She really couldn't understand what this "Aleja" was aiming for. Why did she care?

"No one is forcing you to be here. If you don't like me here, that's not my fault," she said.

"Yes, you're right. No one is forcing me to be here. I'm here because I want to be, I'm here because I want to help you. It's my job."

She softly scoffed. "Your job?"

"That's right. My job, and you're not making it very easy right now. Please, just talk to me. I don't even think you're fully aware of the type of train station this is. You seem confused. People don't come back from this train station. It's a one-way trip here. Very, *very* few people are able to catch a train back. And they're always worse for wear. I can't physically stop you from boarding this train, but it's my job to do everything I can to convince you to leave here. But I can't do that if you keep ignoring me," Aleja explained, an almost desperate tone creeping through her voice.

"There's nothing to talk about. I chose this train station. I bought this ticket. I made this decision by myself. What is there to talk about?"

Aleja sighed. "You really don't get it, do you?"

The roaring ocean could be heard crashing behind them. The salty wind splashed over their faces. It tossed her hair and clawed over her feet. Speckles of the sea dusted over them. It slowly started to bleed over the platform. The cuffs of her pants got damp from the running water. When she looked down, she noticed the water had a tint of red floating through it. A knowing feeling started to dawn on her, but it didn't matter. She was already there; she had already made her decision. There was no going back; there was nothing to go back to. She had to catch this train; she just had to. It didn't matter if she disappointed people by catching it; it didn't matter if people wanted to try to stop her. She had to catch it.

Maybe some people would be cross at her for catching it at such a young age. She wouldn't expect them to forgive her. She knew catching this train was selfish on her part. But she also knew she had to catch it. She had to. She wondered if people would miss her in the future. Maybe they would, but she knew she'd forever live in the past, and all those people were more than welcome to visit her there when they wanted to. Maybe they'd be able to go far enough back that they'd find a version of her that didn't look as sad in the eyes. Though she wondered if a time like that ever existed at all. Maybe it had. If it did she had no doubt they'd be able to find that younger version of her somewhere, and she hoped that version of her could bring them some type of comfort that she wasn't able to anymore.

The station grew colder.

She could still feel Aleja's eyes looking at her, sanding down her neck.

The wind pushed through the reeds behind her and rang through the air. Wet, heavy, and demanding. It was as though the world around her was eating her whole.

She turned around and ran her right thumb up and down her knuckles and bit her lower lip. Her chest felt tight. Her feet felt cold, her body twitchy.

She looked around at the train station.

How had she gotten there?

SHE FELT as if she was trapped in a glass box in a pitch-black room. She could hear other people talking, she could understand the language they spoke, to a degree, but she couldn't see them or feel them. She was incapable of being heard by them, no matter how hard she screamed. Sometimes she would feel something as thick and durable as clay being poured over her. It would pull and tug at her body, forcing her to change her shape and become something she never used to be. It always used to feel as though someone else had come along to her little part of the dark room and tipped it over her, but then she came to realize she was the one who poured it over herself. And she never knew how to stop.

.   She wanted so desperately, so furiously, to be made out of the same substances as everyone else. She wanted to see herself reflected in everyone else. It was as if she were a light bulb that blew its fuse and was being crushed between the fingers of *supposed to be* and *not enough*.

Never enough.

She couldn't remember the last time she and Aleja had spoken. She couldn't remember the last time she walked outside comfortably. She couldn't remember the last time she looked at herself in the mirror and was proud of who she was and who she loved. They were all so distant in her memories that she questioned if she ever actually had those thoughts and hadn't just dreamed it all up. Maybe it would've been for the best if she simply had dreamed it all up. Perhaps then her unwavering desires for change and love and assimilation wouldn't have corroded her heart so much.

She tried not to blame herself too much, for where is one supposed to go when the world tells them that they aren't enough? That they're a failure?

What happens when one loses who they are, who they're supposed to be, to who they are expected to be?

It was better to just not think about it at all, really. The lingering thoughts led to self-doubt and a special type of pain that would be near impossible to heal from. But think about it was all she could do; as much as she didn't want to blame herself, blame herself was all she managed to do. Drown in it all was all she managed to do.

After all, how could she not think of those warm and meandering summers past where she and Aleja would walk along the grainy shores of a forgotten beach, talking of what never was and what may never be?

After all, how could she not think of the yearning and the burning that would crash against her stomach and heart like a midnight ocean storm as she watched Aleja hold hands with a man and run kisses down his neck?

After all, how could she not think of the way her nose stuck out too far or her neck stretched up too high?

After all, how could she not think of all the ways she was destined to forever be a nobody—a mawkish and noticeable nobody?

She knew she would forever and always be trapped behind everyone else; she would forever and always be less than and never enough. That was her reality—how could she be expected to not think about that?

HER TOES had turned purple.

The water from the ocean continued to rise and flow from behind her. It crashed against her knees and ran off the edge of the platform like a waterfall. For a split second she thought of letting go and allowing the current of the ocean to push her off the edge of the platform so that she might be cradled by the black nothingness below. She decided against it, though. She was too set on boarding the train to allow herself to disappear from the platform.

She felt a hand touch her back.

"Aleja is her name, right?"

She nodded her head. "It was her name, yes."

Although she did not turn around, she could tell that Aleja's face was glossed over with melancholy.

"Is that... is that why you wanted to see her before you boarded the train? Is that why I look like her?"

She shrugged.

"Was there anything you wanted to tell her?"

"I don't know," she confessed. "I think when I still saw her, I had told her everything I wanted to. She was my only real friend, and I loved her so much, so much that it hurt. I feel as though she sucked almost every one of my secrets right out of the marrow of my bones and held them tightly in her chest. I feel like once she left, she took a part of my life with her. Once she was gone my secrets didn't feel like my own anymore. They felt like a story I might have once read to her or a movie we saw one too many times."

Aleja moved next to her, the water still gushing past them, and gripped her arm firmly and reassuringly. "She seems like a very special person. I can see why you would have loved her so much."

She turned her head to the side and looked at Aleja. "I would've done it again in a heartbeat. I would have fallen in unrequited love with her every day for a million years if it meant I could've been a part of her life. Even if it hurt, I was glad I loved her when she was alive and I had the chance to."

"Then why are you here?" Aleja whispered. "Being here will get you nowhere."

"Nowhere is still better than where I was. I can be somebody nowhere, but I was nobody back there. I can't handle being nobody, a useless, disappointing nobody."

"I'm sure that Aleja didn't think you were a nobody."

"I guess I'll never know."

The ocean continued to run over the platform. A moth landed on her head.

THERE HAD been a place across the river and under a large willow tree where she and Aleja would go every once in a while. Most of the time they would lay on the grass for hours, not saying a word, but there were rare occasions where they would drowsily whisper the words of their cracked-open hearts.

She would always be able to smell Aleja's soap and perfume blending into the smell of the grass; she would try to remember that smell. It always helped to keep her heart pumping, one beat at a time.

One month before Aleja had passed away, they had gone there. It was a particularly warm day that gave their bodies a light covering sheen of sweat. She had been star-fished out on the ground, the prickly and itchy grass to her back and her face to the sky, when Aleja first spoke.

"I can't wait to get out of this town. I want to move to a big city and get an apartment filled with weird and wacky clothes."

She laughed. "That sounds like a pretty nice idea."

"It's all I want."

"Why a big city, though?" she asked. "Do you want to go out there and become somebody?"

"Oh God, no!" Aleja exclaimed as she sat up. "I want to go to a big city so I can finally be a nobody. I'm tired of being a somebody, and as long as I stay here in this town I'll always be a somebody. People will know my face and my name and my achievements and my loves. I hate it. Being a somebody is overrated. I want nothing more than to be a nobody, a featureless face in a crowd filled with other featureless faces. Being a nobody seems like the biggest blessing on earth."

She held up her hand to block out the light, but through the gaps in her fingers she saw Aleja sitting up, straight and proud, and she had never seen a more determined person in her life. She had never seen a more beautiful person in her life. Her heart clenched; she realized that as long as she walked this Earth, Aleja would never be the complete nobody she wanted to be, because Aleja would always move her world—she would always be the biggest somebody to her.

Maybe that would be okay.

SHE DIDN'T know how long she and Aleja had been standing at the train station. She was sure it must have been hours by that point, but Aleja still stood beside her, holding her arm. The ocean had started to slowly stop running over the platform—it was but a mere stream. She moved forward to the edge of the platform and sat down. Her legs hung over the edge, dangling over the never-ending pit of darkness and nothingness. She could feel the draft from below tickle the bottom of her feet.

"I'm so lost," she whispered. "I was so sure coming here would give me some direction. But now I don't know. The train hasn't come yet. I've been waiting so long, but this train still hasn't come here for me. Maybe I'm not supposed to be here either. The one place I thought I might belong and be able to be somebody in seems to have rejected me too. I... I don't know what to do. I don't know where I'm supposed to go."

Aleja came and sat next to her.

"Why did you come here?" Aleja asked.

She pushed her head forward and placed it on her knees. Her back and shoulders began to shake as she cried.

Aleja softly put a hand on her back and ran it up and down in a soothing manner. They could hear the flow of the ocean behind them and the crickets chirping in the reeds.

"I came," she sobbed, "because I have nowhere else to go. I want to be here. I'm so alone and broken at home. I don't want to be there anymore. I'm so terrified to spend another day there, let alone my whole life."

"This train only comes when you are ready for it to," Aleja whispered. "I've heard it rumbling around the corner for a while now,

Miss No-Name. I think you want to board it, I think you're ready, but I also think that deep down there is a part of you that wants to leave this place and go back home."

She sat up and let out a grim laugh. She wiped the tears from her face. "Go back home to what?" she asked bitterly. "Go back home to a world where I'm called a pervert? Where I have no friends? Where people will think I'm a failure and a disappointment? Where I'll never be able to find love? Where the only person who cared for me is gone? Where people will think I'm a nobody?"

Aleja's eyes were filled with sympathy. It was as if she was looking at a tiny duckling that had been separated from its family, covered in mud and unable to see. "There is more to your life than that."

"How would you know?"

"Because for the most part you're only telling me what other people think about you and have made you think about yourself. That's not your life."

"But it is. I've got nothing to offer the world that it hasn't already been given. I just don't."

"You can't even remember your name. You can't even tell me of the good things you've done," Aleja stated. "It seems like you remember other people's opinions more then you remember who you are."

"What else is there to life? What does it matter how I view myself if everyone else will think something else?"

"It matters a lot," Aleja said. "You're not living your life for other people. Who cares if you don't have friends? Who cares if you all you can manage to do is fail? Who cares if you disappoint people? Who cares if people hate how you dress or that your hair is short? Who cares if you're nobody? Being somebody is overrated. The world needs more nobodies. You don't owe the world achievements. You just get to live. You can fall over every day, but you still deserve your life. Nothing will change that. Yes, maybe you won't make any friends, and maybe you won't achieve anything meaningful, and it'll hurt, but it's okay. You still deserve to live. You still deserve to try, and you deserve your life."

She kept her face hidden by her hands. "I'm scared."

"I know you are," Aleja said soothingly.

"What if as soon as I go back I regret it? What if I make the wrong decision?" she cried. "I don't know… I don't know what I want. I don't know what I'll regret and what I won't."

Aleja placed a hand on her knee. "How about I make a deal with you? If you give me your train ticket, I'll hold on to it for you. I'll keep it safe and never let anyone steal it. And if one day you decide to come back here, your ticket will be ready and waiting."

"You'd do that for me?"

"Of course I would. It's my job. I may not know you, but I care about you. I know you think boarding this train will fix everything for you, but it won't. It really won't."

She gripped her ticket tighter. It felt as though it was glued to her hand. She wasn't sure how she was supposed to hand it over and go back to her life knowing nothing would happen. She still wouldn't be doing enough, and she knew she wouldn't suddenly start doing more. She knew once she went back she wouldn't suddenly fall in love or find friends or become attractive or intelligent or somebody. She knew if she went back she would still be lonely and stupid and ugly and loveless and without achievements. She would be going back to nothing. Did she want to do that? Did she want to reenter a world as gray and dark and stormy and clogged as the one she had left?

What would she really be going back for?

Why did she have to go back? Just because someone told her to? Just because she was having small doubts? That wasn't any reason to go back.

"What're you thinking about?" Aleja asked.

"I don't know, really. I just can't see any reason to go back. I really can't."

"How about going back to give yourself a chance for once?"

She shook her head. "That just seems stupid. I know nothing will get better if I go back. Nothing will miraculously change. I'll be in the exact same spot I was in right before I left."

"Maybe so," Aleja said. "But you don't want to be here, trust me. This place is very predictable. We know what will happen here. But back home there is no such thing as predicable. Change is an ever-flowing current. Sometimes you can get so stuck in something that you believe it'll never move or change, but then one day, out of the blue, things will start changing. It may take many years, but change is an inevitable force that will wash over everyone. I know things can change. But if you stay here, if you board that train, change is something you will briefly taste for a second and then never again. After that one lick of change, you will never see any form of change again. Ever. But if you go back, you have the opportunity to taste any small type of change each day. It is a magical blessing. Don't throw it away. Please."

Her eyes began to prickle with tears desperate to run out of her eyes. "What if I can't wait that long, though?" she whispered. "I don't think I'm strong enough to. I've used all my energy up. I'm dry of determination."

A small smile slid across Aleja's face. She cradled her cheeks and met her eyes. "I don't believe that for a second. If you truly had lost all your will and strength, that train would've been here already. You're still fighting. You're still strong, and I believe you have the strength to go back home."

The ocean began to roar and rumble again. A large wave crashed over onto the platform, slamming into their backs. She tensed in response to it. The water sprayed over them and ran over the edge. She expected the force of the frosty sea to push her off the edge, down into the black pit of nothingness, where she would not have to think or make another decision again. But as the second wave crashed against her, she realized there was hardly any force behind it. The water felt solid and sharp against her skin, but it had the force of steam.

Even in that world, it appeared she was stronger than she originally believed.

FOR MOST of her life, she had felt she was slowly moving through a frozen garden. The footpath was covered in snow and ice. The flowers were dead, and the trees had crashed to the ground. The sun, covered by the clouds, prevented her from knowing if she was ever heading in the right direction.

The footprints of others would always be covered by the freshly fallen snow. No matter what direction she looked, she would find nothing but the white abyss of loneliness she had seen her entire life. Some days her eyes would play a trick on her and she would convince herself she saw a shadow in the distance. Finally, she would think, finally I have found someone who sees what I see, who feels what I feel, who is as lost and confused and cold as I am. But whenever she would try to run toward the shadow, she would lose sight of them and have to once again face the reality that she was alone in that frozen garden, where not even the flowers or the bees would be able to greet her.

Eventually she stopped walking around. She had no will left to move around in circles seeing the same thing every day, day after day.

So she stayed still; she let the frozen world consume her. She let the ice eat away at her heart and spit out the burned pieces of it.

She then went to the train station, to a world that was equally as cold, but that coldness had a door she could walk through to set herself free so she would never have to feel the bitter coldness of loneliness ever again.

What she sometimes thought about the garden was that despite the cold and despite the barren land above, perhaps a vibrant world of flowers and life lay beneath. A world of warmth had never evaded her; maybe it was simply below her. The cruel and blinding pain of chilling loneliness had prevented her from remembering the beauty that might have one day been thawed back to life. And she wondered if she would've been able to see the beauty of it if she kept herself warm by walking through the ice, but she failed to believe in a future when she felt as though she was living in a repeat of the past.

SHE TRIED to think of what life she could have if she went back, but nothing came to mind. She had been at the train station so long she had begun to forget what she had left behind. If she went home, would she get along with her parents? If she went back home, would she find a chance to succeed? She could not say. Maybe things would be okay, maybe they would get better, maybe she had a future, but maybe she didn't. Maybe nothing would change; maybe she would forever be that useless disappointment she was terrified of being. Was it worth the risk? Was going back with a slim chance of things getting better actually worth it? Wouldn't it be better to just stop trying and board the train? She was tired of trying. She was tired of putting on a brave face only to be trodden on by other people.

She turned her head and saw Aleja looking at her. Whether it was the real Aleja or not, the look on her face stabbed her in the heart. She knew Aleja would give her a look of sadness. She knew if she boarded that train that both this Aleja and her Aleja would feel disappointment and betrayal. She didn't want either Aleja to hate her, but was that enough of a reason to go back home and leave the train station?

She had come to the train station because she was tired of being a disappointment to everyone, but was being at the train station a disappointment to the person she held closest to her heart? Should she really go home for a person who was no longer in her life? Should she really continue that life for someone who couldn't even share it with her?

What would Aleja know? She had already detached herself from their world. She had already been saved from its expectations and its requirements and its rules; what would she know about the pain of waking up every day and knowing it was going to be filled with nothing but sadness and torment?

She couldn't pull her eyes away from Aleja's face. She felt as though she was being pulled into her eyes and being locked into her soul, with no hopes of escaping. She didn't mind, though.

Maybe she was supposed to head back home. Maybe she was meant to try to carry on for Aleja's sake—maybe that's what life was about. Living for oneself could become redundant and pointless at times. It was much easier to live for someone else. Maybe that's what she was meant to do. Maybe she was meant to live for Aleja.

"What're you thinking?" Aleja whispered.

Her eyes ran over Aleja's lips. "That maybe I can go home," she replied softly. "Maybe it'll be okay if I can stay strong for Aleja. That's what I'm supposed to do, right?"

Aleja hesitated before she shook her head.

"Why not? You want me to go back; you said it's your job. Why can't I go back if it's for the sake of Aleja?"

"You can't go back for someone else. It'll keep you going for a little while, but not for long. You have to go back for you. What about you do you want to see again? What about you do you want to one day see, or continue to see?"

"Nothing," she said. "Absolutely nothing. I spent twenty years trying to find something, and I got nothing. Not my love, not my skills, not my appearance, not my dreams, not my hopes. Nothing."

"Maybe that's what you can go back for, then—to find your something. Wouldn't that be a wonderful thing to do with your life?"

"Stay back there to find my something?" She had never thought about that. She had always been so consumed by the fact she didn't have a "something" she could be proud of or pour herself into that she never thought of continuing to devote time to finding it. She had always assumed that if you never found it by the age of eighteen, you were just destined to walk around the Earth with a giant hole in your selfhood, a hole so large that nothing could fill it. Maybe she could try to find something to fill it. Something not controlled by other people and their opinions and their approval. Maybe she could find something warm to fill herself up with, something that only she would know about. Something to give her meaning.

"Do you think I would be able to find it?" she asked.

"You'll never know unless you try."

She looked down and took a deep breath. "Do you promise I can come back? Do you promise to never let my ticket go?"

"I do. I promise."

"I might disappoint you. I might come back as soon as I get there," she warned. "I know I can't handle that place. I know I very well might come back."

"That's okay, but don't give up on yourself before you even try," Aleja replied. "I truly don't think you want to board that train. I don't. It would've been here right away if you did. Miss No-Name, I think you just wanted someone to hear you. You've kept your voice, your true voice, hidden for so long. I can't imagine how much it must have hurt, but please know this: I heard you. I heard you crying and screaming and pleading. I heard you. I still hear you, even now; I can hear the pleas of your heart. I know it may feel like no one will ever hear you, but leave here knowing I heard you so clearly—and your voice is beautiful. It's not something you need to be ashamed of."

She flung her arms forward and pulled Aleja into a tight embrace. She tucked her head into the side of Aleja's neck and let out a deep breath. It pushed so heavily out of her throat that it felt like the first true breath she had let out in years. "Thank you," she said.

Aleja smiled and ran a hand up and down her back before slowly starting to stand. Once they were both up, she rubbed Aleja's face.

Aleja looked up at her. "May I please have your ticket?"

She stretched her arm out, then pulled it back again. It had been her decision to come to the train station. She was so sure it was going to set her free.

"It'll be okay, I promise," Aleja assured. "I'll keep it safe."

She extended her arm once again and let Aleja take her ticket. Once the ticket left her fingers, she felt as though a dark cloud she didn't know had been wrapped around her heart started to part.

A large orange cat meandered onto the platform. It had a golden bell around its neck and a tall and curved oil lamp strapped to its back. It lit up the entire platform.

"This is Sho," Aleja said. "If you follow him, he'll take you back home."
She nodded.

Aleja walked over to her and held her hand. "It'll be okay. I hope you find what you need to. It was a pleasure meeting you, and while you can come back, I hope I don't have to see you again. I hope you find what you need back home and don't have to come to this train station again. I believe you will, though; you're so strong."

She bit her lips and looked down, unconvinced.

"There is great beauty and strength that comes from being nobody. And no matter how small and invisible you feel, you must remind yourself you take up space. Your soul and mind and body take up space. Your being is never completely invisible. Don't forget that."

Aleja's warm words wrapped around her. It felt as though ice was being melted away from her mind. "Thank you." She smiled.

"If I ever run across your Aleja, I'll be sure to let her know how you are. I'm sure she'd love to know how you're doing."

Her eyes went wide. "You'd do that for me?"

"Of course." Aleja smiled. "She deserves to know how incredible her friend is. I'm sure she'd be so proud of you for going back."

She blushed. "Thank you."

Aleja brought her hand to her lips and kissed it, staining her knuckles red. "You'd best be off now. So long, Miss No-Name. Thank you for letting me do my job." She bowed and waved goodbye before dust started to appear around her and she slowly faded away.

She only pulled her eyes away from where Aleja had been when she heard a deep and rumbly meow from Sho. He started to pad toward the back of the platform and down the stairs. She hesitantly followed him. Once she reached the stairs, she turned around to see the train station one last time. When she did, she didn't see the small slab of concrete she had before. No. She saw a large station that curved over the horizon. It was engulfed in the rich light of the full moon. It covered the platform like melted stardust. The station was filled with people and those clothed in tuxedos talking to them. She saw the train. She saw people boarding the train. She saw people crying on the platform. She saw people leaving the station, as she was.

Maybe that frozen garden of hers hadn't been as abandoned as she first thought.

She continued to follow Sho down the steps. With each step she took, her vision got blurrier and the world around her darker and darker.

Her right foot crunched down on something, and with that she lost all sight, but she felt her body falling backward into nothing.

Once she opened her eyes, she noticed she was outside, the night sky above her and the feeling of wet grass below her. As she sat up, she heard the faint sound of bells chiming in the distance, then nothing but the swaying of trees in the wind. She looked down at her hand and saw the red smudge of lipstick on her knuckles.

She looked up at the sky and saw the stars that painted it, broken and imperfect but beautiful nonetheless. She let the wind brush through her hair and hug her frail shoulders.

Kiara, she thought, looking at the moon.

My name is Kiara.

B.K. HAYES spends most of her time daydreaming, drinking tea and playing with her cats. When she is not doing that, she is most likely writing stories and being detrimentally introspective. Ever since she was little, she has lived in her mind and in the worlds of fiction. Through her writing she hopes to help people feel less alone and hopefully discover something new about themselves.

Email: bk.books@hotmail.com

Subtle
by Daniel Okulov

"I'M GONNA have some friends over next Friday," I announce, and the sound of dishes clattering from the kitchen interrupts my next sentence.

"What?" my mother calls. "I'm going to need you to watch Matthew. They're no longer allowing me to work from home every day. I told you this last week."

I groan. "That's why I'm telling you ahead of time, so you can figure something else out."

"Honey, no," she says as she appears in the doorway. "A week's notice isn't enough, even if I could find a babysitter. You know you can't have people over when you watch him."

"Except I *won't be* watching him, because I already made plans."

"Justin, this isn't negotiable."

"I can't handle his issues! He hates me! Can't you find someone else to fill in for one night? What if I light the house on fire trying to stop one of his meltdowns? What then?"

Mom pinches the bridge of her nose and exhales. "Honey, I can't leave him with a stranger."

"Well, you can't leave him with me either!"

"*Justin.*"

Now I feel bad, because she looks visibly distressed, but I can't allow myself to give in. "Mom, please," I say. "I just want to hang out here with Jeremy and Kev without Matty crying and screaming any time one of us moves. A normal seven-year-old's tantrums would be a pain in the ass to deal with, but Matty is a different story."

My mother's jaw is clenched, and she shakes her head slowly. "It's very taxing for us to find care for him. You should consider your role in the family before you decide to put me in a difficult position over your disdain for your brother."

"How is it a difficult position if you have a week to find someone more capable than I am?"

She sighs deeply. "Hon, babysitters aren't free, and special needs babysitters ask for even more money."

"We're not exactly poor. And—" I say when she starts to turn away. "Think of it as helping the economy by increasing the job market."

"Justin, honey, I know you want to hang out with your friends, but I just don't know about this."

"Please, Mom," I beg again. "I don't want to have to cancel on them."

She purses her lips in a way that makes me hopeful she'll consider it. She waves me off without another word.

"THE NEW babysitter's coming over to meet Matty soon." Mom surprises me on Monday at breakfast, but her voice is too cold for my comfort.

"What?" I ask. "You mean you found someone?"

"No, hon," she sighs. "I found a *potential* someone, and I want Matty to warm up before I leave him with a stranger." She glances at my brother, who is relentlessly poking a piece of cereal with his finger and chasing it around the table.

"Oh."

Mom looks at me for a long moment, but she exhales and turns away instead of saying anything. Her disappointment is clear, but I can't let her be in control of my life.

"Is it cool if I go out for a drive tonight?" I ask.

"I'd like you to stay and meet the sitter."

I point my thumb behind me to the hallway. "I'll buy milk if you let me go. I know we're running out."

She looks exasperated, but she says, "Fine. Grab some cash from my wallet."

"Thanks, Mom."

I ONLY have one class on campus on Wednesdays, and I wait around for a dreadful half hour until Jeremy and Kev walk out of their classes after two o'clock and head to the dining hall. They make small talk entirely composed of sex jokes until Jeremy gets his food, and we loiter at one of the tables outside.

"We still on for Friday?" Jeremy asks as he picks at his garden salad with a spork. I hate the cafeteria food, along with the entire campus, and watching him attempt to eat it is making my stomach do cartwheels.

"Yeah," I say, wrinkling my nose at Kev lighting his cigarette. "My mom found a babysitter who's apparently good with disabilities or some shit."

"Oh damn," Kev says. He keeps clicking his lighter, but it fails to work, and I resist the urge to snatch it out of his hand. "She hot?"

"I don't know. We haven't met."

"Well, shit, dude, don't get my hopes up." He chuckles.

I squint at him. "The point of a babysitter is to watch the kid so that we can do our own thing."

Kev shrugs. "Doesn't mean I can't hope your mom hired a babe. Do you think she'd, like, make us snacks or something?"

"Dude, I told you I don't even know who it is, and it's a babysitter. Not a maid or a servant."

"Okay, chill." He laughs through a cloud of smoke. "I'm just asking."

I grimace at the smell and wave my hand in his face. "Yeah, I decided to skip out on the meeting on Monday. I mean, I kind of begged my mom into hiring someone in the first place, but that doesn't mean I want to interact with another person who's essentially replacing me but is getting paid for it, you know?"

Jeremy shakes his head. "If I had my way with my parents like you do with yours, I would've been in Hollywood by now, hitting it big on the next superhero movie."

I grin at him. "I don't think they hire vegans," I tease.

He feigns a pout, and Kev playfully jabs him in the shoulder. "Don't worry," Kev says, "I didn't think they hired homos either, but there's plenty of those in famous films, so I'm sure you stand a chance against the meat-eater-dominated industry. Don't get me wrong, though. If it were up to me, they'd ban both of those from film. Tough luck getting in my next movie, Jeremy. You dirty vegan."

"I don't think those things are comparable," I say.

"Since when do you care?" Kev jeers. "It's just a joke." He grabs Jeremy's plastic salad dish out of his hands before he finishes it. He tosses it in the trash can several feet away.

Jeremy gawks at him. "You're buying me a new fucking salad."

"You were nearly finished with it!"

"I don't care."

"Great, I was gonna go back to the dining hall anyway."

I zone out of their banter and take a calculated step away from them.

"Hey, Justin." Kev shakes my shoulder. "You coming back to get food with us?"

"Nah," I say slowly. "I'll catch you guys later. I've lost my appetite."

KEV BRINGS over a shitty thriller for Friday night that I've never heard of before, but he convinces us it's gory enough to still be enjoyable despite its questionable ratings. I don't have the patience to argue with him and neither does Jeremy, so we load up on popcorn and start the movie early, before my mom leaves. The exposition is unclear and difficult to keep track of, and I'm bending over backward trying to understand the plot before I give up and decide to just enjoy the bloodshed.

"Pause the movie," I say about thirty minutes in, jolting Jeremy's shoulder when he fails to reach for the remote. "Dude, pause it. I'm gonna go get more popcorn."

Jeremy obliges, but he makes sure to groan loudly while doing it. Once he pauses it, I rise and start up the stairs. One of the guys pelts me in the back of the head with a popcorn kernel just before I leave, and I hear them snicker upon my departure.

"Mom!" I yell as I reach the door, and I glance around once I'm out of the basement. "Mom!" No response, so I head to the kitchen to heat up the bags myself. I rifle through the cupboard for a minute without finding any popcorn. I stand up and head out of the kitchen with a disgruntled sigh. "Mom! Where are the—"

I nearly run into someone as I round the corner, and the person instantly backs up several steps. "Whoa, sorry," he says.

"Who the hell are you?" I ask, studying him once my shock subsides. The guy looks like he can't be any older than me; he's a bit shorter, with brown skin, dark eyes, and a hairstyle that resembles a bird's nest. Raven hair falls over his face and nearly obscures his eyebrows when he raises them.

"I could ask you the same question," he says. "But I'm gonna go ahead and assume you're Justin." He flicks his thumb behind him toward the living room. "Mrs. Ramones left earlier than she planned and told me to let you know when you came up. I'm watching Matty, and I was gonna ask if y'all could maybe keep it down? That'd be cool, I think. We'd appreciate it."

I stare at him, and he looks away and clears his throat. My mind takes a moment to buffer. "You're, uh…."

"Dakota." He holds out his hand. I hesitantly take it, and he pulls back after a few seconds. "Keep it down while you're up here if you can," he requests, before he turns around to head back down the hallway.

I'm a little dazed by the suddenness of the interaction, but I forgo my trip to the kitchen and head back to the basement with nothing.

"Took you a while," Kev mutters as soon as I descend the stairs and enter the room. He notices my lack of snacks and throws his hands up. "And with nothing to show for it too. What the hell, dude. Did you eat it all coming back down here?"

"Sorry," I say. "I couldn't find anything." I head toward the couch and sit down between them. "Well, I did find the babysitter. Turns out my mom left early."

"Oh fuck." Kev perks up, and Jeremy snickers behind me when I give Kev a look. "Is that why you took so long? Were you—"

"No." I roll my eyes.

Kev latches onto my arm and shakes it. "Well, who is it?"

"A guy."

"Oh," he says. He lets me go. "Huh, I probably should've considered that possibility."

I scoff. "Yeah, maybe." I lean back into the couch and prop my feet up on the table. "I couldn't even tell if he's in college or high school, so good luck getting him to make you food."

"I can be very persuasive," Kev says. He grins. "But maybe you were still—"

I shove my hand in his face and ignore him before I tap Jeremy's arm. "Just play the damn movie, dude."

He does, and by the time the credits roll an hour later, I realize I zoned out of most of what's been happening on screen for almost the entire thing. Kev is making strange noises to accompany the end credits, and Jeremy is egging him on.

Stretching my arms over my head, I yawn and stand up. I ignore their shenanigans and begin the trek upstairs. Kev's on my heels, and Jeremy is idling somewhere behind him. I instinctively walk into the kitchen, and I stop when I see Matty sitting at the dinner table and quietly thumbing some colorful toy. Dakota is standing at the stove over a pot, squinting at the label on a blue box of macaroni.

"What're you doing?" I ask, and Dakota looks at me, slightly startled. I don't recall seeing his wide-framed glasses earlier. He settles down after a moment and focuses back on the box.

"Mrs. Ramones said to cook him mac 'n' cheese, so that's what I'm doing." He shoves his fingers under the flap to rip the box open.

"He eats that shit all the time," I say. "It's not healthy."

Dakota shrugs. "Take that up with your mom."

"Oh hey," Kev says as he appears in the doorway behind me. I look back to see him nod to Dakota. "You're the sitter?"

Dakota barely spares him a glance. He takes the cheese packet out of the box and dumps the shell pasta into the water. "Yes. Hi."

"Cool, cool. How old would you be?"

Dakota grabs a wooden spoon to stir the pot. "Are you asking my age?"

"Yeah, that's what I said."

"Weird phrasing," says Dakota. "How old *would* I be, as if you mean in the hypothetical future."

Kev scoffs. "Okay, okay, whatever. Semantics. How old are you?"

"Nineteen."

"Oh shit." Kev laughs and bumps my shoulder. "Homeboy is barely older than you. At least he's not younger, or that would've been more embarrassing. Having a babysitter younger than you, imagine that—"

"Jesus, Kevin, shut up," I groan.

"You in college?" Kev addresses Dakota again. "We go to the community college here."

"I take online classes."

"What year?"

"Sophomore."

"University?"

Dakota sighs quietly and glances at my brother, who's been warily eyeing Kev every couple of seconds. "Can you please settle down or go somewhere else? I'm watching Matty, and I don't like being interrogated while I'm working."

"Got it," Kev says. "That's fair. Lemme just grab some juice and we'll be on our merry way. Okay?" He takes a straight path to the fridge and jostles past Matty's chair, hitting it loudly as he veers too close. Matty tenses up, and I prepare myself for the wailing noise he's about to emit.

Dakota drops the spoon and rounds on Kev before Matty's shrieks even pierce the air. He grabs him by the shoulders and pushes him away fiercely but silently. Then he heads back to the table.

Matty is making an ungodly noise, and I yank Kev by the sleeve to direct him out of the kitchen. Dakota slowly sits down near Matty, and I think I hear him softly speaking to him, but I turn the corner before I see what else he does. I'm already getting a headache from the commotion, and Jeremy appears out of the living room with a daze in his eyes.

"What's going on?" he asks, and I push Kev toward him.

"Matty had another meltdown 'cause Kev got too close to him."

Jeremy twists his mouth. "Yeah, I figured."

"Sorry." Kev rubs the back of his neck. "Forgot about that kiddo."

"Yeah, whatever," I say. I glance at the clock on the wall. "It's getting late; you guys should probably head home. My mom wanted you gone before she got back, and she's due home in thirty."

Jeremy looks at his watch. "Isn't she usually only back at eleven?"

"She said she'd be two hours early tonight. I told you," I lie.

"How're you gonna sleep with all that racket?" Kev laughs, and I roll my eyes.

Jeremy pats his shoulder and gives me a sympathetic look. "We'll see you tomorrow, dude, deal?"

"Yeah," I say. I rub my eyes to will my migraine away. They leave quickly, but the splintering ache in my head doesn't subside even when the door closes. I'm about to head upstairs, but I halt when I realize the change in the atmosphere.

There's no screaming.

I run to the kitchen with a fleeting thought about Dakota tranquilizing my brother to make him shut up. Maybe it's just the adrenaline from the thriller movie my mind just glazed over, but his tantrums never stop this fast. I'm nearly sprinting when I get to the kitchen doorway, only to see them both sitting quietly at the dinner table.

"What did you do?" I ask through the panicked heartbeat in my ears, and Dakota turns to give me a discerning look with no verbal response.

Matty tenses up slightly, but he has his fingers wrapped around a green object, and Dakota has something similar in his hands too. An array of toys is scattered around the table.

I approach quietly and take a seat in the chair next to Dakota. He doesn't look at me, and I observe how he interacts with Matty. He isn't saying anything, but he taps his fingers gently on the table. Matty sits still before he mimics the sounds Dakota tapped out.

"Matty," Dakota says softly. "You wanna say hi to Justin? He isn't here to be loud with his obnoxious friends anymore."

Matty giggles and reaches for the red chain by Dakota's knuckles. Dakota doesn't move, but he slowly looks over at me.

I stare at him. "How did you get him to calm down?" I whisper.

Dakota raises his eyebrows again and squints at me. He either doesn't hear me or ignores the question entirely as he stands up to go to the stove. He turns the gas off and starts draining the pasta, and I don't want to repeat my query in case it disturbs Matty. I sit and quietly glance between them every so often for a couple of minutes, until Dakota finally sits back down and places a bowl of macaroni next to Matty.

"Hey, sport," he says. "Now I don't really approve of you eating so late, but Mom's orders. Think you can eat dinner and play for another hour before going to bed?"

Matty doesn't respond for several minutes.

"Matty," I say, "you have to—"

Dakota leans his knuckles against my arm to cut me off.

I grimace at him. "What? He isn't going to eat unless you make him."

Dakota sighs and has the nerve to ignore me. He doesn't say anything and taps his fingers on the table close to Matty. I roll my eyes.

"Matty." I raise my voice. Before I can get another word in, Dakota pushes me enough to make my chair shift slightly under me. It's not a shove as much as it is a request for me to stop. I stand up abruptly. "Fine," I say. "Good luck getting him to fucking eat."

"Chill," Dakota chides. The fact that he doesn't bother to even shoot me a warning glance is somehow more infuriating than if he had, because I feel ignored.

I stare daggers into the top of his head as he quietly taps his fingers near Matty again. Matty reaches for the spoon after a calculated eternity, and I bet Dakota feels really smug about his success. Matty puts the spoon down after one bite and sits still.

"Matty," I scold.

Dakota reaches behind his back and swats around until he hits my arm and pushes me away again.

"Fine!" I say. "Have fun sitting here for an hour while he eats."

Dakota makes some strange noise that sounds like arrogance to me. I back out of the kitchen and make my way down the hallway and upstairs.

Maybe this was a bad idea, but at least I can relax knowing that Matty is being watched by some abrasive guy with the magical power of stopping his conniptions.

I FIND out the annoying way that Dakota will be working here every school night by Mom breaking the news to me on Monday only an hour before his arrival, so I don't have time to plan anything to do to avoid him. I can put up with lurking around the house or going out if he's here only every Friday, but the thought of his snobbish presence occupying five-sevenths of my week is exasperating.

I'm still brainstorming ideas of how to get out of the house without being bored out of my mind by the time he shows up.

"Hey," Dakota says when I open the door. He's wearing a gray flannel shirt and an awkward smile. A teal bag hangs over his left shoulder.

I wordlessly gesture him in, and he stalls for a moment before entering.

"Is Mrs. Ramones—"

"In the living room." Once I close the door, I head straight upstairs. Dakota seems to pace by the shoe rack for a minute before I hear him talking to my mom. Their voices fade out as I ascend the stairs and go to lock myself in my room.

I recline in my computer chair and close my eyes. The distant sound of the front door slamming signifies my mother's departure. I didn't have any plans of what to do tonight besides assignments, but it would be more comforting if I knew I wouldn't have to linger in the kitchen to cook dinner while Dakota and Matty are around.

By the time I muster up the nerve to go downstairs and grab some food, it's nearing seven o'clock. I leave my phone on my desk and go to the kitchen. Dakota's cooking something for Matty again, and he greets me casually when I walk in. I ignore him and open the freezer to get out a bag of frozen fruit. I pour it into a bowl and avoid his prying eyes.

"Are you sure that's all you want to eat?" Dakota asks. "You can have some of the spaghetti I'm making."

"I'm fine," I say.

"That's not really dinner, Justin."

"Whatever," I say on my way back down the hall.

I head upstairs to find my phone buzzing uncontrollably on my desk. There are thirty-seven unread messages sitting in my inbox from the group chat with Jeremy and Kev. I scroll through them without really reading anything until my eyes fall on one text where Kev throws around several colorful insults directed at me for not responding.

The sour feeling in my stomach germinates, and I don't bother texting back. My notifications keep going off with more texts from them, and I decide to shut down their plans of seeing a movie this Friday by lying and saying I'm busy. They keep sending messages, but I mute the chat and barely refrain from throwing my phone against the wall.

NOTHING BUT the same basic routine traps me for the next week and a half. All I do is go to the few day classes I have and spend the rest of my time on online assignments and making a point of avoiding Kev and Jeremy whenever I'm on campus. In the evenings, Dakota and I barely speak to each other. I have no desire to communicate with him, and he doesn't seem to mind that. I prefer to think of it as us calmly existing in a blissful state of mutual ignorance. This doesn't stop me from feeling unnerved whenever I pass by him and Matty sitting in near silence in the kitchen or living room. Matty's smiling more often than not when he's with Dakota. I feel inadequate.

ON THURSDAY, my mom decides to carpool to work with her friend so they can go out to some restaurant and stay out late. I resist the urge to take the car out for a spin until around eight, when the boredom of letting an essay about Renaissance art drain the life out of me nearly makes me homicidal. My feet propel me out of my room and down the stairs until I'm grabbing the extra set of keys and slipping on my shoes and jacket. I halt right before opening the door and decide to head down the hallway and look into the living room, where the TV is playing some kids' show at a low volume.

Dakota and Matty are sitting on the floor together, surrounded by several dozen colored papers with scribbles all over them. Dakota is folding some complicated shape out of paper.

"Hey," I say hoarsely, then clear my throat when Dakota looks up at me. "I'm going for a drive."

"Cool," he says. "Have fun." He looks down for a moment before handing my brother an origami swan. Matty takes it slowly and grins to himself.

"Okay," I say. "Bye."

"Say 'bye' to your brother, Matty," Dakota whispers. He makes an exaggerated waving motion with his fingers, and Matty languidly mimics it.

I turn around and head out the door.

The air outside is frigid, and I sit in the driver's seat and wait for the windows to defrost before I go anywhere. Driving helps me focus and let go of my thoughts, but I figure I'll probably circle into some parking lot and sit there on my phone until I run out of battery.

Hours pass me by as I get lost on the road. Not lost, but entranced enough in driving that I notice it's close to eleven and I still haven't stopped, despite taking the same loop on and off the highway repeatedly. I eventually pull into the parking lot in front of the pharmacy and turn down the rock music to sit and scroll through my phone.

Several unread texts from Jeremy sit in my inbox, and they're all bullshit about getting together and going to one of the events on campus. I can't bring myself to reply and tell him and Kev that I'm uninterested. I can't bring myself to ask them whether they want to come over tomorrow. The baseline opening of a post-hardcore song I like comes on the playlist, and I crank up the volume until it drowns out my imminent migraine. I nearly rear-end a pole when I swerve out of the parking lot and head home.

My fingers freeze in the short distance between the driveway and the front door, so I have trouble getting the key in. The door jerks open and I nearly drop my keys.

"Had a nice excursion?" Dakota asks. He steps aside to let me in and closes the door behind me.

I shrug. I turn away to hang up my jacket and take off my shoes. I glance at him quizzically when he doesn't move. "Where's Matty?"

"Asleep. He got a little hyperactive when some TV show came on earlier, so I put him to bed and he conked out."

"Oh, okay." I glance at Dakota, and we stare at each other until he rubs his neck and breaks eye contact. "What've you been doing since?"

"Hmm? Nothing. I was just coming downstairs when you decided to take five minutes jiggling the lock."

"It's cold out," I explain. "I still can't really feel my hands."

"Wear gloves next time," Dakota says.

I shake my head and dig my phone out of my pocket. "My mom said she'd be coming home late. What're you gonna do for now?"

"Probably just wait in the living room."

I frown at him. "All right. I'm gonna…." I wave my hand aimlessly. "I have a headache. I'm gonna go take some pills and lie down or something."

Dakota nods and follows me once I walk down the hall, but he heads into the living room while I go to forage through the kitchen cupboard. I can't recall where the ibuprofen is and search through several drawers before giving up. With Dakota out of the way, I boil some water to make coffee and hope the caffeine might mellow me out.

Once I have a mug of heavily sugared coffee in my hand, I decide to go upstairs. I impulsively stop in the doorway to the living room instead. Dakota is slouching on the couch with his nose buried in a sketchbook. The TV is quietly playing some idiotic drama film.

I convince myself that I'm just too exhausted to go upstairs. I sit down on the opposite side of the couch, leaving almost a full cushion between me and Dakota. "There's coffee in the kitchen if you want some," I say.

Dakota glances at me for a millisecond before he resumes sketching. "Thanks, but caffeine does weird things to me. Did you find the pills?"

"No, but coffee tends to help me for some reason." I try to crane my neck to see his paper. "What're you drawing?"

He adjusts his position to further obscure his sketchbook from me. "I don't really like people watching me draw."

I frown. "How come?"

"It's the—" He cuts himself off. "Maybe I'll show you later."

"All right." I don't know why I feel an ambiguous sense of disappointment. I sip my coffee and flick my eyes between him and the boring film on TV every so often.

Dakota catches me off guard when he speaks up after several minutes of tense silence. "Where are your, uh, your friends? I haven't seen them around in the last week."

I take a breath and study him for a moment. He looks up at me inquisitively when I fail to answer, before he goes back to drawing. I sigh again.

"I don't know, I just don't really like hanging around people that I can't be genuine with, you know?"

Dakota snorts softly. "Yeah. I know."

My jaw clenches from the sudden rush of anger and frustration in my gut. "I'm just tired of feeling judged indirectly."

He hums. "Did they say something?"

"God." I tug at my hair. "They've *been* saying things. It just took me ages to finally snap."

"Just the final straw, then?"

I shake my head. "I don't know. I guess it was fine when it was just passive comments, but I saw a text from Kev where he said that if I don't answer, then I'm acting like a homo faggot killjoy, and I just—" I take another deep breath and force myself to take a sip of my coffee. I nearly choke on it and put my mug down, wiping my mouth. Why the fuck am I telling Dakota this if I can't even bring myself to look at him?

"Are you okay?" he asks.

"I'm sorry," I exhale. "I don't even know why I'm telling you this."

"Shit's hard," Dakota says. "I get it. You have to cut people like that out of your life. We all have to."

I chuckle humorlessly. "They're, like, the only people in my life, and now I'm bored as hell."

"Tough shit. Get better friends."

I rub my eyes and finally look over at him. He's still sketching something, but he puts his journal off to the side and looks at me. He's about to speak, but a knock on the front door interrupts whatever he's about to say. I faintly hear the lock jiggling.

"I'll get it," Dakota says. "Just stay here. I'm sure it's your mom."

I follow him into the hall anyway. He tries to usher me back into the living room, but I push past him to go upstairs. I hear him unlocking the door for my mom as she thanks him for saving her from the cold, but all I want to do is sleep.

NEITHER OF us acknowledges what I said over the next two weeks. I have the odd feeling that Dakota might be trying to say something anytime we're in the same room for a minute, but Matty always distracts him. Matty. The only reason Dakota is here is because he has a way with Matty that I don't. Envy isn't something I'd want to admit to, but Dakota interacts with Matty so easily that I feel incompetent sometimes.

Mom leaves the car at home again on Thursday. It's gotten warmer outside, and I go for a drive for several hours to clear my head. Windows down, music blaring, thoughts lost to the wind. I can almost ignore the sixty unread messages from my "friends" collecting dust in my phone.

When I get back home past eleven, there's no one in the living room. I head to the kitchen to see Dakota standing alone at the sink with his back to me.

"Hey," I say.

Dakota stalls for a moment before he briefly glances over his shoulder at me. "Hi. Have a good drive?"

"I guess. Is Matty asleep again?"

"Yep."

I idle and stare down at my feet before I muster up the nerve to say, "Can I ask you something?"

"Shoot."

I lean against the doorway as I watch him diligently slice into an apple over the sink. "How come you're so good at understanding Matty?"

Dakota doesn't answer, and I listen to the scraping sound of him peeling the apple. I wait for a response, but he doesn't offer me one because he's too busy arranging the apple slices in a bowl. I'm about to repeat the question when he turns around and leans back against the counter, fiddling with the bowl in his hand.

"I can't stand eating unpeeled apples." Dakota shoves a slice in his mouth and chews before continuing. "But I also can't stand it when they get brown, so I have to eat them fast."

I stare at him as he chews and says nothing else. "Did you hear my question?"

Dakota seems to ignore me again and continues on whatever spiel he has in mind while he picks at the apple pieces. "If I peel the inedible covering off a slice of ham and I accidentally nick a chunk out of it with my fingers, I'm not inclined to eat it."

"So you have weird eating habits? So do most people."

Dakota shakes his head and holds his finger up to me. "I don't have a particularly good memory. I often can't recall how to spell the name of a teacher I've known all semester, which is annoying as hell. But I can quote and dissect the vast majority of Mercutio's speeches from *Romeo and Juliet*, to the point that it's a little embarrassing and I have to stop myself from gushing about it. I've never been in a play."

I'm not sure how to respond, but he pauses to continue eating as he seems to contemplate something. I don't know whether to say anything or just walk away, but he suddenly captivates me with more words.

"My cats like me more than they like anyone else, because I tend to prefer their company to people. I have a habit of picking up the fat one and lying down with him on my chest because the pressure makes me feel calm. When I get too excited, I can't always control my movements or my voice. I sound awful when I reach the higher octaves, so it's embarrassing sometimes."

I squint at him and cross my arms over my chest. "Why are you telling me all of this?"

Dakota chews the last apple slice and carefully places the bowl in the sink. He takes a deep breath. "Because when you asked me why I understand Matty, I was tempted to answer by asking, 'Why don't you?' Because he's your brother, so naturally you'd be predisposed to understanding him."

I shake my head. "But he's—"

"But"—Dakota talks over me—"I know that it's too difficult for some people to comprehend how we think and behave, even if the way I'm describing myself to you now doesn't seem that odd. I get Matty because I have quirks and needs that I can't explain to people, because I go through meltdowns and need to stim sometimes, because I know how it feels when the people around you can't make an effort to understand what it means to be autistic. Contrary to your presumptions, Matty isn't difficult for me to deal with. He's just an ordinary kid. Like me."

"Wait," I say. "What do you mean?"

"I mean what I said. I'm autistic."

"But you're…." I frown.

Dakota looks up at me with a judgmental expression. "I'm what?"

I swallow. "You're normal."

"Well," he scoffs, "Matty's normal too. But if by 'normal' you mean that I'm like you, that I can function socially without any difficulty, then you're mistaken. I just had to teach myself to suppress the parts of myself that people think are abnormal. Granted, there's still a ton of shit about me that people condemn for other reasons. I guess you know what that's like."

I rub my jaw. "Okay. I mean, that's fine…."

Dakota laughs. "Of course it's fine. I love being autistic. It doesn't make me, or Matty for that matter, any different or less human than you."

"But you *are* different than Matty," I say. "His symptoms are more severe, he can barcly talk—"

Dakota spreads his hands on the edge of the counter and hoists himself up onto it. "All autistic people are different, 'cause it's not so much a spectrum as it is clusters of symptoms. Some of us are better at pretending to not be autistic than others, but that doesn't make us less autistic."

"But there's no way that you're—"

"None of us are the same, but for all intents and purposes, I guarantee you that you've met other autistic people who are 'like me,' okay?" Dakota says. He turns his head away with his hand latched onto the back of his neck.

I open my mouth to say something, but I close it for lack of any good response.

"Listen," he sighs. "It's pretty exhausting to explain, no matter what you're like, to someone who doesn't and will never understand it. My point is that I understand Matty because I've been where he is, and making an effort is something that comes to me more naturally. You have the capacity to understand him too. You just have to make an effort."

"I have been," I counter. "I've been around him for seven years, and yet you're better with him than I am after knowing him for a few weeks."

Dakota shrugs. "Then maybe you give up too easily."

"I've been trying," I seethe.

Dakota stretches his arms over his head. He sounds skeptical when he says, "Sure."

"I have been."

"Okay," he says. "You seem tense. Maybe you should call up your friends and go do something fun with them."

"I can't do that."

"Tell me why."

I sputter. "Because I don't want to talk to people who make jokes at my expense."

Dakota nods. "I get that. They don't know. They don't understand. So they lash out and make jokes out of their ignorance instead of trying to communicate with you honestly. What your friend said to you may be hurting you now, but imagine having an older brother like him for your entire life. That would suck, right?"

I turn around and storm upstairs without a word.

I DIDN'T think I'd go from passively disliking Dakota to despising him within one interaction. I'd actually been starting to enjoy his company and almost considering him a friend. I've never been so committed to avoiding someone before, especially a person who's nearly a constant presence in my house. I limit my trips downstairs to only the kitchen and don't bother to stop whenever I walk past him and Matty.

Dakota always has to get at least a single word in to me, whether it be "Hi," or "Say 'hi' to your brother, Matty," or "Justin, there's extra stir-fry on the stove if you want it."

When he says that last phrase on Tuesday while we're all in the kitchen, I finally snap.

"Why are you being so nice to me if you clearly think I'm a dickhead?"

Dakota stares at me. "Can you maybe lower your voice and not curse around Matty?"

"Why do you care? He can't understand me, anyway."

Dakota sighs. "He can."

I shake my head. "Whatever."

"Your homophobic friends came by earlier. I told them you were busy moping."

I whirl around to glare at him. "You *what*?"

He holds his hands up in surrender. "Kidding. Chill. I told them that I'm your mom now and I grounded you."

I stare at him, unsure of how to respond. "Are you serious?"

"God," Dakota says. "I'm bad at taking jokes, but you need to lighten up too, man. Yeah, they stopped by, but I told them you're doing schoolwork, and I happened to be holding a kitchen knife, so I think they took my vague gesture as the threat it was. And yes, this is serious. You're welcome."

His statement startles me enough to make me freeze, but I force myself to grit out another "Whatever." I go to rifle through the contents of the fridge, and I can almost feel Dakota's judgmental eyes burning into my back. When I turn around, he's not paying attention to me. I can't find anything I'm willing to eat.

"Stir-fry's getting cold," Dakota calls when I start down the hallway.

I ignore him.

IT BECOMES routine for Mom to leave the car at home on Thursdays by the time the fourth week of Dakota's service rolls around. Procrastination takes a toll on me for several hours, and I get zero work done even before thinking about getting out of the house. I usually don't make a habit of reading articles about political correctness and disabilities I don't understand, but it's more informative than my assignments. I decide to be lazy about cooking myself any microwaveables or leftovers and check the balance in my bank account. The vague sense of guilt that's been sitting in my chest for the last week makes me contemplate several redeeming actions, but I force it out of my head. I dawdle in the kitchen to give myself time to make sure I want to eat out before I head toward the door.

Matty's quiet giggles compel me to stop as I pass by the living room, and I look in to see Dakota sitting next to him and showing him something on a piece of pink construction paper. Matty laughs and takes the paper from him with little hesitation. Dakota points to a blue crayon lying by his foot, and Matty reaches over to grab it, leaning on the paper and crumpling it in the process.

Dakota notices me after a moment of me zoning out and watching them. "Hi, Justin," he says.

My mind takes a minute to buffer. "Uh, hey." I gesture down the hallway and toward the front door. "I'm gonna head out and get some Chinese takeout."

"Okay." Dakota nods. Matty shifts and stares curiously at a point somewhere below my eyes.

I clear my throat. "I'm gonna grab something for Matty, since he actually likes the noodles they have there. So you don't have to cook anything for him."

"Is that all right with your mom?"

"Yeah. She left some cash for me earlier."

"You sure? She didn't mention it to me."

I sigh. "He's my brother. It's fine."

Dakota purses his lips, but he gives in once he sees Matty's shy grin. "Okay, thanks."

I slowly start toward the door before I falter. I stop and turn back toward them. The vague sense of guilt from earlier moves my mouth before I can consider my words. "Dakota, do you want me to get you anything?"

He looks slightly astonished. "Nah, I'll be fine. I'm trying to save money."

"It's chill, I'll pay for it."

"Then I'll pass."

I roll my eyes. "Dude, just tell me what you want."

"Nothing."

Turning on my heel, I call out, "Okay, I'll order something random off the menu, and if you don't like it, then you'll only have yourself to blame."

"Justin! Wait," Dakota hisses.

I backtrack and raise my eyebrows at him. "Tell me what you want."

He looks vaguely irritated and somewhat puzzled, toying with an eraser he picked up off the floor. "Something with seafood, preferably nothing with onions."

"Thanks." I smile slyly, and he exhales and shakes his head. Relief floods through me as I head to the car and drive to the nearest Chinese place.

I bring back vegetable lo mein for Matty, seafood lo mein for Dakota, and chicken for myself. Dakota opens the door for me when I'm struggling because of the bag of food tucked under my arm, and he takes it from me to let me inside.

"Thanks for this," he says.

I shrug quietly in response.

Matty's ricocheting through the hall and flapping his arms in excitement before I can even call him over. Dakota grins when Matty latches onto his arm and reaches for the bag. I can't force the smile off my face.

In the kitchen, we eat in near silence, but Matty makes a mess of picking out every sliver of carrot in his food.

"It's one of the only food items where everything's mixed together that he likes," I whisper to Dakota. "This, and the stir-fry you made two days ago."

Dakota snickers softly. "I don't think he liked that either. I think he ate it because I told him he could stay up later if he did."

I shake my head. "I think he just likes you."

Matty prods at his food, but he ends up eating half the portion and rubbing his tummy in anguish afterward.

"You okay, sport?" Dakota asks him.

"He ate it too fast," I say. "This always happens."

Matty whines softly, but it doesn't escalate into a tantrum. Dakota finishes his food quickly, and Matty agrees to be taken to bed. I sit alone at the table and finish up while I listen to their footsteps get fainter as they ascend the stairs.

I'm washing the plastic takeout trays by the time Dakota comes back down and stands next to me. He offers me help with the dishes, but I decline.

"Matty's gone to bed," he tells me. "Do you know when your mom's coming home for sure? She gave me a loose ballpark."

"No idea," I say.

"Damn."

I finish washing the plastic trays and shake the water off them before tossing them into the recycling bin. I dry my hands with the towel and glance over to see Dakota staring absentmindedly at the floor.

"Hey," I say.

He looks over at me. "Hmm?"

I finish wiping my hands and hang the towel on the dishwasher handle. "Can we talk?"

Dakota raises his eyebrows. "I'm listening."

"Do you mind if we go to the living room?"

He shrugs and gestures me toward the door. I walk down the hall and sit on the living room couch. Dakota watches me before he sits down, not quite on the opposite side but not quite next to me either.

I take a deep breath in and let it out. "I'm sorry."

"Okay," Dakota says. "Now I'm intrigued. Please, continue."

I swallow my pride and shake my head. "I've been doing more thinking about it than I've probably ever done in my life because I felt so awful, and I'm sorry for the dumb shit I said. It was out of line, and I hate myself for how I've been behaving. I kept trying to justify it, but I always knew deep down that I fucked up, and the reason I wanted to think I hated you was because you called me out on it and you were right."

Dakota is gradually shifting his contemplative stare between me and the ground. "I appreciate that," he says. "Thank you."

"I'm not done," I explain. "It's just hard for me to say things sometimes."

"Yeah, I know what that's like."

"I've been really lonely recently, and you're the only person I see around on a daily basis. And you understand Matty so much, and I think I might be jealous of that. I don't even know why I told you my problems in the first place, but they felt like they were overflowing and about to tip me over. But it still felt good to get everything off my chest."

Dakota nods silently. I anxiously wring my hands.

"I think I just lost it a little," I say. "With how you explained being autistic, because it's not something I understood, especially with how you compared me to Kev."

"That happens," Dakota sighs. "Maybe I went overboard with it, and for that I'm sorry. But I wanted you to understand how Matty might feel about your behavior."

"I know. I just don't think it's necessarily fair to make a comparison between being gay and autistic," I say. "I mean, they're different things."

Dakota nods. "Maybe, but you're talking to one whole entire bisexual, buddy. And on top of that," he starts, then stops to chuckle at my perplexed expression. "God. Dude. You really don't recognize me, do you?"

I frown. "What do you mean?"

He laughs, but his smile seems slightly askew. "I mean, I remember seeing you around in high school. You were a junior the year I graduated, but I kinda saw you around sometimes when the theater and art kids mingled with the STEM crew. You congratulated me when I won an award for an essay I wrote about intolerance and prejudice affecting young teens."

I stare at him. "I'm sure I'd remember—"

"They got my name wrong," he says. "They said my birth name in the ceremony, and I was really upset because half the reason I wrote that essay is because of how people treat me for being autistic, and the other half was because of how people treat me for being trans and bi."

"Oh."

Dakota makes a face to mock me. "Yeah, 'oh.' I thought you would've figured it out. I remember you approaching me after everyone else and not saying much, but it was nice. I felt the support, even though I don't think you knew anything about me. I guess that's why I was pretty distraught to find out how disconnected you are from your brother."

I rub my face and nod slowly. When I glance at Dakota, he looks conflicted.

"Fuck," he says. "I don't tend to tell many people that I'm a trans guy. Please don't tell your mom, because then she might—"

"What?" I ask. "No, it's fine. I mean, I won't tell her, but that isn't really new to me because I think I remember that kid you were friends with in my grade. He kinda yelled at Kev one day after Kev said some dumb shit, and I was around to hear it, so I realized I knew how he felt and apologized to him on Kev's behalf later. I used to talk to him. I just didn't make the connection who... you were."

Dakota smiles. "That's a relief."

I shrug. "I mean, I'm just ashamed of myself for hanging around bad people and letting them influence me, even though I know better. Like, gay stuff or whatever isn't weird to me. I mean, it's still new, and I guess I know I don't understand you even in that context right now. But I'm willing to, because you were right about me judging you and Matty for your autism, when seeing the way you connect with him was just making me jealous and stupid."

"Damn," he snickers, "I didn't think I'd hear you admit you're jealous of me."

I sigh and sink myself farther into the couch. "I'm just... I'm sorry."

"You should tell that to Matty."

I swallow. "I think you deserve to hear it too."

"Thanks."

I glance over and meet Dakota's dark gaze. He looks away and picks up his sketchbook from the sofa armrest to flip through it. I finally figure out how to speak again once I watch him pick up a pencil. "Can you help me communicate better with Matty?"

Dakota looks at me. "If you're willing to be patient."

"I am."

He smiles. "Are you sure?"

"I really want to try."

Dakota studies me for a moment, but he makes little actual eye contact with me. He gets up and shifts closer until he's sitting with his leg two inches from mine. He hands his sketchbook to me, where it's open to a page with a rough sketch. He flips several pages back.

"Holy shit," I gasp. His drawings depict humanoid figures and faces, most distorted with smudges and outlined deformities. They're expressive and dark, with bursts of color captivating and guiding my eye around the page. "These are amazing."

"Thanks," Dakota says. He's wearing a sheepish smile. He flips the page for me, and I look through the rest of them. "Most of the finished ones are plans for a concentration I'm doing. On, uh, a lot of internalized issues I've personally had and which other people have as a result of prejudice."

"I don't know what to say."

"Maybe something like, 'What the fuck, Dakota, why can't you make one thing in your life not revolve around social justice?' I say that to myself sometimes."

I shake my head. "It's not that. I just didn't know you had this much talent."

"Sometimes," Dakota says as he reaches to take his journal back from my reluctant hands, "when you make an effort to understand people, you find out new things about them."

I scoff and look at him. "I don't really think Matty is this kind of artist. He's seven."

He shrugs. "I guess you'll find out once you connect with him."

I rub my eyes, then contort my spine when I stretch my arms up and yawn. "I don't remember the last time he really smiled before you came. I haven't heard one of his meltdowns in longer than I can remember."

"He's had a few. It happens. I've had them too. I still do, but not often. He's just a kid who needs people to know how to love him."

"I know," I say. "The only time he smiles around me is when I get him Chinese food."

Dakota grins. "I guarantee you that you can change that."

THE HOURS feel longer and fuller when I don't lock myself up in my room every day. I spend enough time on assignments to not feel overwhelmed, but on Monday, I grab my laptop from my room and take it downstairs to where Dakota and Matty are drawing on scattered papers again. When Dakota notices me walk into the living room and plug my computer in, he raises his eyebrows and greets me with a smile.

"Hey, guys," I say. "Do you mind if I chill in here?"

Matty doesn't acknowledge me immediately, but Dakota chuckles. "Sure, but don't step on any of the papers."

I sit down on the couch with my computer in my lap and glance at them playing quietly and giggling from time to time. Something about this seems freer, and it isn't just the size of the room or the atmosphere.

Every day, I start to sit with them and attempt to engage when Dakota encourages me to participate.

When Matty runs up to me to show me the crayon chicken he colored over Dakota's drawing, I beam. Dakota catches my eye and grins at me.

MATTY GOES to bed before Mom gets home on Thursday night again, and I sit on the living room couch while Dakota lies on his back in the mess of papers he and Matty made. He's cleaning up the crayons and markers by balancing the pencil box on his chest and wiggling to try to reach all the drawing supplies with his hands.

"Why don't you just get up and do it more easily?" I snicker.

"Well, if I'm entertaining you, then I must be doing something right." Dakota smiles when I shake my head at his response. "Nah," he says. "I told you I pressure stim sometimes. It just feels nice to have some kind of weight on me."

I laugh. "I didn't really think you were serious about that."

"Oh yeah, I am. And I'm also lazy and tired. Your brother really knows how to drain the energy out of a guy."

"Thank you," I say.

Dakota looks at me. "What for?"

"For helping me communicate with Matty, and for helping me be less of a dickhead."

Dakota hums in a way that sounds like exaggerated arrogance. "Glad to be of service."

We remain quiet for several moments, until he starts wiggling like a worm and I laugh. A thought that's been manifesting in my head for the past few weeks pokes at me, and I decide to take a chance at voicing it.

"Would it be weird for me to say I kinda like you?" I ask. My gut clenches with regret as soon as the question leaves my lips, and Dakota doesn't move.

"If I'm being honest, yes. Very," he says. "That's something to explore another time."

I swallow the lump in my throat. "Explore? So I have a chance?"

He chuckles. "Maybe you do."

"This is new to you? I mean, I know I've been subtle, I guess, but I really do admire you."

"Social cues and I aren't great friends, Justin," Dakota says. He turns on his side to see me better, promptly spilling all the drawing supplies off his stomach. He looks down. "Fuck. Oh well." He sits up and begins gathering all of them back into the box. "I guess I've been a little confused, but yeah. You can't be subtle with me. It flies over my head most of the time."

"But you're not surprised?"

"I am, kinda. I mean…." He pauses to think. "It's complicated, and we have a lot to sort out. Understand my hesitation."

"Okay," I say. "That's fine."

Dakota shoots me a bright smile. "Wanna see some of the sketches I drew earlier?"

"Yeah."

He jumps up and grabs his journal off the sofa armrest and sits down next to me. He flips through it and lands on a detailed page of a moody-looking guy whose face is partially obscured by colors. I stare at it.

"That's me," I say.

"Egotistical much?" Dakota laughs, and I give him a knowing glare. "Yeah, it might be you. Don't be offended by the rainbow color palette. I'm just proud of you coming to terms with—"

I pinch his arm, and he yelps and swats at me.

"I'm kidding," he says. "Kidding!"

"What do the words say?" I ask. There are small letters that I almost didn't notice scattered across the page, and I squint at them.

Dakota clears his throat. "It says, 'They say that hatred and intolerance come from fear. But I don't believe that's really the case. At least, I refuse to accept that it's that simple. I don't think you are ever scared of a person you love because they're different. I think it's more than being scared of a person who is tangible evidence that your worldview is skewed. I think it's more than being scared of the unknown. People are afraid to realize that by accepting the humanity of those who are different, they must reconsider why they themselves are human as well.' That's what it says."

"Makes sense," I say. "But it's also too deep, and a little tacky."

Dakota scoffs. "Let me ponder philosophy without your judgment."

"You can have all my judgment if you put your words all over my face."

"It's not really your face," he assures. "You just inspired it."

"That's fair."

We sit in silence while I flip through his other pages.

"Seriously," I find myself saying after a minute. "Thank you."

"What for? Capturing your beauty?"

I try to hide my smile but give up when he notices it. "No," I say. "You make me consider things that I never could—no, that I actively *avoided* thinking about before."

"Yeah," says Dakota. "Being as oppressed as I am has that effect on people." He laughs when I scoff. "Not really," he clarifies. "I mean, millions of people like me exist in the world. It's just hard juggling our identities when we're so judged for the few we can openly display. But it's not like I exist as an example of how to behave right. I'm just living my life."

"Yeah, well. You kinda changed mine," I say.

He chuckles. "That's a little dramatic."

The fear I used to have of speaking my mind feels nonexistent, replaced by an overwhelming sense of relief. I shrug and meet his eyes, no longer bothering to contain my euphoria. "You told me not to be subtle."

DANIEL OKULOV is a part-time writer and full-time neurotic from the Washington metropolitan area. Despite considering himself a semireclusive goblin, he is active in online support groups for other LGBT and neurodivergent people, and he advocates for self-acceptance and recovery. He strives to challenge social issues and represent minorities in his writing without limiting himself by genre. He loves his pets more than socializing with new people, but that doesn't stop him from being a hopeless romantic with a soft spot for heartwarming relationships and happy endings.

Someone Else's Star
by Arbour Ames

THERE WERE three of them.

Each looked about the same, except for the helmet. Each had those long, gangly limbs, the slim bodies, the slender necks decorated with thin black necklaces. Their skin was pale, but it had a strange tint to it, like they were sickly or perhaps put dye on their skin that never quite faded.

When they first arrived, people joked that they might be aliens. Their mannerisms were odd. Their style was a mixture of a biker gang and nineties space punk. Their helmets were slick and black, the darkness broken with smooth lines glowing with different colors. One glowed blue. One glowed pink. One glowed green. That was the only way to tell them apart.

"What's the significance to the colors?" asked Kelly Banks one day, curiosity finally overcoming his apprehensiveness. He leaned across the counter as he served the pie—apple, which was Goulcrest's famous flavor.

"They're the colors of our souls," said Blue very seriously.

Kelly tried to laugh, but he didn't know if Blue was joking or not.

There were three of them, and they arrived on the bus. Each had a duffel bag. They didn't offer names, and they didn't offer explanations. Green bought a single hotel room at the Parallel Inn with one queen-sized bed. They spent four hours in that room. Then they came out, and they went into the Hive, which is where Kelly Banks worked, which is where Goulcrest's famous apple pie was made. Blue ordered a slice of this pie. Green ordered a milkshake. Pink ordered a glass of water with three slices of lemon. They settled at the counter in front of their orders, but not a single one of them took off their helmet to eat.

"Anything wrong?" asked Kelly Banks.

"No," said Green. The helmet synthesized their voice and made the words come out strange and robotic. "Nothing is wrong. Thank you for the sustenance."

Kelly Banks tried to laugh. He told them to call him over if they needed anything else.

They didn't need anything else. After an hour of sitting still at the counter, not one of them saying a word unless spoken to, they all got up, paid the bill with a generous tip (each on separate tabs), and left. Fletcher

Simon left the Hive too and went after them, carefully ensuring he stayed out of their sight. He was a quiet boy—definitely on the small side—and was rather invisible, so townsfolk liked to send him after the newcomers. Little towns like Goulcrest ran off big gossip, and Fletcher Simon was usually the provider of that gossip.

He crept after them for hours. They walked around town, stopping to look at shops through the decorated glass windows, and then they went back to the hotel. That was all they did. Fletcher returned to the Hive.

"Well?" Kelly was finishing his cleanup of the diner, and as Fletcher walked in he threw his towel over his shoulder. "Anything?"

"Nothing exciting." Fletcher took a seat at the counter and arched his back, trying to ease the pain that always crept up about this time of the day. "They walked around some, but that was it."

Kelly put a piece of pie in front of Fletcher and dropped a scoop of homemade vanilla ice cream on top of it. "You hear names?"

"No. They didn't talk. Far as I know, the only times they've talked was when they were here and when they got their room at Parallel. Can I have a fork?"

Kelly handed him a fork.

"They don't have any mode of transportation either," said Fletcher as he dug into the pie. "I guess they travel by bus everywhere. They look like bikers, don't they?"

"Sure do," said Kelly. He rubbed at his chin. "I can't imagine anyone will be very happy with this news."

"Well, nothing I can do about it."

Kelly grabbed a napkin and reached over the counter to dab lightly at Fletcher's cheek. "You're making a mess."

Fletcher grinned at him. "It's part of my charm."

"Your charm is making a mess of the diner I just cleaned up?"

Fletcher shrugged. He scraped his fork against his plate. "Who do you think they are?"

"The newcomers? I don't know. Aliens?"

Fletcher laughed. "Yeah? What planet are they from?"

"Mars. For sure."

"Everyone's from Mars. Make up something better."

Kelly's smile was quick—just a flash, like all his smiles were. They were the kind of smiles you could miss if you liked blinking too much, but they were also the kind of smiles worth keeping your eyes open for. "I can't help it," he said, "If they're from Mars. Already decided."

"Fine," said Fletcher. "Then what do they look like under those helmets?"

"Big, big teeth. Their whole head is just one big mouth." Kelly put his fingers up against Fletcher's face, his thumb touching the corner of Fletcher's mouth, his middle finger on Fletcher's forehead. "They can open up their mouths this big. All teeth—rows and rows of them, like a shark."

"Yeah?" Fletcher felt the warmth of Kelly's fingers and wanted to bring his hand up too to touch Kelly's, but he was shy. "And where are their eyes?"

"They communicate by sounds and smells and tastes." Kelly took his hand back and grabbed the towel from his shoulder. "That's all they need. Who needs eyes?"

"What are their names?"

"Oh, that's easy." Kelly grabbed Fletcher's fork, put it into his mouth, and licked away the last of the pie. "Green, Blue, and Pink, of course."

"Yeah," said Fletcher, who felt quite breathless. He slid off the stool, and his legs wobbled, weak, beneath him. "Yeah, of course."

FLETCHER FOLLOWED the newcomers again. He woke early, got ready in a few minutes, and kissed Mrs. Banks on the cheek as he slipped out the door.

"Not gonna wait for Kelly?" she called after him.

"Let him sleep!" Fletcher called back.

The newcomers left their room at 7:00 a.m. sharp. They stood in front of the Parallel for twenty minutes after that, none of them speaking to one another. They just stood and looked around at their environment and sometimes at each other. And then they went their separate ways.

Fletcher panicked for a moment. Blue was headed toward the city limits. Pink sauntered toward city center. Green seemed to be headed downtown. Who was he supposed to follow?

He followed Blue. Other people could observe Pink and Green, he reasoned. They were walking through the town, and everyone in Goulcrest was just about as nosy as Fletcher was. News would spread without Fletcher's help.

He zipped up his hoodie, and he went after Blue.

If Blue came from Mars, they sure moved gracefully for being on a planet with a gravity three times their usual. They moved gracefully to anyone's standards, really—Fletcher didn't often have to run to keep up with anyone, but this time he was almost loping, and Blue seemed to merely be gliding.

They went deep into the forest. Not once did they stop for a break, but Fletcher had to, and then he had to rush to keep up. He was lucky he knew how to track people, or he would be out of his job, if one could even call it that.

Suddenly, then, Blue stopped moving. They stood in a small clearing, stock-still, head cocked like they were listening. Fletcher got a chill up his back. He imagined, underneath that helmet, that big monstrous mouth Kelly described. But nothing happened. Blue didn't move. They stood there, unwavering. If they had eyes somewhere under there, Fletcher thought they would be unblinking too.

Nothing.

Fletcher pulled himself up the nearest tree, settled into its branches, and waited.

"WHERE HAVE you been all day?" There was still one more person in the diner, and as Kelly served them their pie, they leaned toward Fletcher with great interest.

"Following our new residents," Fletcher said. He collapsed into a booth and waved one hand. "Pie. Pie!"

"It's coming. Calm down." Kelly took his sweet time in plating a thick slice of apple pie. He dropped it onto Fletcher's table and then slid into the booth too. His leg pressed against Fletcher's thigh. "Spill the beans."

Kelly was, in all sense of the word save for the actual occupation, a bartender. Everyone told him everything. Fletcher sought out gossip, but people surrendered their secrets to Kelly voluntarily. Fletcher was no less immune to this than anyone else.

He took a big bite of his dessert and chewed for several long moments.

"Fletcher." Kelly's voice had almost dropped to a whine.

"What did Green and Pink do?"

"Walked around. Nothing." Kelly rolled his eyes, clearly put out by the information. "They went back to Parallel about an hour ago."

Fletcher absorbed this. Then he said, "Blue went into the forest and just stood in one place. I think they're looking for something. Or waiting for it."

Kelly shivered. He was so close that Fletcher felt this shiver in every part of his body; logically he knew Kelly sat so close so they could speak without being overheard, but he couldn't help but hope for another reason. "Creepy," Kelly said.

"Maybe." Fletcher stacked a mouthful of ice cream onto a mouthful of pie and tried to fit all of it into his mouth. "They could just be normal people."

Kelly's expression was so disbelieving that Fletcher almost laughed. "What? They *could*."

"No, Fletcher, they couldn't. First off, who the *hell* acts like they do?"

Fletcher did laugh this time. He shook his head and shrugged. "I don't know! Maybe they're just weird!"

"*Second* off," said Kelly, louder now, "when have you *ever* not found at least *something* after two days, Fletch? Gimme a break."

That was a good point.

"And *thirdly*."

Oh. So he was still going.

"Who the hell comes to Goulcrest looking like that?"

"You're very passionate about this," said Fletcher, crossing his arms and leaning his back against the booth.

"Damn right I am!" Kelly took Fletcher's fork and scooped some pie into his mouth. "It's been two days and we don't know anything! If it keeps going like this, Mrs. Carrigan is gonna start making stuff up!"

Fletcher laughed again. "What do you think she'll say this time?"

"Probably something like they're raging homosexuals trying to find a place to spread their sinful ways."

"She's *awful*."

Kelly finished the last of the pie. "Yeah, no kidding." He wiped at his mouth and glanced over at Fletcher. "Why do you think they're here? You never said."

"I said I think they're looking for something."

"Yeah, but what?"

Fletcher watched Kelly wipe the plate clean with his index finger. "For answers to the universe."

Kelly stuck his finger in his mouth. "So you think they're aliens too."

"I don't know." Fletcher's hands twisted in his lap. "I just know they've lost something."

Kelly looked at Fletcher for a long time. His expression was unreadable. He said, "You have me," and then he said, "You have my mom."

Fletcher wanted to cry. A terrible bitterness was in his mouth, and something akin to jealousy twisted like a knife in his stomach—or perhaps that was dread.

"Fletcher," said Kelly softly, "you have me." He reached over to touch Fletcher's hand, and Fletcher let him. The bitterness evaporated, and something fluttered deep in his stomach. Kelly always knew what to do. He *always* knew what to do.

He leaned his head on Kelly's shoulder and closed his eyes. "I know," he whispered, "I know."

"FLETCH." KELLY'S hand was on Fletcher's arm, shaking him. It took only a moment for Fletcher to wake and gather his bearings.

"What's going on? What's wrong?"

Kelly's angular face was lit beautifully with the moonlight streaming in through the window. Fletcher still hadn't gotten used to how suddenly and overwhelmingly handsome Kelly had become in puberty.

"I had a dream." His voice was a soft, low rumble.

"You—what? Like a nightmare?" Fletcher rubbed at his eye with one hand and started pulling back his covers with the other. "You can stay in here with me, if you want—"

Kelly waved one of his hands. "It wasn't a nightmare. I think… I think it was a message."

Somehow, Fletcher was paying even more attention than before. He leaned toward Kelly. "What do you mean 'a message'?"

"The new people in town. The helmets? I think they're trying to tell me something." Kelly chewed on his bottom lip, and Fletcher had to struggle to take his gaze away from that.

"What are they trying to tell you?"

"I think they're connected to my dad. Where he was before Goulcrest or maybe… maybe to his death."

"He died in an accident, Kelly." They'd had this conversation many times before; when Mr. Banks died three years prior, Kelly tried proving it wasn't an accident in any way he could, convinced for some reason that his dad was too *smart* to just die in an accident.

Unfortunately, it didn't matter how smart anyone was when there were drunk drivers involved. Fletcher had come to terms with that when his own parents died.

Kelly, though, dismissed Fletcher's words with another wave of his hands. "Either way, I need to ask them about it,"

"Right now?"

"Why not?"

Fletcher sputtered. "It's three in the morning!"

"Almost four, actually. And if I'm right, *they'll* thank *us* for showing up at their door. If not, brush it off as a mistake. We got the wrong door, no big."

Fletcher had no idea how to reply to any of this.

"I want you to come with me. Will you?"

Fletcher searched Kelly's eyes—those amazing brown eyes he'd come to love with all that he was. "Yeah," he said. "Of course. I have your back."

Kelly grinned. "You always have."

Fletcher slid out of bed. He was dressed and ready to go in five minutes, and together he and Kelly slipped out Fletcher's window.

The night was quiet. Only the gas station was still open, and even then Fletcher doubted anyone was awake in there. Goulcrest was too far off the interstate for anyone to bother driving through it.

They reached the Parallel in ten minutes and were up to the second floor in a couple of minutes after that. Kelly's fist hovered next to the helmets' door. He looked back at Fletcher.

Fletcher said, "Are you sure about this?" and Kelly chewed on his lip again. "You don't have to." *We can go back*, he wanted to say. *We can go home and forget about all this. We can live our lives.* But he didn't say any of this, because Kelly already had a determined set to his mouth and was bringing his knuckles toward the door.

Immediately, it opened. Green stood in the doorway, blocking Fletcher's view into the room.

"Hi," said Kelly. "I got your message. I think you knew my father."

For a long moment, Green didn't move. Fletcher was distinctly reminded of Blue in the forest. Then Green stepped aside and opened the door wider. Kelly let out a relieved sigh.

"Thank you." He moved to enter the room, and Fletcher started after him, but Green held up a hand in Fletcher's face, stopping him.

"I'm going in with him," Fletcher said.

"Fletch."

"No. I'm not letting you go in there alone. That's ridiculous."

Green's hand was still up. Fletcher swatted it away.

"We don't know anything about them, Kelly."

Kelly looked between the room—perfectly normal, from what Fletcher could make out—and Fletcher's imploring face. "It's okay," he said finally, offering one of his quick smiles. "If anything happens, you can tell everyone how I died." And then he winked and stepped past Green. Green tilted his head at Fletcher.

"Don't you dare hurt him," Fletcher said.

Green closed the door.

FOR HOURS, Fletcher waited. He tried sitting right outside the door, but then he took to pacing, too restless to stay in one place. He thought about Kelly, about his easy laugh and his sincere eyes, the way he'd always been there for Fletcher and Fletcher had always been there for him. He thought about how, when his parents died, Kelly didn't stop fighting until *his* parents took Fletcher in and became Fletcher's legal guardians. He thought about how they basically came out together—Fletcher as trans, Kelly as bi, and Kelly's parents threw a big celebration for both of them, like Fletcher was just as important as Kelly was. He thought about how often Kelly snuck into Fletcher's room or Fletcher snuck into Kelly's room and how late they stayed up together, talking about everything and nothing, strengthening their friendship with every word, Fletcher falling deeper with every word.

They were a love story—that's what they were. Fletcher was the hero and Kelly was his knight, and when they were both ready, they'd ride into the sunset together.

Fletcher glanced at the window at the end of the hall. It was getting lighter outside, which meant it was probably around seven. Kelly had been in there for ages. What was Fletcher supposed to do if Kelly never came out? How could he report that? How did he tell the police that Kelly voluntarily went into a room with people who were probably aliens and never came out? What would they even say to that?

He moved toward the door and lifted one hand. Before he reported anything, he was going to raise some hell. Make some noise. He would—

But the door was opening and then Kelly was standing there. Behind him, Blue, Pink, and Green stood rigidly against the far wall.

"What happened?"

Kelly just took Fletcher's hand and pulled him away from the door, away from the room, away from the Parallel Inn.

"Kelly? What happened?"

They walked in silence most of the time, but Fletcher couldn't help but ask again. He didn't like what those hours did to Kelly; he didn't like the hard look in Kelly's eyes, or the way his other hand was clenched at his side, or the way he refused to answer any of Fletcher's questions.

"Did they hurt you?"

At last Kelly responded, but it was just a shake of his head.

"Are they connected to your dad?"

Kelly pushed open the front door of his house, and Fletcher stumbled after him. "Mom!" Kelly shouted into the house. "Are you up?"

"It's only half past seven. She might—"

"I don't care." His tone was sharp. Fletcher shrank back from it. "Mom! Get up!"

A moment later, they could both hear Mrs. Banks's chair rolling toward them. She rubbed at her eyes and squinted at them.

"How early is it? What were you two doing out?"

"You *knew*."

She stopped rolling her chair toward them. All traces of sleep were gone from her eyes now, and she blinked at Kelly with a mixture of shock and horror. "I don't...." The words cracked, and she took in a shuddering breath. "I don't know what you mean, sweetheart."

"Bullshit. You knew. You knew who they were when they arrived and you didn't tell me."

"When who arrived, Kelly? What are you talking about?"

"Stop lying!" he shouted. "Just stop! You should have told me when Dad was still alive! How could you keep this from me?"

"Your father—he didn't want you to have a part of any of this. He wanted you to have a normal life."

Kelly's entire body shuddered. He took a big step away from his mother, almost colliding with Fletcher. "So you admit it. All of it is true."

"I don't know what they told you, Kelly, but—"

"They told me enough."

This was a Kelly completely different from anything Fletcher had ever seen before, and it terrified him.

"You and Dad never told me *anything*, and now Dad's past is catching up with him. With *us*."

"He was going to tell you when he was ready, Kelly, but he wanted you to have a normal childhood, and if you were ready—"

"If *I* was ready?" Kelly scoffed. "Are you kidding me? What the hell is that supposed to mean? What did 'ready' look like to him? And when he died, what? You thought I would just never find out, is that it?"

Mrs. Banks sniffled. She pressed a hand to her mouth, and the tears rolled down her cheeks and over her fingers. Then the sobs came, suddenly, violently, shaking her shoulders and wrecking her throat.

Kelly watched this all apathetically. "I know who they are." He was calm—deadly calm. "I know who they are, and they know who I am, and they've invited me to go with them."

"Kelly, Kelly." Mrs. Banks couldn't seem to come up with any other words.

"And," Kelly said, "I think I'm going with them."

"Kelly, *please*."

But Kelly walked away, and his mother was a blubbering mess behind him, and Fletcher still looked between them, wildly and hopelessly confused. Did he comfort Mrs. Banks, who'd basically became his mother when she took him in? Did he go after Kelly—his best friend, his knight?

He floundered, floundered, floundered, and then he ran for Kelly's room.

KELLY WAS sitting on the floor with his back against his bed, his legs stretched out in front of him. Fletcher sat cross-legged next to him. They didn't say anything for a while. Fletcher was afraid to. Usually the silence would be comfortable, but today, like it was earlier, it was stifling. It had never been like this with Kelly.

"So…." Fletcher reached over to Kelly's hands and started playing with his fingers, like he always did. Kelly, like he always did, let him. "Are they aliens?"

Kelly jerked away. His laugh was short and harsh. "Are you kidding me? That's what you're asking me?"

There was a lump in Fletcher's throat. He tried to swallow it away. "Are you really going with them?"

"Well, why shouldn't I?"

Why shouldn't he? What was Fletcher supposed to say to that? Shouldn't the answer be obvious? *Why* shouldn't he? Because of Fletcher! Because he would be leaving Fletcher behind—Fletcher, who had always been there for him, who had always supported him, who had never once let him down. How could he be okay with that?

"Well?" said Kelly. He was actually expecting an answer. He wanted to know Fletcher's thoughts. Maybe he even wanted Fletcher to convince him to stay.

"Well," Fletcher repeated, his confidence solidifying, "what about me?"

Kelly shot him a look.

"I mean, what about us? You and me."

The look turned disbelieving. "You're asking me to give up learning my heritage so I can... what, be with you?"

All the air rushed out of the room. Kelly laughed again, just as harshly as before.

"You still don't get it, do you?"

"Kelly—"

"This isn't your story, Fletcher. You aren't the hero of this book. You can't expect a happy ending or a grand adventure because your story hasn't even *started* yet. This is mine. This is my story. The helmets came for my father, not yours. They want *me* to go with them, not you. I'm not your side character, and I for damn sure am not your love interest."

Tears burst from the corners of Fletcher's eyes, and he grabbed at his chest, struggling to breathe. He wondered if he looked like Mrs. Banks now, blubbering, pathetic. He choked out, "Did you ever love me?" and Kelly's lip curled.

"That isn't the point, and you know it. The point is, you've warped me into this dream boy you'll have your happily-ever-after with, and you forgot that I have dreams too! Dreams that aren't limited to what a kid who's still in high school thinks I should be doing."

At this, he pushed to his feet and stomped out the door, apparently done with the conversation, done with Fletcher, done with everything they'd done together.

MORE TIME passed—hours passed. Fletcher waited in Kelly's room for a long while, and then he moved to his own room and he waited there. Mrs. Banks eventually stopped wailing and wheeled back to her bedroom, where, Fletcher imagined, she stretched herself across her bed and cried herself back to sleep.

They were both worried about Kelly, but neither went to the other, too afraid and too aware that their reasons for wanting Kelly to stay were too different: Fletcher yearned for the romance he thought blossomed between them; Mrs. Banks wanted her son to stay young, innocent, and nearby. If they spoke, perhaps one of them could convince the other that their way of looking at the entire situation was wrong, that Kelly *should* be able to go with these helmets and live out his dream.

"He'll be back," Fletcher whispered to himself. "He'll be back." He stood and went to his desk, then traced his hands over the pictures he'd pinned up. Him and Kelly on one of their many trips to the park, him and Kelly arm in arm at the beach, him and Kelly taking a selfie during a hike in the forest. He touched Kelly's image, trailed one finger over the line of Kelly's jaw.

You've warped me into this dream boy you'll have your happily-ever-after with, and you forgot that I have dreams too!

He shook his head. Kelly was his dream boy, sure—as in, he was everything Fletcher always wanted. But Fletcher didn't *warp* anything. He knew Kelly better than anyone. They'd been living together for years. They'd been best friends since they met, and Fletcher fell in love with him only two years after that.

Warping things? What was that supposed to even mean? There was nothing to warp. There was nothing about Kelly that *needed* warping. He was the perfect person to love because of that: he was considerate and gentle, and he was a good listener, and he always kept his door open when Fletcher had nightmares about finding himself alone in the universe.

"Come on, Fletch," he would whisper, holding Fletcher to his chest, "You know you always have me."

Fletcher stepped back from his desk—from the pictures. He rubbed at his mouth and blinked a few times. What could he possibly be warping about Kelly?

He could ask him about it when he got back. They'd always been able to work things out before. Like all other friends, they'd had fights, but they'd always been able to work things out afterward. Kelly would come back, and they would talk, and they would hug afterward, and maybe Fletcher would pass out in Kelly's room, curled up in Kelly's arms.

But then again, it had never been like this before. It had *never* been like this before. Kelly had never said things like this before. Fletcher had never felt more unimportant than he did when Kelly put him down, when he said that it wasn't Fletcher's story, that him loving Fletcher "isn't the point."

Didn't that mean, then, that Kelly never loved him? Didn't that mean he didn't want anything between them?

Fletcher swore under his breath and checked the time. It was getting late into the day, and Kelly still wasn't back. Should he go and find him? Should he be the one who tried to make up their friendship? Was he supposed to be apologizing for something, or was Kelly the one who needed to apologize?

God. He just wished those alien-looking helmets had never come to Goulcrest. He wished Kelly's parents had told him whatever it was they needed to tell him early on, and he'd rejected it. He wished everything was back to normal, when Fletcher was pining and Kelly seemed to encourage the crush.

Kelly: his hero, his knight, the boy of his dreams.

Was that what he meant? Was that what he meant when he said "warped"?

How well did Fletcher know him, really?

How was it that he didn't recognize Kelly in those last moments before he left?

NIGHT CAME and went. Fletcher slept restlessly, and then he rose early. He glanced in Kelly's room. Untouched. He headed downstairs. Mrs. Banks was seated at the window, staring out onto the street. Fletcher couldn't get out the door without also getting her attention.

"Going out?" The words were toneless.

"He didn't come home last night."

"No." She looked down at her hands. "No."

"I'm going to go find him. I'm sure he's still here. You know how sometimes he needs his alone time." Even as he said this, he knew it was a lie. Kelly sometimes needed alone time, but it wasn't ever away from his family. He never needed time away from his mom or from Fletcher. It was only ever from the other people in Goulcrest.

"I know," said Mrs. Banks, accepting the lie.

"I'll bring him back home with me and we can all talk, okay?"

"Yes, okay."

He stopped with his hand on the doorknob. "I love you."

This time she didn't answer. A tear slid down her cheek.

"I know it doesn't mean much," said Fletcher, and he tried not to let her silence get to him, "but I do love you. And you know how grateful I am for everything."

Still nothing. Fletcher couldn't help but think that in Kelly's voice: *nothing*. He thought most of what he thought in Kelly's voice; if his thoughts weren't in Kelly's voice, often he thought about how Kelly would react to what he was thinking.

Kelly was just that kind of person. When he wasn't present, he consumed thoughts. When he was present, he was loud and he demanded attention. Where Fletcher blended in, Kelly shined. He couldn't help it. When once he'd tried to go with Fletcher on one of his newcomer missions, he botched it and immediately announced he would stick with the diner. He would accept secrets, he said, but he wouldn't take them.

Fletcher left the house and walked down the street with his hands in his pockets. In his head, Kelly said, "*Nothing.*"

He stopped by the gas station and went inside, where he purchased a small bottle of sweet tea and a bag of salt-and-pepper chips. The clerk wouldn't tell him anything if he didn't spend any money.

She greeted him by his deadname, not paying attention to the visible wince she got in return. "What kind of information are you looking for today? I know you never eat this stuff."

"Have you seen the newcomers? The ones with the helmets?"

She pursed her lips. "Maybe I have."

"Come on, Mrs. Carrigan. I already bought tea. *And* chips." He shook the bag at her, like it would prove his point better. "You have to know something."

"I do. I saw the blue one head into the forest."

"How long ago?"

She shrugged. "Ten minutes. Headed the same way the last time he went."

"And have you seen Kelly?"

"Kelly Banks? No. Should I have?"

Fletcher shook his head. "I was just wondering."

"Anything the lovely citizens of Goulcrest should be in on?"

He suddenly hated her. He hated everything she was, everything Goulcrest was, everything this town made him be. He was just a *kid*. Why was it his job to gather gossip? Why was it his job to follow people around, putting himself in danger just so the old ladies in the Hive had something to giggle about?

"No," he said, "nothing at all."

He continued his journey, this time headed into the forest. He went to the same clearing Blue went to before. They were standing, like before, in the center with their head tilted up to the sky. Fletcher had no qualms this time about walking right into the clearing too.

"The universe is bigger than you think it is." Blue's voice was robotic and almost monotonous. "It's growing bigger. That is the way of the universe. No matter how much we struggle toward order, we always end up moving toward destruction. With every breath you take, the stars get farther and farther away."

Fletcher swallowed.

"It would be selfish," said Blue, turning to face Fletcher, "to hold someone back from reaching those stars just because you've decided that they're your sun."

There was an ice on Fletcher's skin he couldn't get rid of, no matter how furiously he rubbed at his arms. "Where is Kelly?"

"He's already on his way to the stars for which he's always yearned."

No. No, it couldn't be. Fletcher struggled with picking the right words. "So... so why are you here?"

"I stayed behind to pay my last respects. Kelly's father was my mentor and my friend. They told me to meet them here, and they never came. They died before they could come. Do you know where?"

"Where Mr. Banks died?"

Blue nodded.

"Up the highway. About a mile from here. We put up a cross." His words shook with approaching tears, and he tried to clear them from his throat. "Can you tell Kelly something for me?"

"I might. If he wishes to hear it."

"Tell him... tell him I know he doesn't need my permission, but that I hope he finds what he's looking for."

Silence for a moment. Then Blue reached up, brought their hand to the back of their head.

"He had a message for you, as well."

Something clicked. Then there was a hiss, like air being released. Blue pulled away the helmet and Fletcher stared, openmouthed, at Blue's true face. He couldn't move. He could barely breathe.

"Your story is coming," Blue said. "Be the person you need to be when it arrives."

Fletcher's heart tried to hammer its way out of his chest.

"Until then," Blue said, "keep your dreams alive."

ARBOUR AMES is trans, gay, sad, and stuck in a town in the middle of nowhere that somehow has absolutely no good attributes. They love to procrastinate on the writing that might actually make them money and instead spend time writing fan fiction that should probably never see the light of day but gets published online anyway. Arbour has weaknesses for fluff (both in fiction and on animals), horror movies, and existential memes. If ever one were to sneak a peek into Arbour's life, they would probably see Arbour binge-watching superhero television shows instead of doing something useful with their life. Feel free to send over an email if you find yourself curious about their terrible fan fiction, if you want rants about superheroes, or if you're just in the mood to get a response that is somehow sarcastic and awkward at the same time.

Contact them at buglebane@gmail.com.